Mango Gold

A Mango Bob and Walker Adventure

by

Bill Myers

www.mangobob.com

Chapter One

I'd only gone about twenty miles after leaving the Florida farm where I'd spent the last three months tending goats in exchange for an RV site when my phone chimed with an incoming call.

I figured it might be Zoey.

She had been there at the farm with me. Living in her fifth-wheel trailer parked in the site next to mine. We'd been traveling together for almost six months, moving from park to park hiding out from the virus.

I had assumed that when our time at the goat farm was up, we'd travel together to another RV site, as we had done in the past.

But Zoey had a different plan. She said we'd spent enough time together and she was heading to upstate New York to stay at a friend's vineyard.

I could go where ever I wanted, as long as it wasn't with her.

You might think my feelings would have been hurt when she said that, but they weren't. We were just traveling companions and not in any kind of relationship. I enjoyed her company and hoped she enjoyed mine, but we both understood we would eventually part ways.

That day had finally come when we left the goat farm heading in different directions.

Still, there was a chance she was calling to tell me she had changed her mind.

I answered on the third ring.

A woman's voice, not Zoey's, said, "Walker, I hear congratulations are in order."

The voice sounded familiar, but I couldn't place it. "Uh, what are you talking about?"

"Walker, it's me, Anna, your favorite real estate agent. You haven't forgotten me have you?"

I smiled. Hearing her name brought back a flood of memories. Most of them good. We had met during a hurricane on the treasure coast. Both of us were camping at Sebastian Inlet State Park. Her site was next to mine. I was in my motorhome and she was in a tent.

When the hurricane came ashore, we joined forces to try to survive the howling winds and rising waters. Neither of us had been in a cyclone before and as the power of the storm increased, we both feared for our lives. Pelted by debris and hundred and fifty-mile winds, we found refuge in one of the park's concrete-walled restrooms and huddled there until the storm passed.

Soon after, we hit the treasure beaches with our metal detectors and made some amazing finds. One that changed her life.

"No Anna, I haven't forgotten you. How are you doing? Selling a lot of houses?"

After the hurricane, Anna moved to Englewood, where I was living at the time. I was afraid she was moving there to be near me, but I was wrong. She'd gone there to get a job selling real estate. And apparently, she was good at it.

"Walker, I'm doing great and yes, I'm selling a lot of houses. That's why I'm calling you. I wanted to make sure you're going to be at the closing tomorrow."

"Closing? What closing?"

"You know, for the place your wife is buying. You're supposed to sign the papers tomorrow afternoon."

I paused, thinking that maybe I had misheard her. Then just to be sure, I said, "Anna, you're joking, right? You know I don't have a wife."

She laughed. "She said you'd say that. Something about wanting to keep it a secret until you got back in town. But she showed me the ring, the wedding photos, even her driver's license with your last name on it.

"Frankly, I never thought of you as the marrying kind. But I guess I was wrong. This Abigail woman sure seems to have won your heart. She said you proposed on a cruise. That you got down on one knee and did the whole romantic thing."

I started to tell her it never happened. That Abigail wasn't my wife. It was true we had once pretended to be married, but only because the case we were working on required it. When it was over, we walked away as friends. We never got married. We never even got close. We were just friends. Nothing more.

But if she was pretending we were married and had gone to the trouble to create fake documents, it might mean she was working on another case that involved me. Or maybe it meant her mind was slipping and she thought our pretend marriage was real.

Either way, I needed to find out.

"Anna, what time is the closing tomorrow?"

"Two-thirty. In my office. You remember where it is?"

"Yeah, on 776 in Englewood, right?"

"That's the place. I'll see you there tomorrow. Don't be late and be sure to bring your checkbook."

She ended the call before I could ask about the house I was supposed to buy and how much it was going to cost me.

I needed to find out, and quickly.

To do that, I had to call Abby. But I wasn't going to call her while I was driving. I wanted to be parked and seated on the couch with Mango Bob before I dialed.

I knew that trying to get any sense out of her while driving a six-ton motorhome on narrow back roads in Florida traffic wasn't something I wanted to do.

Checking the GPS, I saw the small town of Palatka was just ahead. Figuring it had a Walmart, because every town does, I told the GPS to take me there. The parking lot was sure to be RV-friendly.

I was quickly rerouted and six minutes later, I pulled into Walmart and headed to the far edge of the lot, away from all the other cars. Finding a row of empty spaces, I pulled in and parked. After killing the motor, I grabbed a bottle of water from the fridge, and settled down on the couch.

Almost immediately, Mango Bob, the big-headed bobtail cat that lived with me, came trotting up from the back bedroom and hopped up on the couch beside me. I gave him a few pets and pulled out my phone.

After taking a sip of water, I punched in Abby's number and waited for her to answer.

She picked up on the fourth ring.

"Hi Walker, I figured you'd be calling. I guess you heard from your Realtor friend."

"Yeah, I did. She wanted to be sure I'd be at the closing tomorrow for the house my wife was buying. I assume you're the wife?"

"Yep, that's me. Your new bride. You'll be there, won't you?"

"No Abby, I won't. We're not married and we're definitely

6

not buying a house together. So unless you give me a really good reason, I'm not going to show."

The truth was, I already had a pretty good idea about what was going on. It had to have something to do with Boris Chesnokov, our mutual friend in Key West. It was rumored he had once been the boss of Florida's Russia Mafia. Some said he still was.

No one dared to ask him if the rumors were true. But a lot of people, including me, believed they were.

When Chesnokov asked you for a favor, you didn't decline. Not if you wanted to stay healthy.

"Abby, I'm waiting. Tell me what's going on."

She hesitated, then said, "Walker, we can't talk about it on the phone. I'm in Venice. How long will it take you to get here?"

I didn't answer right away. I wasn't sure whether or not I wanted to get involved in another one of Chesnokov's schemes. The last two had gotten me awfully close to being on the wrong side of the law. People were killed. There was talk I had been holding the gun that had fired the fatal shots.

I might have been.

Abby interrupted my thoughts by repeating her question. "Walker, how long will it take you to get to Venice? I'll tell you everything when you get here. It's important you don't miss out on this."

I wasn't so sure.

"Abby, I think you're trying to get me mixed up in something I'm going to regret. In fact, I already regret it. You've been telling people we're married. People who know me.

"You shouldn't be doing that. Not without talking to me first. You definitely shouldn't have signed papers with Anna making her think I'm buying a house with her as my agent. She'll be on the hook when the deal falls through. She doesn't deserve that."

I took a deep breath. I'd made a decision, one that I was sure to regret.

"Abby, I guess I have to come to Venice whether I want to or not, to straighten this thing out. It'll take me four hours to get there. But you have to promise you won't be telling anyone else we're married or that we're buying a house together. I don't need you digging that hole any deeper."

I had close friends in the area and didn't want any of them to get caught up in whatever scam Abby was running.

"Don't worry Walker, I won't say a word to anyone until you get here. I've got a site reserved in your name at Oscar Scherer State Park. We'll meet up there this afternoon."

She ended the call before I could ask any more questions.

Chapter Two

I called Abby right back. As before, she answered on the fourth ring.

"Walker, I know what you're going to ask me. But please don't, because you won't like the answer."

I doubted she had any idea what I was wondering about but I decided to see what she'd say. "OK smarty pants, if you think you can read my mind, tell me what I was calling about."

I waited to see if she'd get it right. She supposedly had the 'gift'. An ability to read minds and see the future. I was a disbeliever when I first heard about it, but after seeing her in action on at least three separate occasions, I was starting to think that maybe there was something to it.

What she said next confirmed my suspicions.

"Walker, you called to ask why you should stay at Oscar Scherer State Park instead of at your reserved site in Mango Bay."

She was right. That was why I called her.

I had a site at Mango Bay RV resort in Englewood, just south of Venice. It had been my home base for more than two years. No matter how often or how far I traveled, my site was always there when I returned. If I was going to be in town, that's where I was going to stay.

She had known the question I was going to ask. But I still needed to know the answer.

"Abby, good guess. Tell me why I should stay at Oscar Scherer instead of Mango Bay?"

She took a deep breath before she answered. Then said, "Walker, you're not going to like this. I called Mango Bay last week and asked about your site. I was told the place was under new management and they had decided to eliminate the free sites the previous owners had set up, including yours. They had tried to contact you, but weren't able to. So they gave your site to someone else. Someone willing to pay the going rate.

"The office manager told me that they've moved your Jeep to a parking place just outside the front gate. They'd appreciate it if you'd come pick it up.

"I told them you would, later this week. We'll get the Jeep tomorrow."

I was stunned by her answer. I knew the owners of Mango Bay personally. I'd helped them buy the park and they had promised me a free site for as long as I wanted to stay there. I couldn't think of any reason they would have rented it out without first telling me.

Apparently, Abby again knew what I was thinking.

"Walker, I'm sorry to have to tell you this, but your friends Polly and Buck, both succumbed to the virus. With their passing, their daughter Lucy inherited the park.

"It was more than she could handle. She turned it over to a management company and moved back to Tampa. She still owns the park but has nothing to do with the day-to-day operations.

"The management company was doing what it thought was in her best interest - clearing out the deadwood – sites that weren't generating any income. Including yours."

Again, I was stunned. Not so much about losing my site. I could live with that. But the passing of Polly and Buck was hard to take. Even though they were both in their late seventies, they had been among the first people I'd met when I moved to Florida, and we had spent quite a bit of time together. I felt bad about not staying in touch while I had been away. I should have called and checked up on them.

I felt bad that I hadn't.

"Walker, there's nothing you could have done. The virus hit the park hard and took out a lot of good people. I'll tell you more when you get here. Remember, Oscar Scherer State Park. Get there before four."

She ended the call.

This time I didn't call her back.

Chapter Three

I didn't get back on the road right away.

Instead, I sat in the Walmart parking lot for almost half an hour thinking about the loss of my friends. It was one of the hard parts about living on the road in an RV. You meet a lot of people along the way, mostly in passing, but once in a while, you meet people that become a part of your life.

Buck and Polly were at the top of that list. They had taken me in, had shared their lives with me, and had asked nothing in return. I should have stayed in touch with them as I traveled. There was no reason not to. But I hadn't.

Now they were gone.

After thirty minutes of feeling guilty about their passing, I let Bob know we were getting back on the road. I moved up to the driver's seat, started the motor, and tuned the radio to a country music station.

The RV's fuel gauge showed the tanks were less than half full, the gas in them at least four months old.

Fresh gas was in order.

I pulled up to the Walmart fuel island and was shocked to see the price per gallon was almost a dollar more than it had been the last time I filled up. There'd been a presidential election since then and I guess the new guy's energy policy was responsible. Or maybe it was something else.

Whatever the reason, it was going to cost me money.

With the tanks full, I pulled out of Walmart and headed for Oscar Scherer, on Florida's west coast, just north of Venice. As I settled in for the lonely drive, Garth Brooks'

"The Dance" played on the radio.

It set the tone for the drive ahead.

Four hours later, I pulled into the park and called Abby.

She answered immediately.

"Walker, you here?"

"Yeah, at the front entrance."

"Good, check in and head to your site. I'll be in the space next to you."

I wasn't in the mood for conversation, so I ended the call. After checking in at the ranger station, I got my campground pass, and headed to my site, number twenty-two.

Like most of the ones at Oscar Scherer, the one assigned to me was a gravel-surfaced back-in pad. It was level, with water and electric hookup, and under a canopy of shade trees. There was no sewer connection. The bathhouse was close by.

As soon as I pulled in, I saw Abby step out of a small Class B camper van parked in the site next to me. She smiled and waved as she walked over to my door. I killed the engine and went outside to meet her. She wasn't wearing a mask and I wasn't sure whether I should be wearing one or not. The science wasn't settled.

I didn't care either way. If a business wanted me to wear a mask, I would. No problem.

I'd already had the virus, so in theory, I wasn't going to get it again, and wasn't contagious. But I hadn't kept up with the news at the goat farm and I was somewhat out of the loop when it came to the current PPE protocol. I had a mask in my pocket, but since Abby wasn't wearing one, I didn't put mine on.

She didn't seem bothered. She walked up, gave me a big hug, and said, "I'm glad you made it. I've missed you."

She stepped back, looked me over, and said, "You look good, but you smell like a goat. Maybe you ought to shower before we talk."

I smiled. The goat smell was still with me. I wasn't sure a shower would help much.

Still, after the long drive and the quickee sailor showers I'd been taking in the RV to conserve water, a long hot shower sounded good. I pointed to the campground bathhouse. "They have hot water in there?"

Abby nodded. "Yeah, they did this morning. You're not going to shower in your RV?"

"No, too much trouble. I'd have to move Bob's litter box out of the stall and get him situated before I can turn on the water. It'll be easier to use the one in the bathhouse."

She nodded. "Okay, shower there. But be quick. There's something I need to show you outside the park and we'll need to go and be back here before they close the gate."

I went to my RV, and after grabbing what I needed, I let Bob know I'd be gone for a few minutes. He didn't seem to care, he was more interested in the wildlife outside our bedroom window. After locking the door behind me, I headed to the men's side of the nearby campground bathhouse.

Like most Florida State Parks, it had roof-mounted solar panels to heat the water. Early morning, the water would be cold, but I knew from past experience, by mid-afternoon it would be close to scalding.

After getting the cold and hot mixture just right, I stepped under the spray and took my time trying to get rid of the goat smell. I was hoping the Irish Spring soap I used would get the job done. I wasn't sure it would.

After the shower, I toweled off and changed into clean clothes. When I got back to my RV, Abby was standing in front of it, holding a young kitten that looked a lot like Bob. At first glance, I thought it was him, but then remembered the last time we were together she'd gone to EARS and adopted one of her own. An orange tabby with a bobtail – it could have easily passed as a clone of my Bob.

I smiled, trying to remember the cat's name. Then it came to me. "It's Buddy, right?"

She nodded, "Yep, that's it. Buddy. He's grown a bit since the last time you saw him."

He had.

"Has Bob seen him yet?"

She shook her head.

"I don't think so. I brought him over to your window, but Bob didn't come up to see us. Maybe he's in the back, sleeping."

Abby and I had traveled together long enough for her to know that Bob spent most of his day sleeping in the RV's back bedroom. Usually up under my pillow. That was probably where he was now, unless he was still looking at the wildlife out the window.

I wasn't sure how he would react when he saw Buddy, especially if Abby was planning on bringing him into my RV. I asked her about it.

"Is he fixed?"

"Yeah. He was hard to live with when he wasn't. The vet said it was the best thing for him. I'm not sure he'd agree, but ever since, he's been a lot happier. Maybe they ought to fix males of all species. What do you think?"

I smiled. "Some of us might put up a fight."

She laughed. "No doubt. So, you ready to take a ride?"

I was.

She took Buddy into my RV and introduced him to Bob. Surprisingly, he didn't seem to mind. He looked at the kitten, sniffed his butt, then went back to his bed. Buddy followed.

We watched them for a few minutes, then Abby asked, "You think he'll be okay if we leave him here?"

"Probably. They don't seem to mind each other's company. And there are plenty of places to hide in here if they want to get away from each other."

She agreed with my assessment. "Okay, let's leave him here. We'll take my van."

Before going out, I made sure to leave the overhead fans running so it would stay cool inside for the two cats. After I locked the door, I followed Abby over to her camper. The last time I saw her, she was driving a rental car and had made no mention about buying an RV. I guess things had changed since then.

Hers looked to be one of the newer class B campers on the market. A Winnebago Travato built on a Ram ProMaster chassis. Silver and still showroom shiny.

"When did you'd get this?"

"Right after I got Buddy. I needed a way to take him with me when I traveled and it was a lot easier to have a camper than to try to find motels that would take cats. I'd come into some money and decided to spend it on a camper.

"It was before COVID hit. Right before prices on these things took off. I've been living in it ever since."

She got in on the driver's side and I took the passenger seat. Looking back behind me, I could see the van had a kitchen, two beds and a bathroom in the back. It was a pretty nice setup for such a small vehicle.

With her at the wheel, we headed out of the park. She had promised to tell me more about why I was in Venice and I figured it was a good time to ask. "So Abby, tell me what you've got me into. Why are you pretending we're married and why am I supposed to be buying a house?"

Instead of giving me the answer, she pointed to the road ahead and asked a question of her own. "You ever been to Casey Key?"

Chapter Four

"Casey Key? It's on the gulf between Venice and Sarasota, right? Not too far from Oscar Scherer? Are we going there?"

She nodded. "Yeah, we are. There's a house there you need to see."

We turned out of Oscar Scherer onto US 41 north. As soon as traffic cleared, Abby pulled into the far left lane. At the first light, she took a left onto Blackburn Point road and stayed on it for a mile until we crossed the swing bridge over the bay. Five hundred feet beyond, the road dead-ended at Casey Key. A narrow barrier island where the rich and famous live.

On our left, large mansions behind gated walls blocked our views of the white sands of the Gulf of Mexico. On our right, similar-sized homes tucked behind even taller walls hid the views to Blackburn Bay.

The road we were on was a narrow blacktop, the surface scarred by constantly blowing sand. There were no shoulders on either side. If you wanted to pull over, you'd be out of luck. Fortunately, there was almost no traffic. No cars behind Abby forcing her to go faster than she wanted to.

We'd gone about a half-mile when the road curved and Abby slowed to a near stop. She pointed to a wall on our left with a for sale sign on it. Behind it, a three-story mansion. Next to it, a smaller but equally impressive home. All behind the same wall.

"Is that what I'm buying?"

She laughed. "You wish. No way you're not buying that.

It's way out of your price range. They're asking eight point nine million."

"Then why are you showing it to me?"

A black SUV had pulled up behind us and tapped its horn. It wanted us to move along.

Abby waved to the driver, and slowly took off down the road. Four hundred yards ahead, she pulled into a driveway on the left and stopped. The black SUV kept going north. She pulled back out onto the road, and drove back to the walled estate with the for sale sign, and parked in the driveway.

"Abby, why are you showing me this place if I'm not buying it?"

She pointed at the gate that kept us from getting onto the property. "This place was built by Tony Ducks. You may not have heard of him, but you've probably heard of his boss. John Gotti.

"Ducks worked for him. As a hitman. He made his reputation when he took out Paul Castellano, head of the Gambino family.

"Gotti rewarded him with a lucrative loan sharking operation in New York. It made him quite wealthy. When the feds turned up the heat on the Gambino family, Tony Ducks came to Florida and built this house. In fact, he built three other houses on this road. The first one, he sold to Steven King."

I stopped her. "Stephen King? The writer? He bought a house from a mafia hitman?"

She nodded. "Yeah, he did. It's a few doors down from here. But we're not going to bother him. He doesn't like visitors."

She continued. "So Tony Ducks built his compound here.

He moved in and did his best to keep a low profile. But he was still working with the Gambino family. When winter set in up north, some of his associates, including Gotti himself, came down here and stayed with him. They'd often have business to discuss. One of the things that came up was suggestions on what Ducks could be doing in Florida to help the family out up north. Ways to bring in more money. Or clean up what they had.

"Tony followed through on some of their suggestions and in the process built up even more wealth for himself.

"Eventually, the feds learned of his activities down here, and he needed a safe house where he could operate unseen. Something low profile, out of the way, and unlikely to attract the attention of the FBI.

"It had to be easy to get to, easy to lose a tail if followed, and if necessary, easy to escape from. Tony wanted it to be on the water with a place to park a boat.

"He turned the search over to a trusted friend, and after a few dead ends, a place was found that fit the bill. The owner didn't want to sell, but for enough money, he agreed to lease it. That worked for Tony, as it didn't create a paper trail. An agreement was reached. Paid in all cash, no questions asked.

"Not wanting to attract attention, they left the property pretty much as it was. No new buildings, no contractors, and no one but Tony's own people allowed through the gate. The place was remote enough that it was essentially invisible to all but those that knew its location.

"Tony continued to live in the big house but ran his Florida operation out of the safe house. The feds never knew it existed. And still don't.

"But they eventually caught up with Tony. He was arrested and charged with several felonies, including money laundering and racketeering. After a long court battle, he was convicted on all charges and sent to federal prison. The feds seized all his assets, including the house in front of us, and everything else he owned.

"The only thing they didn't get was his safe house – because they didn't know about it. It went back to the man he leased it from.

"That man died ten years later, and the property went to his only daughter. She had moved away from Florida and had no interest in ever moving back. She listed the property and it was sold to an investor.

"To make a long story short, the investor went broke, the property went back to the bank, and a few months later, the bank itself went under.

"It wasn't until recently that assets of the failed bank were reacquired by another bank and the safe-house property was finally listed for sale again."

"Our mutual friend in the Keys knew about its past along with some secrets it might still hold and wanted to buy the place for himself.

"But he also knew that if he put his name on the deed, the feds, who've been keeping an eye on his activities, might become curious about why he was buying such a remote place. They might start an investigation.

"Our friend didn't want to risk that, so he needed someone he could trust to buy the place and put it in their name.

"That's where you come in."

Chapter Five

We were still sitting in Abby's van, parked in front of a Mafia hitman's former home. I had a few questions about the story she'd just told me.

"So Abby, let me get this straight. You've signed me up to buy a killer's secret hideaway. Tell me again why I'd want to do that."

She smiled. "You'll be helping out a friend, that's why. And you'll be making a good investment."

She paused then continued, trying to convince me to go along with the plan.

"Like I said before, Boris wants the property. But because the feds are watching him, he can't put it in his name. If he does, they'll wonder why he's buying it and start looking into the transaction. If they find out it belonged to Gotti's hitman, someone who was later convicted of money laundering, they might want to search the place to see what they can find.

"Boris doesn't want that. He's afraid they might come across something that links back to him. Something he'd rather they not know about.

"So he needs someone he can trust to buy the place and hold it for a few years. He's decided that person is you. You should be honored."

I wasn't so sure. "Honored? Because he wants to use me as a patsy? Sure, I can understand why he thinks it's a good deal for him. But what about me? Why would I want to get involved? Is he at least going to front me the purchase price?"

She shook her head. "No, he can't do that. The money has to come from you. The feds always check when a buyer pays cash for a place, and that's what you'll be doing. Paying cash, because there's no time for you to get a loan. Living in an RV and not having a job, you probably wouldn't qualify for one anyway.

"So without a loan, the feds will want to know where the cash came from. If it looks like someone behind the scenes gave it to you, they'll suspect money laundering. If they can prove it, you could end up in federal prison and I'm pretty sure that's not on your bucket list."

It wasn't.

"So when you buy the place, you'll have to pay for it yourself."

I could think of a lot of reasons I wouldn't be doing that. But instead of giving her a list, I decided to play along. I wanted to learn more.

"Okay Abby, let's say I agree to this crazy scheme. The problem is, as you noted, I'm just a poor guy living in an RV. I don't even have a job. What makes you think I have enough money to buy anything? Especially a house?"

She smiled. "Walker, I checked. You're not poor. You have plenty of money in the bank."

I did, but I didn't know how she knew.

"You checked? How could you find out what's in my private bank account? How do you even know where I have an account?"

She smiled, and this time, she reached over and patted my leg, just above my knee. "Walker, you'd be surprised at how easy it was for me to find out where you have accounts and how much money you have in them. For someone with my skills, it was child's play. The only thing I couldn't get into was your safety deposit box. I suspect you have more stashed away in there. As your wife, I probably should have a key."

I shook my head. "Abby, you're not my wife. We're not married and you're not getting a key to my safety deposit box. And since you still haven't bothered to tell me how much I'm supposed to be paying for this place, I'm not sure I'm going to be at the closing tomorrow."

She could see I was a little upset about her having gained access to my bank balances, so she tried to calm me down. "Walker, take it easy. This is actually going to work out in your favor. You'll be investing in a prime piece of Florida waterfront real estate. It's sure to go up in value. Not only that, it'll give you a place you can call home where you can park your RV when you're not on the road."

She lowered her voice and whispered, "It's only going to cost you six eighty-five."

I wasn't sure I heard her correctly. "Did you say six eighty-five? As in six hundred and eighty-five thousand? Is that what you said? I can't spend that kind of money."

Shaking her head, she smiled and said, "Walker, yes, the price is six hundred eighty-five thousand. And yes, you can afford it. In case you haven't been keeping track, as of yesterday, you had just under eight hundred thousand in your savings account. I assume most of that came from the legal settlement with your former employer."

She was right. The money had been awarded to me by a big corporation with lots of government contracts. They had paid me not to talk about certain financial misdeeds I had discovered while in their employ.

My attorney at the time said I'd be a fool not to take them up on the offer. So I happily accepted the money and put it in a savings account, planning to use it to fund my RV lifestyle.

If I were to spend most of it on this property deal, it wouldn't leave me much of a cushion. If I ran out of cash, I'd have to get a job. Something I wanted to avoid at all costs.

"Abby, that won't leave much to live on."

She smiled again. "Walker, don't worry about money. It won't be a problem. When you see the property, you'll understand why. It's on a private bay with direct access to the Intracoastal and the Gulf of Mexico. There's no way you're going to lose money on this deal."

I wasn't so sure. But I did know that waterfront property in Florida was almost always a good investment. If it had the kind of frontage she said, it might be worth looking into. The money in my bank account was just sitting there, doing nothing, drawing almost no interest. Investing it might make more sense.

And as Abby suspected, I had a safety net. Two rolls of gold coins and almost fifty thousand cash tucked away in my safety deposit box.

The truth was, I could afford to invest in real estate if the right property came along.

"Okay Abby, maybe I'm interested. But I need to know more. When can I see the place?"

She shook her head and tapped an imaginary watch on her wrist. "Not today. It's too late. It'll be dark in an hour. We need to get back to our campsites. Maybe pick up dinner on the way. We'll look at the property in the morning. I promise."

Grabbing dinner and heading back to the campground sounded like a good idea. But checking out the place before I bought it made more sense.

"Abby, we have an hour before it gets dark. There should be plenty of time to go see the place. Let's go there first."

She shook her head again. "Walker, I'm telling you, we don't want to go out there this late in the day. It'd be dark when we got there. You won't be able to see anything. It'll be better if you see it in the daylight."

I wasn't buying it. For some reason, she didn't want me to see it. I wondered why.

"What do you mean it'll be dark when we get there? How far away is it?"

She thought before she answered, then said, "It's not that far. It's just that the roads leading to it are unpaved and there are no streetlights. It's kind of dangerous driving around there at night."

I didn't like what I was hearing.

"The roads aren't paved? That doesn't sound good. What else are you not telling me?"

She hesitated for a moment, rubbed her neck, and finally said, "Tony Ducks, the hitman who had the place? He gets out of prison next month."

She paused, then added, "There's a rumor he hid something there and has plans to get it back."

Chapter Six

"Are you trying to get me killed? You want me to buy a place that a mafia hitman feels is his? He gets out of prison, finds out I own the place, and he comes looking for me? I get killed, and then you, being my fake wife, end up with everything? Is that your plan?"

I was being a bit overly dramatic. I really didn't think Abby was actually setting me up to be knocked off by a hitman, but from the outside, it might look that way.

"Walker, you know me better than that. I'm not setting you up. No one is looking to see you get knocked off. The guy's been in prison for twenty years. He's old. Almost eighty. When he gets out, I'm pretty sure there will be a lot of other things he'll want to do before he starts thinking about the houses he used to own in Florida.

"Even if there was a reason for him to come back to the property, he wouldn't want to do anything while there that could put him back in prison.

"Really, there's nothing to worry about. He won't come looking for you."

She sounded like she knew it for a fact, but we both knew there was no guarantee he wouldn't want to visit some of his old haunts after he got out.

But maybe the situation wasn't so bad. Like Abby said, after being in prison for twenty years and getting out at the ripe old age of eighty, he probably had other things on his mind. At least that was my hope.

Abby started her van, put it in gear, and carefully backed

out onto Casey Key road. As we left the driveway of the gated compound with the for sale sign, I knew some of its secrets and how they might affect my future welfare.

It took just a few minutes to leave Casey Key and turn onto Blackburn Point Road. At the light at US 41, Abby took a right into the parking lot of a strip mall. We passed an Ace Hardware store, a Dollar Tree, and a Pinch-a-Penny pool supply. She slowed when we got to a Publix grocery store and found a parking spot between it and a Chinese take-out. After killing the motor, she turned to me and said, "I know you have a lot of questions, and you should. Spending that much money on a place you've never seen is crazy. Even I know that.

"But here's the thing. There are a lot of people looking for waterfront property with the kind of acreage this place has. If I hadn't jumped on it and made an offer as soon as it came on the market, it would be gone by now.

"It really is a good deal. Even if Boris didn't want it, it would be a good investment. But don't take my word for it. Call Anna, your real estate friend. She knows the market and she knows what the place is really worth.

"Call her, ask her straight up if it is something you should buy. Tell her you want the truth. Call her now while I get dinner. You want Chinese or something from Publix?"

The deli in Publix almost always has take-out meals. You got your choice of a meat, two veggies, and a dinner roll. If you hit it on the right day, they'd have fully cooked ribs. Since it'd been three months since I'd eaten meat, ribs sounded good to me.

"If Publix has ribs, get them. Along with cowboy beans and coleslaw. And Hawaiian rolls. If they don't have ribs, get something from the Chinese place. Something with meat in it."

Abby nodded and reached for the door. Before she could get it open, I said, "Wait. Forget all that. Get whatever you want. I'll eat whatever you get. Need any money?"

She smiled. "Ribs it is."

Leaving me in the van, she headed across the parking lot and into Publix. I figured she'd be gone at least ten minutes, maybe more. Plenty of time to call Anna and see what she thought about the place I was supposed to buy.

Even though she was the real estate agent and stood to get a decent commission, I was pretty sure she'd be straight with me. She had been in the past.

Her number was still on my call list from earlier in the day. I hit dial and waited for her to answer.

It rang eight times before she picked up. She sounded slightly out of breath when she said, "Hey Walker, I was kind of expecting you to call. You get cold feet?"

"No, not yet. But I do have a few questions about the place."

I took a breath and continued.

"As you probably know, I haven't seen it yet. In fact, I didn't know I was buying it until you called this morning. I just got into town and Abby has been telling me about the place. It sounds interesting, but she said I should call and see what you think. She said it won't hurt her feelings no matter what you tell me. If you think it's a bad deal, she wants you to let me know.

"So tell me. Am I getting into something I'm going to regret? Is it worth what I'll be paying?"

Before she answered I could hear what sounded like a glass with ice cubes being set down on a wooden table. She was probably sipping on something to help her relax after a long day working with clients.

"Walker, you saved my life once and I'll never forget that. So

31

no matter how much money is involved, I want you to know that I'm not going to lie to you just to get a commission. I wouldn't do that.

"So here's what you need to know. Waterfront property in Florida is really hot right now. It seems like everyone from up north is coming down here, and waterfront is what they want. But there's not much for sale. And what there is, has been priced sky-high if it has a nice house.

"When it comes to vacant land, especially property with any kind of acreage, developers are snapping it up as soon as it comes on the market. They know that as long as they can get the zoning right, they can build it out and make a fortune.

"That's what makes the place you are looking at unique. It has a hundred and eighty feet of waterfront on five acres, with three buildings with a well and septic already in. On top of that, it has a deep water dock with electrical service. The place is a developer's dream and is why I have three full-price backup offers if you bail out.

"If you decide it's not for you, it won't hurt my feelings. I've got people standing in line to buy. In fact, if I had the money, I'd buy it myself.

"But it's not perfect, far from it. It's in a flood zone, so it'll be hard to get insurance. The main house may not be livable, and it's definitely not up to code. The two other structures on the place should be torn down. And most importantly, it's not zoned for multi-family and may not ever be. So it'll be hard to develop.

"The truth is, if it weren't for the fact that it has water frontage on a protected bay with a permitted deep water dock, it wouldn't be worth anything close to the asking price. Especially considering the location.

"But with the frontage and acreage, it's a very unique

opportunity. In fact, there's nothing else like it on the market close to the price. In my opinion, as an investment, it is a very good deal. If you bought it and held onto it for a couple of years, you should have no problem making a decent profit when you sell.

"But like I said, it's not perfect and not move-in ready. No one's lived there for at least ten years. What used to be the main house needs work. The grounds are overgrown and the neighbors are a bit odd.

"You should definitely go and check it out before you decide whether you want it or not. Promise me you'll do that first thing in the morning. Then after you see it, if you want to back out, it'll be okay. Just let me know before closing so I can contact the next person on the waiting list."

I told her I would and thanked her for her opinion. I had just ended the call when I saw Abby heading across the parking lot carrying two grocery bags. I hoped there were ribs in one of them.

I stepped out of the van and went over to see if she needed any help.

She didn't.

Chapter Seven

Abby opened the van's sliding door and put the grocery bags on the floor. She shoved them up against the fridge so they wouldn't fall over as she drove. After getting back in the driver's seat, she turned to me. "So, what did Anna say?"

"I'll tell you over dinner. Did they have ribs?"

"Yep. Hot off the rack. Along with cowboy beans and Hawaiian rolls. And wine."

She put the van in gear and headed out of the parking lot the same way we had come in. When the light at US 41 turned green, she turned right and headed south. A half-mile later, she pulled across the highway into the entrance of Oscar Scherer. The gate was open and when the ranger saw the pass taped to her windshield, he waved us through.

Staying below the posted speed limit, she kept on the main road until we reached the first camping loop on our right. She made the turn and followed the arrows that eventually took us to our campsites. I was happy to see that my RV was still there.

After getting her van backed into her site, she turned to me and asked, "We eating at your place or mine?"

I didn't have to think long before answering. "Mine. There's a lot more room and both our cats are over there. We need to check to make sure they haven't torn the place up."

Abby nodded at the grocery bags. "You get the food. I'll bring the wine."

I reached behind my seat and picked up both bags. One was warm to the touch and heavy. The other, not so much.

With food in hand, I walked over to my RV with Abby close behind. From inside, we could hear two kittens meowing in harmony. Bob and Buddy. I hoped they were okay.

I unlocked the side door and opened it just wide enough to make sure neither cat was waiting to get out. I was pretty sure Bob wouldn't try a runner but I didn't know if Buddy would or not. He was still young and foolish.

From what I could see, neither cat was near the door. I opened it wider and let Abby go in first. As soon as she stepped in, she said, "Wow! What a mess."

Going in behind her, I could see that every toy that Bob owned, along with the remnants of the plastic bag that held his organic catnip was spread out over the floor.

Bob was sitting on top of the couch, giving himself a bath, trying to look innocent. Buddy ran up to Abby, meowing constantly, telling her all about the fun he'd had. His eyes were as big as saucers, it was obvious he had gotten into the catnip.

After he rubbed his head against her ankle, he turned and ran to the closest toy, a stuffed mouse. He quickly snatched it up and ran back to Abby and dropped it at her feet. Then he turned and went back for another toy and did the same thing. While he was making his third trip into the field of toys, Abby pulled out her phone, and snapped off three quick photos of her little Buddy carrying a stuffed toy in his mouth.

After putting her phone away, she bent down and picked him up. He struggled to get away, but she held tight. She kissed him on the head and then carried him over to the couch and sat. Still holding him, she began to stroke his back while saying his name, doing her best to talk him down from his catnip high.

Bob watched, still acting like he was totally innocent. I knew better. He was the only one who knew where I kept the catnip and it had to be him who had gotten it out.

I asked him about it.

"Bob, you did this, didn't you? You got out all your toys so you and Buddy could play, then you found the catnip and got him high. You shouldn't have done that. He might not be used to it like you are."

Bob looked up at me, yawned, and blinked his eyes. It was like he was saying, "It's not my fault the kid couldn't handle a little bit of the good stuff."

While Abby helped Buddy come down from his high, she had me set the table with plates, silverware, and glasses, then had me unpack the food.

She had done well at Publix. Inside the grocery bags were two fully cooked and still warm half racks of ribs, a pint of cowboy beans, and a pint of coleslaw. Before touching the food, I went to the back bathroom and washed my hands.

When I came up front, Abby was pouring two glasses of wine. Buddy was on the couch, apparently sleeping it off. He'd probably wake up with a kitty hangover. It would be Bob's fault.

With the cats out of the way, Abby and I sat down to eat. We were both hungry and didn't say much through the first half of the meal. After we finished off the ribs, she asked me the same question she had asked back at Publix. "What did Anna say?"

I put down the roll I had just bitten into, wiped my hands, and told her.

"She thought it was a good investment, but said I should definitely go out and see it before we go to closing tomorrow. She said after seeing it, if I wanted to back out, it would be fine with her. She had at least three full price back up offers."

Abby smiled. "See, I told you it was a good deal. Even if Boris wasn't involved, it's the kind of place I thought you'd be

37

interested in. Just wait until you see it."

I was hoping she was right. The more I thought about the idea of investing in Florida real estate, the more I liked it. I had just spent six months on the road and it was getting almost impossible to book a site for my RV. All the campgrounds were full and with so many snowbirds flooding into Florida, finding a place to camp was going to get harder and harder.

Now that I had lost my permanent site at Mango Bay, I knew it was time to find a new place I could use as my home base. Somewhere I couldn't be kicked out of or be turned away whenever the next virus hit.

Owning my own private piece of paradise would be the way to go.

After dinner, we cleaned up and sat on the couch with our cats in our laps. I had a lot of questions about the place I was supposed to buy, but also questions about Abby's immediate intentions. She had been telling people we were married and I wondered how far she planned to take it.

Instead of waiting to find out, I asked, "Are you spending the night here with me?"

She looked surprised. "Why are you asking?"

"Well, we're supposedly newlyweds, and we haven't consummated the wedding yet. If we're going to do that tonight, I need to know. I've got to get the bedroom ready."

She reached over and patted my knee. "Walker, don't worry about it. I'm staying at my place tonight. And will probably keep staying there until you at least get the goat smell out of here."

I started to tell her why the place smelled like it did, but she stopped me. "Yeah, I know. You spent the last three months on a goat farm. There was a woman there with you. I don't care about that, but I think you should have at least gotten her to wash the sheets before she left."

She smiled, picked up her cat, and said, "Do yourself a favor. They have washers and dryers over in the bathhouse. Use them. We'll be leaving around eight in the morning. If you get the bedding washed, maybe I'll stay longer tomorrow night."

She headed to the door, carrying Buddy who was still sleeping. As she stepped outside, she waved goodbye, leaving me and Bob to think about what she had just said.

It was definitely time to wash the sheets.

Chapter Eight

The inside of my RV did smell like a goat farm, understandable since I'd spent the past few months tending to goats. But now that I was away from the farm, it was time to get rid of the smell.

Abby said I should start by washing the bed sheets using the washers and dryers in the campground bathhouse. That would have been a good start, but I figured I should do more than just the sheets. I should wash everything, including my clothes, towels, wash clothes, basically anything that wasn't bolted down.

It'd take a lot of quarters to wash everything, but I was ready. I kept a zip lock bag full of them in the driver's door pocket. It came in handy at toll booths or whenever I needed change.

I stuffed the bag of coins into my pants pocket and headed to the back bedroom. There, I stripped the bed and stuffed the sheets into one of my pillowcases. I gathered up my dirty clothes and crammed them into a second case.

Looking like a hobo with the two pillowcases over my shoulder, I headed outside to make the short trek to the bathhouse. When I got there, I was happy to see that the two washers were not in use. I dumped my sheets into one and my clothes into the other. After buying a box of Tide from the wall-mounted vending machine, I poured half into each washer. Then filled the coin slots with quarters to get them started. With everything up and running, I went back to the RV.

Bob was still sitting on the couch, dozing. He wasn't too

interested in what I was doing. But I knew as soon as I came back with warm bedding from the dryer, he'd come alive. It was one of his favorite games – to play hide and seek under the warm sheets as I tried to fit them on the bed.

It was a contest he always won. He had claws and wasn't afraid to use them. I'd play until he drew blood, then I'd bail, leaving him to enjoy his time hiding under the warm sheets.

While I waited for the washing machines to do their thing, I got out my laptop and checked the park's internet connection. Most Florida State Parks don't have WiFi and Oscar Scherer was no different. No internet, at least none supplied by the state.

For me, it wasn't a problem. I had a portable hot spot from AT&T. It gave me internet no matter where I was. Just plug it into a DC power port and when the two lights on the little device turned green, I had WiFi.

I fired up the hot spot and checked my email. There were fifty-seven unread messages – mostly spam. A few looked to be important. I flagged them for later review.

I checked YouTube, Facebook, and a few others sites, just to make sure there was nothing important I'd missed while I was at the goat farm.

There wasn't. Just the typical 'look at me', 'see what I can do' posts, along with nasty replies from basement trolls.

After powering down the laptop, I gathered up the towels and washcloths I'd missed on the first trip over and headed back to the laundry room.

When I got there, the first loads were on the final spin cycle. Not quite done yet. While waiting for them to finish, I checked the lint filters on the two dryers. One was clean, but the other was full of what looked like red and yellow yarn. I figured someone had used the machine to dry a sleeping bag or blanket. I cleaned the filter and put the yarn in the nearby trash can.

When the washers finally spun down, I unloaded each and put the damp clothes and sheets into the two dryers. It cost me another eight quarters to get them up and running.

After putting the load of towels I'd brought over into one of the unused washers, I fed in more quarters and started it up. With all the machines humming, I figured I'd have at least a half-hour before I needed to come back and check on the loads.

Back at the RV, the goat smell was still pretty strong which meant I needed to do more than just run everything through a washing machine. I needed to do some deep cleaning. The good news was I had a tub of lemon-scented disinfecting wipes, a broom, and a small mop, along with some mild liquid detergent. The bad news was there was no one else around to use them. Just me.

I opened all the windows so the smell of disinfectant wouldn't overwhelm either me or Bob. He took it as an invitation to hop back up on the top of the couch, and lean against the screen so he could take in the sights and smells of the tropical oasis outside.

It wouldn't be long before he'd be chattering at some unseen rodent on the ground below us.

With the windows open and Bob out of the way, I went to work. I wiped down all the cabinets, countertops, and sinks, and then swept and mopped the floor. Even though the inside of the RV was relatively small, it still took me thirty minutes to get the job done.

After depositing the trash I'd collected into the dumpster next to the bathhouse, I checked the dryers. They had ended their cycle, but everything was still too damp to take back to the RV. I reluctantly plugged in another eight quarters to get them up and running again.

Rather than stand and wait for the dryers to actually dry, I headed back to the RV.

Inside, it no longer smelled like a herd of goats. At least not to me. I thought about calling Abby and asking her to come over and give me her opinion, but decided against it. Women typically didn't like it when men asks them to smell something. At least not in my experience.

With twenty minutes before my clothes would hopefully be dry, I decided to get out my laptop again and see if I could find anything about the place I was supposed to be buying.

My plan was to enter the property address into Google and see what came up. But I didn't know the address. Abby hadn't given it to me and I hadn't seen the paperwork that would list it along with the price I was supposed to pay.

There were two people who did know, though. Abby and Anna. I could call either one and they'd tell me. But Anna, my real estate friend sounded tired when I spoke to her earlier. She might have been tucked in for the night. I didn't want to wake her if she were sleeping.

Abby was my second choice and even though she was right next door in her RV, I didn't want to bother her - mainly because I was a little embarrassed that I didn't know the address of the place I was about to pay more than a half-million dollars for.

Rather than call either woman, I thought about it for a few minutes and came up with a plan. As the selling agent, Anna would have the property listed on her web page. I could go there, search for a place that matched the general description, and hopefully find the listing.

Even if there were a lot of properties, the place should be easy to find. Anna had said there weren't many others like it on the market.

I entered her name along with the word 'real estate' on Google, and a link to her website popped up. I clicked on it and it took me to a page that had her photo, a brief bio, and her current listings.

Scrolling through them, I quickly found a property described as 'Rare waterfront acreage in Grove city'. I clicked to learn more.

Unfortunately, the details were scant. Just a general description of the place and three photos. The first showed a rusty front gate, with a 'keep out' sign.

The second showed a long boat dock with a caption that read, 'Coast Guard approved deep water dock with direct no-bridge access to the Gulf."

The third was an aerial view with the legal borders outlined in red. You could clearly see the place was located on a small bay just off the Intracoastal waterway, with Stump Pass directly across from it. A canopy of trees hid whatever was at ground level, including any structures that might have existed.

There was no address listed, just GPS coordinates.

I copied those and entered them into Google. The resulting screen showed a large-scale map with a red icon at the center. It gave me my first real understanding of where the property was, and why it may not have had the curb appeal expected of a place costing more than a half-million dollars.

Before I could zoom in to see more detail, I remembered my laundry. I needed to check on it before I got too involved with the map and satellite view.

Chapter Nine

Walking into the laundry room, the first thing I saw was an older woman folding clothes. Looking closer, I realized they were mine.

I smiled. "Ma'am, I think those are my clothes."

She looked up and with a sheepish grin, said, "I'm sorry, but I couldn't help myself. I'm camping here with my husband and well, it's been a while since we spent so much time together in such close quarters. I needed to get out of the trailer and get some fresh air.

"I was walking the loop and decided to check out the laundry room. When I came in and saw the dryers were done and they had clothes in them, I couldn't walk out, knowing the clothes were going to get wrinkled. So I took them out and started folding.

"After raising four kids and doing their laundry for twenty years, checking the dryer became something of a habit. If it was full of clothes, I'd get them out. I couldn't let my kids leave the house wearing anything wrinkled.

"So when I came in here and saw the dryers were done, I couldn't help myself. I started folding. I hope you're not mad."

I smiled. "Me? Mad? Not at all. In fact, I should be paying you. It's probably the first time they've ever been properly folded. So thank you. But now that I'm here, you don't have to keep doing it. I can take over."

She nodded toward the washer as she continued to fold. "Are those yours too?"

"Yes ma'am. They are. I guess I need to put them in the dryer."

Still folding, she said, "You do. If you leave them in there too long, they'll mildew. You don't want that."

I smiled, thinking about how she was giving me the kind of advice she probably gave the children she'd raised.

Rather than be offended by her words, it was nice that she felt comfortable enough around me, a total stranger, to treat me like family. Maybe folding my clothes created a bond between us.

Not wanting to break it, I put the wet clothes in the now-empty dryer, filled the coin slots with quarters, and started it up. Then I moved to the folding table and joined in on the action. The woman had thankfully skipped over my underwear, leaving them for me.

I folded each pair and stacked them on the table. My creases weren't nearly as sharp as hers, but she didn't mention it, nor did she refold any of the things I had done.

With both of us working, the pile of clothes got smaller and smaller. When we got to the sheets, I told her there was no need to fold them. I'd be putting them on the bed as soon as I got back to the RV.

She smiled. "Young man, you should always fold sheets. And towels, too. It shows a bit of class. Doesn't matter if you are going to use them right away or not. It's the right thing to do."

I wasn't going to argue. I nodded and helped her fold the bedding. It was probably the first time the sheets had been folded since new. And probably the last time unless I ran into the woman again.

After everything was done to her satisfaction, I turned to her and said, "My name's Walker. I'm in the RV, right across the road."

She smiled. "Walker? That your first name or last?"

It was a question I got asked often. I gave her my standard answer. "Last. First is John, but everyone calls me Walker."

"Okay, Walker, I'm Carol, Carol Davis. My husband and I are down here from Pensacola, looking for a place to buy. What about you? You here on vacation?"

Since moving full-time into my RV more than two years earlier, I'd never thought about it being a vacation. But I could understand why some people would think it was. I didn't have and didn't need a job, had plenty of money in the bank, and could travel as much as I wanted. Still, it wasn't a vacation. It was just the way I lived.

Rather than tell her this, I just said, "No, not a vacation. I down here buying a place. Supposed to close on it tomorrow."

"Really? You found a place to buy? We've been looking in Venice for months, ever since our home in Pensacola was destroyed by Irma. We haven't found anything. Everything we look at is either too expensive or already sold by the time we ask our agent about it.

"If we don't find something soon, we'll have to move into an RV park and live in our trailer full time. I'm not looking forward to that. Especially during hurricane season. Not after seeing what Irma did to our house.

"The other reason we're looking for a place down here is to be closer to our Cassie. She's our youngest, just out of college. We thought it might be nice to live close to her, maybe help her get started in her new career."

When she paused, it felt like I was supposed to ask about her daughter. I think social norms require it. When a parent mentions a child, you're always supposed to act interested. Whether you are or not.

One way is to ask a follow-up question. Which I did.

"Cassie, huh? Nice name. She's just out of college? What was her major?"

That seemed to be the right question because the woman, Carol, brightened and said, "Paleontology. The study of bones. She was always digging in our backyard and on Dad's job sites. Looking for dinosaur bones. She never found any, but it stuck with her. When she got to college, it was the only degree she was interested in. She's smart and driven, and we hoped she was going to go to medical school, but old bones are what fascinated her."

She paused, probably thinking about Cassie and seeing her little girl grow up. I took the opportunity to ask another question.

"So now that she's got her degree, does it mean she's got a job digging up dinosaur bones?"

Carol shook her head. "No, she took a temp job with Miami U, here in Florida. Doing fieldwork for them at Little Salt Spring near North Port. There's a lot of history there, but no dinosaur bones. Cassie would be the first to tell you, there were no dinosaurs in Southern Florida. The oceans covered most of the state while the dinos were alive. She's finding bones, but not dinosaurs.

"Still, she says she's happy and for us, that's all that matters. Now, if we could just find a place to buy around here, we'd be happy too."

I nodded and when I did, Carol said, "If you don't mind, tell me about this place you're buying. How'd you find it?"

I laughed. "This is going to sound crazy, but I haven't seen it yet. It may not even have a house on it. Truth is, I didn't even know I was buying it until this morning when I got a call from my Realtor. She told me to be at the closing tomorrow and bring my checkbook."

Carol shook her head. "I don't understand. How could you be buying a place you haven't even seen? How could it be closing tomorrow?"

I thought about how crazy my answer would sound if I told her the full story. So instead of giving her all the details, I left out the part about the pretend wife and the mafia hitman. "A friend knew I was looking for a place, and when this one came on the market, she thought it would be perfect. I was off-grid at the time and she couldn't reach me, so she contacted my Realtor and convinced her to write a full-price offer in my name.

"The seller accepted, and well, it looks like I'll be buying the place tomorrow."

"Really? You're buying it sight unseen? I'd never do that. You must have a lot of trust in your friend. And your Realtor."

I nodded. "Yeah, I do. I've worked with both of them before and things went well. Hopefully, it'll go the same way this time."

Wanting to change the subject, I asked, "So you're not having any luck finding a place?"

"No, and our Realtor hasn't been much help. She rarely returns our calls and when we do reach her, she says she's too busy to show us anything. She tells us to do a drive-by and if we like a place, give her a call.

"Usually when we call and get through to her, the place has already been sold. We don't want to move back to Pensacola, but we might have to if we can't find something here."

I nodded. "Venice is a hot market right now. All the snowbirds and COVID refugees moving down from the north are snapping up everything as soon as it is listed.

"Maybe you should consider looking in Englewood. It's eight miles south and has everything Venice has except the crowds and crazy traffic. It has more beaches, more waterfront homes, and prices haven't gone up near as much there. You should check it out."

"Englewood, huh? You think we could find something there?"

"Probably. You could talk to my Realtor. She's in Englewood and is pretty good at finding places."

Carol smiled. "What's her number? I'll call her."

I pointed to the stack of nicely folded clothes and said, "Her number is in my phone back in my RV. If you're going to be here for a minute, I'll take these clothes over and come back with it."

She smiled. "I'll be here. There's another load in the dryer that needs to be folded."

Chapter Ten

Carefully balancing the stacks of recently folded laundry in both arms, I headed over to the RV. I had left the door unlocked and was able to get inside without dropping anything. Bob was on the couch where I had left him, but when he saw me walk in carrying warm sheets, he hopped down and trotted back to the bedroom. He knew the games were about to start.

I followed and carefully set the stacks of folded clothes on the bed. Opening the closet door, I put the shirts on the top shelf next to the camera and computer gear I kept there.

There wasn't room for underwear and cargo shorts, so I stacked them on the floor below the hanging clothes. I was sure Carol would not have approved. Feeling guilty, I picked them up and took them to the bathroom. I cleared a shelf in the linen closet and stacked the shorts neatly next to the socks and underwear. I was pretty sure this would meet her approval.

When I got back to the bedroom, Bob had created a cozy little nest on top of the warm sheets. He was laying on them, purring loudly while making biscuits.

Normally this would be when we'd start the game. I would flap out the bottom sheet and as it settled down on the mattress, he would tuck up under it. He'd hide there in ninja mode, waiting for me to try to pull the fitted sheet over the mattress corner. When I dared to do this, he'd strike out, and if I weren't quick enough, he'd get into me. We'd repeat the process until I was bleeding or got tired of trying to make the bed with him not letting me. I'd give up, tell him he won, and leave him under the sheet. I'd come back and finish the job later when he was off somewhere else.

Being that the sheet game was one of his favorite things, if I hadn't promised Carol I would be right back with Anna's number, I would have stayed and played it with him.

Seeing how he looked pretty content just laying on top of the warm sheet, it probably bothered me more than him that we weren't going to play. Frankly, I kind of enjoyed the game - as long as he didn't get his claws into me.

I let him know I was going to be gone for a few minutes, and with phone in hand, headed back to the laundry room.

Carol was still there waiting for me. She was sitting in one of the plastic chairs along the back wall, reading a tattered copy of People magazine. When she saw me come in, she looked up and said, "You made it back just in time. Your dryer is almost done."

She put the magazine in the empty chair next to hers, stood up with a groan, and walked over to the dryer. The timer showed four minutes were left until the load was done. I wasn't sure that meant the clothes would actually be dry. The first loads had taken two full cycles, and this one being mostly towels and wash clothes would probably take even longer.

While waiting for the load to finish, I pulled out my phone and scrolled down the list of recent calls until I found Anna's number. I turned to Carol and asked, "You have a pencil?"

"No, not on me, but I do have my phone. What's the number?"

I called out the digits as she entered them into her contact list. When I was done, she said, "I'll call her first thing in the morning. You want me to mention your name?"

I couldn't think of a reason for her not to, so I said, "Sure, tell her that Walker said to call. She can thank me when I see her tomorrow afternoon."

I was about to tell Carol more about Englewood, about the small-town feel, and how things were pretty laid back most of the time. But before I could, the dryer dinged, telling me it had completed its cycle.

I walked over, pulled open the door, and reached in to feel the towels. As I suspected, they were still damp. I closed the door, put another four quarters into the slot, and started it up again.

Carol watched as I did this, then said, "Looks like you've got it under control. My husband is probably wondering where I am. I need to get back before he comes looking. I'll leave you here with the clothes, but you have to promise you're going to fold those towels and not just roll them up like a heathen."

I smiled. It had been a long time since anyone called me a heathen. Especially in regards to how I handled my laundry. I didn't want to break the streak, so I said, "I promise. I'll fold them."

She nodded, thanked me for Anna's number, and left me standing near the dryer, wishing the towels would get done quicker.

Rather than go back to the RV, I took a seat in the same chair she had been sitting in, picked up the People magazine, and gave it a look through.

It didn't take me long to get through it. It was filled with articles and photos about people I didn't know. I put the magazine down and checked the dryer. It showed twenty minutes until the load was done.

Without anything else to read, I pulled out my phone and checked my messages. There was just one and it was from Abby. She said she'd be at my door at seven the next morning and expected me to be ready to go with her to look at the property.

I didn't text her back, not wanting to wake her if she were sleeping.

For the next twenty minutes, I killed time checking local news and weather, along with a few websites. Remembering that the property I was supposed to buy was in Grove City, I used Google to find out more about the place.

I learned that Grove City wasn't really a city. In fact, it wasn't anything more than a name on a map. There was no actual city, no main street, no stores, no government, nothing. Just a name a developer had come up with a hundred years earlier when he hoped to sell lots in what he described as a lemon grove paradise.

Unfortunately for him, the lemon trees were killed off by a rare arctic cold front that brought sub-freezing temps to the area. Without the groves, the area never really developed. Homes were never built, paved roads and city water was never put in, and there were not many reasons for anyone to want to live there.

Even a hundred years later, the population was just a handful of people, most of whom lived in mobile homes and traveled unpaved roads to get to them.

The only redeeming factor was that some of the land touched the waters of Lemon Bay which flowed unimpeded into the Gulf of Mexico. Much of that land had been bought by developers with dreams of turning the area into the next Venice.

So far it hadn't happened.

It seemed that the place I was supposed to buy had been overlooked or had been unavailable to them. I would have to ask Anna if it had anything to do with the mafia hit man's ownership.

The dryer finally beeped telling me that hopefully, my

towels were dry. When I checked, they were close enough. I'd hang them on the shower rod in the motorhome and let them air out overnight.

Keeping my promise to Carol, I folded them and took them back to the RV.

Bob, having given up hopes of playing sheet, met me at the door. He followed me to the bathroom and watched as I unfolded and hung the towels. Before letting me leave, he nudged his food bowl, telling me that it needed to be topped off. It was nearly empty and even though he usually doesn't eat much during the night, I didn't dare ignore his request.

I knew that once the kibble reached what he considered a dangerously low level, he would continue to tell me about it until I resolved the situation.

Not refilling the bowl before going to bed meant I'd have to listen to his cries all night long. I'd been through that before and had no desire to repeat it. I grabbed the kitty food and topped off his bowl.

He rewarded me with a snort, then headed off tail high, knowing that he had gotten me to do his bidding for him.

While he was up front at the window checking the goings-on of small critters scurrying about in the night, I quickly made the bed without his assistance. It was after midnight when I finally slipped under the covers.

I didn't wake again until morning.

Chapter Eleven

I hadn't bothered to set my alarm the night before. Abby had said she would be at my door at seven, and I figured when she knocked, that would be my wake-up call. It wouldn't take me long to get ready. All I would need to do was put on shorts, socks, and a tee and I'd be good to go.

But Bob had a different plan.

He was up well before seven and he wanted me to join him. Apparently, he had been woken by a large sandhill crane that had squawked as it wandered past our campsite. He wanted me to see it so he had come to my bedroom and used his ear flicking technique to wake me.

The first time he'd done it, almost two years earlier, I was in a deep sleep and hadn't felt the first tap of his paw against my ear. Had I felt it and responded, the rest of my day would have gone much better.

But I didn't feel that first tap back then, and Bob decided that perhaps he should try a little harder. He tapped my ear again, with more force and a bit of claw. That one got my attention. When I snapped my head to get away from his paw, his sharp claw dug into my ear lobe. The pain along with the blood taught me that whenever Bob tapped my ear to wake me, I shouldn't ignore him.

I didn't think he meant to draw blood that day, but it proved that he could, whether he intended to or not.

So when he tapped my ear wanting me to get up and check out the sandhill crane, I opened my eyes and said, "Okay Bob, that's enough. I'm awake."

I threw off the sheet, sat on the side of the bed, ran my hand through my hair, and looked around for my shorts. Usually, they are either on the side table by the bed or hung on the bedroom doorknob. I liked having them close in case I needed to get them on quickly.

But they weren't in either place.

That's when I remembered I had stacked my cargo shorts along with my underwear and socks in the bathroom pantry.

I made my way there, took care of morning business, and dressed. I had just finished brushing my teeth when I heard a knock at the door. It had to be Abby. Bob didn't know that and he did what he usually does when someone knocks. He runs and hides under the bed.

I went up front, opened the door, and saw her standing there holding Buddy. She smiled and said, "Glad to see you're up. Hope you don't mind me leaving Buddy here today. It'll be safer than taking him with us."

I figured she meant that having a cat riding along can be a challenge if you are making several stops and opening and closing the doors a lot. A young cat like Buddy might be tempted to get out and do a little exploring. If he left the van, it might be a while before we could coax him back in.

"No problem. Bob will enjoy the company. But to be on the safe side, I'll hide the catnip."

Abby took a seat on the couch with Buddy while I moved the catnip from the lower drawer near the sink to a higher more secure location. While I was doing it, Bob came up from the back to see what was going on. He knew the sound of the catnip drawer and wondered if I was opening it for him.

I let him know I wasn't. "Bob, you've got company today and I want you to play nice. Abby and I will be gone for a few hours so you'll be in charge here. Just promise me you two

60

won't tear the place up."

He looked up like he understood what I was saying, but I doubt that he really did or even cared. All he knew for sure was that having Buddy around would give him someone to play with while we were gone. As long as Buddy didn't eat all his food, he wouldn't mind.

He jumped up on the couch, trotted over to Buddy, and playfully swatted at him. The younger cat swatted back and soon the games were afoot. After the playful swats, both cats jumped down from the couch and took off. Bob led the way to the back bedroom with Buddy following close behind.

Abby looked at me and said, "Don't worry. They'll be fine."

She was probably right, but I was always a bit worried when I left Bob behind. I was responsible for his well-being and didn't want to put him in a situation where he might get hurt.

After grabbing my hat, wallet, sunglasses, and keys, we stepped out of the RV. The weather was cool, the campsite was well shaded, and the forecast said the temps wouldn't get above seventy. The cats would be happy inside, especially since the windows were open. As long as they didn't bust through the screens, they'd be okay.

Abby went over to her van, unplugged from shore power, and after making sure she hadn't forgotten anything, we headed out. She was driving, I was in the passenger seat holding on.

As soon as we left the campground and got on US Forty One heading south toward Venice, she asked, "So, McDonald's or Burger King?"

I hadn't had time to eat and knew both places had pretty decent breakfast biscuits. But since we were in a camper van, I knew we wouldn't be using the drive-through. I also knew it would be a lot easier on Abby if she didn't have to cross four lanes of traffic to get into a place.

"Burger King is on this side of the road. It's just up ahead and the parking lot is easy to get into. I vote we go there."

She nodded, "I was hoping you'd say that."

After pulling in and parking on the far side of the lot, she turned to me and said, "Get me sausage egg croissant, no cheese, and a small coke. I'll wait for you here."

I smiled, knowing that her tastes in breakfast foods were pretty much the same as mine. Simple and quick. I opened the door. "I'll be right back. Don't leave without me."

She smiled. "I never leave a man behind, especially if he's bringing me food. Just hurry, I'm hungry."

I was hungry too and happy that there was no line inside at the counter. Most of the people buying breakfast were going through the drive-through. It was usually faster that way. Stay in your car and have food delivered to the take-out window.

When traveling in an RV or camper van, you don't have that option. Most drive-thrus were too low and too narrow for an RV. If you forgot and tried to go through one, you could rip off your roof, peel off your side wall, or just get stuck. It simply wasn't worth the risk.

Still, there were advantages to being in an RV even at a fast food joint. You could park in the lot, go inside, get your food, then go back to your camper and eat in the comfort and privacy of your home. You could wash up in your own bathroom and if you felt like it, take a nap or watch a little TV before you drove off.

Since most fast-food places have free WiFi extending out into the parking lot, you could stay awhile and surf the web in the privacy of your home on wheels, if you wanted to.

We didn't do any of that. I went in, got our food, and went back out to the RV, happy to see it was still in the parking lot. As promised, Abby hadn't left without me.

Inside the van, we moved to the back and sat on the twin beds, and ate our croissants. We washed them down with our cokes and then got back out on the road.

Abby said that with snowbird traffic it would take us almost an hour to go the twenty miles to Grove City. It wasn't that there were a lot of cars, it was just that most of the retirees out in the early morning were in no real hurry to go anywhere.

The locals who had places to go and jobs to get to would jockey around the slower-moving cars making traffic feel like a game of frogger. Move the wrong direction at the wrong time, you'd get squashed.

Many of the snowbirds didn't know their way around town. They'd miss a turn and come to a full stop unexpectedly in the middle of the road, or go for miles with a right or left turn signal on, leaving others to guess whether they were planning to turn at some point in the future or had turned in the past and wanted us to know of their accomplishment.

It was a relief when we left busy US Forty One behind and turned onto Englewood road, also known as State Road Seven Seven Six. It was four lanes wide and smooth with almost no traffic. The posted speed limit was forty-five and the few cars around us were easily doing that and more. Abby stayed in the right lane, out of their way, and drove with a smile on her face.

But then things got weird.

Chapter Twelve

After going about five miles on Englewood Road, Abby slowed and hit her right turn signal. Apparently, she decided we needed to make a stop. Looking ahead, the only place on our side of the road was Babe's Ace Hardware. Maybe she needed something for the van.

She pulled into the driveway and parked near the front door. After killing the motor, she turned to me and said, "We're going to need hedge cutters and a pruning saw. Heavy-duty ones. And you'll need work gloves. Don't cheap out. Get the good stuff. I'll wait for you out here."

Abby was like this. Taking it for granted she could give me orders and I would follow them. Of course, it was my own fault. She'd learned I almost always did whatever she asked of me. Not because I was a pushover or afraid of her. It was hard to be afraid of someone that was barely five feet tall in heels.

I usually did what she asked because there was almost always a good reason behind her requests. Still, it didn't hurt to ask about this latest list of goods she wanted me to buy.

"Hedge cutters and a pruning saw? Why?"

She was ready with her answer. "The driveway. It's overgrown. I don't want to scratch my paint."

Before I could say 'Okay, that makes sense', she continued. "You're going to want to cut everything back because if you don't, you'll tear up your RV when you take it over there tomorrow.

"So go inside, get clippers and gloves. I'll be waiting out

here."

I smiled. "As you wish my dear."

She should have known better than to send a grown man like me into a hardware store, especially an old-fashioned one like Babes. Inside, it was wall-to-wall tools and screws and nuts and bolts and paint and lots and lots of shelves filled with gadgets that needed to be looked at.

Being located in Englewood and so close to the beach, the store also had fishing and boating gear, and even RV accessories. All of which I had to check out.

Fifteen minutes later, I was in the outdoor section trying to decide which Weber barbecue grill I liked best. The Genesis II was nice, but at a thousand dollars, it seemed like a lot of money just to grill burgers. The smaller Webers made more sense, but the bigger one had my attention.

It was about then that someone tapped on my shoulder. I turned expecting to see a store employee, but instead, it was Abby. She was shaking her head when she said, "I don't see you carrying a hedge cutter? Are they out?"

I was caught. She had sent me to the store to get clippers and gloves and I had failed her. I had gotten distracted by all the other things vying for my attention. I came up with what I hoped was an acceptable answer to her question.

"Abby, they're up front. I was back here looking for gloves. Maybe you can help me find them."

Still shaking her head, she took my hand and led me up front to the garden department. There, she quickly located a display of shears and pruning saws. Next to them, a rack of work gloves."

Without saying anything, she picked up a Fiskar hedge cutter and a matching Fiskar Ultrasharp lopper. She handed both to me, then she grabbed a pruning saw and two pairs of leather work gloves. Size small for her and extra-large for me.

Without giving me time to get distracted by the other garden tools on the same rack, she grabbed the sleeve of my shirt and led me to the checkout. The cashier rang up the purchases, I paid, and we headed outside.

After I put the tools in the back of her van, I climbed into the passenger seat and sat there quietly. Abby started the motor and pulled back out onto Englewood road.

I figured I was in for it. I had spent way too much time in the hardware store, knowing she was waiting for me outside. I deserved whatever she was going to say.

But instead of getting mad, she said, "So you're thinking about getting a grill, are you? Does that mean you'll be cooking me burgers and steaks sometime soon?"

I nodded. Relieved that she wasn't too upset about my loss of focus in Babes. Since she'd mentioned the grill, I figured it was a safe subject to talk about.

"Yeah, I think having one would be nice. I just have to figure out which one I want and where to put it. I don't think any of the ones I saw back there will fit in my RV."

She smiled. "If you buy the place we're going to look at, you'll have plenty of room for a grill. You can get the biggest one you want. And if you're nice to me, I might even show you how to cook steaks without burning them."

We continued to talk about grills and steaks and burgers until we reached the light at Placida road. It was about halfway through Englewood. A large Publix grocery store was on our right, sharing a shopping center with Bealls clothing. Across the way, another shopping center with a Winn-Dixie and a Pet Supermarket. I had shopped these places before and knew where we were.

But when Abby turned right onto Placida road, I was quickly

out of my element. I knew the road would eventually take us through Grove City and end up at the toll bridge leading to the island of Boca Grande, but I'd never driven it myself.

A mile beyond the turn, the retail establishments of Englewood were replaced by boat storage yards and small engine repair shops. Two miles beyond those, the area turned into a retail desert. No stores, no shops, just tropical landscape and peek-a-boo views of Lemon Bay.

Eventually, we came to a series of streets heading off to our right. All with state names. Michigan, Georgia, Arkansas, Mississippi, Pennsylvania, and others. It was almost like the person in charge of naming them had pulled out a map and named the streets after the states he had visited.

I never did see a 'Welcome to Grove City', sign, but Abby said the state streets were part of it and the road to the property was just two miles ahead.

After passing a Dollar General Store, Abby slowed and turned right onto an unnamed and unpaved road. The surface was typical of dirt roads in Florida. Crushed seashell on top of hard-packed sand.

We traveled about a hundred and fifty yards, passing two older mobile homes before Abby slowed again. Ahead of us, the limbs of a Brazilian Pepper tree had grown out over the road far enough that they would scrape the side of her van.

Abby didn't need to tell me to get out and start cutting. I knew what needed to be done. I grabbed the lopping shears, along with my gloves, and headed over to the offending branches.

The sharp blades of the shears made quick work of them. I cleared a path wide enough for her van. Instead of getting back in with Abby, I walked ahead and cleared away other branches that were in the way. There weren't a lot of them, but the ones that were could definitely have done damage to her camper.

After about twenty minutes of clearing away brush, we came to an iron gate that spanned the road. The gate appeared to have been originally painted white, but most of the white had flaked away revealing a light coat of reddish rust.

A sign hanging from it read 'Private Property. No Trespassing."

Abby pulled up close, killed the motor, and got out. She locked the van doors and walked over to me. "What do you think so far?"

I pointed at the rusted gate. "This is it? This is what I'm supposed to be paying more than a half-million dollars for?"

She nodded. "Yep, this is it. But don't worry, it gets better. A lot better."

As it turned out, she was right. It got a lot better.

Chapter Thirteen

The gate was locked and we didn't have a key. But that didn't stop Abby. She hitched up her pants and climbed over. She almost got stuck at the top and I was tempted to help her by giving her butt a push but decided against it. If she wanted me touching her butt, I was sure she'd tell me. She had once before and we weren't anywhere near a gate back then.

After she landed safely on the other side, it was my time to climb over. I'd had a lot of experience climbing over cattle gates in my youth, and knew that the only thing you had to worry about was how well the gate hung on the hinges. If they were weak, the gate could fail when you put your full weight on it. If you were on top when the hinges gave way, you could end up on your back with the heavy gate on top of you.

I wanted to avoid that.

Abby didn't weigh enough to put any stress on the hinges, so her getting over without a problem didn't count. It might be a different story for me. I weighed around one-eighty almost twice her weight.

So before I climbed up on it, I put my full weight on the bottom crossbar. As expected, the gate shifted downward. But not enough to worry about. At least that's what I thought.

Using the second crossbar as a step ladder, I hoisted myself up over the top and jumped down onto the other side where Abby was waiting.

She shook her head. "Took you a while to get over. Are you getting too old to do this kind of thing?"

I knew she was joking. I was only three years older than she was, with both of us being in our mid-thirties and in good physical shape. I could have gotten over it a lot faster. The next time I definitely would, but on that first try, I wanted to be sure the gate could hold me.

I didn't have to explain it to Abby. She already knew why I took my time. I was being careful. I had been badly hurt in an accident a few months earlier and didn't want to re-injure myself.

She pointed to the trail leading away from the gate. "The road on this side is not nearly as overgrown. When we come back tomorrow we won't have much to clear away. We'll just have to watch out for snakes."

I looked at her shaking my head. "This place just gets better and better. Snakes?"

Smiling, she said, "Alligators too. There might be some around and it's mating season. You know what that means."

I did. Gators were a lot more active during mating season. They'll leave the safety of their underwater hidey-holes and head up onto dry ground looking for a little loving. When they found it, you didn't want to be in their way.

Abby turned and headed up the path that once was the driveway leading into the property. Not hearing me following her, she stopped and said, "Come on, there's something up here you need to see."

I quickly caught up and we walked in the middle of the old driveway until it opened into a wide clearing. In the center, sat a military-style Quonset hut. The kind used by the military for barracks or airplane hangers.

The one in front of us still had its army issue olive drab

paint scheme. The flat front of the structure had two windows covered with hurricane shutters. A metal door was strategically centered between them. A single wooden step led to a deck in front of the door. The entire structure sat on a dirt berm raised about four feet above the surrounding ground.

Abby nodded at the building. "There's three of them on the property. The guy who originally owned this land bought them when they closed down the Army Airfield in Venice after World War II. They were being sold as military surplus. He thought they would be cheaper to put up than any barn he could build.

"He bid on five and won the three that are here. The one in front of us is the biggest. The other two are smaller.

"He had to disassemble each one over at the airbase, load the parts onto a flatbed truck, and then cut a road to get the pieces back here.

"One of the ones he bought had been the officer's quarters, so he put it up first. His winning bid included the interior walls, the furniture, and fixtures, even the hardwood flooring. With a couple of friends, they put it together and ended up with what you see in front of you.

"It turned out a lot nicer than the farmer thought it would, so instead of using it as a barn, he decided to make it his home.

"It wasn't fancy, but it was well built and designed to withstand high winds and even the occasional hurricane."

She paused to take a breath while I thought about what she had just told me. Instead of having a real house on the property, the place had an old World War II Quonset hut pretending to be a house. That probably turned off a lot of potential buyers who were looking for a move-in-ready place. That, along with the possibility of having to avoid gators and snakes at their front door.

I turned to Abby to ask what the Quonset hut was like

inside, but before I could get the words out, she said, "I haven't been in it yet, but supposedly it's livable. Or at least it was, at one time. It has a kitchen, two bedrooms, and two baths.

"The other two huts are over by the water. One was used to store farm equipment and the other was set up as a workshop. The workshop is locked and I don't know what's in it. There's an old boat under the other hut."

She paused again, then said, "What I do know is when Tony Ducks needed a place to run his business without the Feds knowing about it, he convinced the owner of this property to lease it to him. I'm not sure how he did that, but I suspect it involved money and maybe some threats.

"In any case, Tony got the lease, put up the gate out front, and brought his guys in to update the main building. He added air conditioning, modern appliances, a TV, and even a satellite dish. He had the boat dock rebuilt, ran shore power to it, and made it ready for his go-fast boat.

"He set up one of his guys as the caretaker and came out here when he needed to do things in private. Or take his boat somewhere.

"When he learned the feds were about to close in on him, he ordered his guys to leave town. He didn't want them to be caught up by the FBI and forced to testify against him. After that, the property sat idle for a few years. Eventually, it went back to the daughter of the original owner. You know the rest of the story."

I wasn't sure I did. Abby had said that at some point the property had been sold to a developer, who eventually went bankrupt, and the bank had taken it back. But that's all she'd said. No mention of the Quonset huts.

So far, I wasn't impressed. The place looked to be just a few acres of overgrown brush possibly inhabited by snakes and gators. I couldn't see spending over a half-million on it.

"Abby, I think this is way overpriced for what it is."

She nodded. "Yeah, that's what I thought the first time I saw it. But something changed my mind and I think when you see what I'm going to show you next, it'll change yours too."

She turned away from the Quonset house and took off down a recently cleared path through the trees. I followed, being careful where I stepped. If there were snakes or gators around, I didn't want to disturb them.

Chapter Fourteen

I could hear the boat before I could see it. A low rumble of diesel motors at idle. At first, I thought the sound might be coming from an airplane. There are a lot of private pilots in the Venice area, and they often follow the coastline when they take their single-engine planes out for a spin.

These prop-driven planes make a lot of noise, especially when they fly low as they often do. But there was no aircraft overhead, at least none that I could see through the palm trees that partially blocked my view of the sky.

Abby was about fifteen steps in front of me when she stopped and said, "You'll want to see this."

I caught up with her and saw why she had brought me this way. We'd come to the edge of the property, clearly defined by a concrete seawall between us and what looked like a protected bay of calm water. It looked to be about two hundred feet wide. On the other side, dense tropical foliage, with no signs of human activity. No houses, no boat docks, nothing to suggest the land had ever been developed. That in itself was unusual for waterfront property in this part of Florida.

Again, Abby gave me the answer before I could ask the question. She pointed across the bay and said, "It's preserve land. It can never be developed. It'll always be that way. You'll never have neighbors on that side."

She turned and pointed down the seawall, "Your side of the bay has a dock. A big one. And there's someone there waiting to see you."

She took off along the edge of the seawall heading toward the sound of the motor. The wall followed the natural contour of the property. As it snaked around a slight bend, I got my first glimpse of the boat dock. As Abby had said, it was big. At least 12 feet wide and forty feet long. Made out of what looked like poured concrete with car tires serving as bumpers hanging off each of the supporting rails.

More surprising than the size of the dock was the boat tied up to it. It was at least fifty feet long, painted a brilliant white with deep blue accents. It had two decks with a row of dark tinted glass on each level. Solar panels on the top along with an array of antennas and a rotating radar arm suggested the vessel was well equipped for long-distance hauls.

Calling it a boat was not a fair description. It was clearly a yacht, an impressive one at that. The name on the back was Charon. Maybe a woman's name. Maybe not. I'd have to look it up later to see what it meant.

A folding walkway had been extended from the boat to give easy access to the main deck from the dock. Abby was a few steps ahead of me when we reached what in the olden days would have been called a gangplank. She stopped and nodded toward a man on deck dressed in all white. He nodded back but said nothing.

I stopped beside her and said, "Nice boat. I assume it belongs to our friend from Key West."

She smiled. "It does. And he wishes to speak with you."

Our friend's name was Boris Chesnokov. I'd helped him out of a mess several months earlier, and he was very appreciative. Money and support, any time I wanted it, even if I didn't ask. He was quite generous when he wanted to be. But I had heard that he could be ruthless as well, when the situation warranted.

Obviously, staying on his good side was the healthy choice. Those who didn't, discovered the difficulty of swimming in concrete overshoes. I didn't actually know whether that was true or not, but those that crossed him often disappeared.

Abby whispered, "You'll want to hear him out. Listen carefully to what he says, then decide whether you want to buy the property or not. He isn't going to force you to do it. If after your talk, you decide not to buy, just tell him. He has a backup person ready to step in, but he needs to know before you leave the boat today whether you'll be at the closing or not."

I nodded. "Good to know I have options. The backup buyer will make my decision easier."

Had Abby not shown me the long water frontage along the protected bay, I wouldn't have wanted the property at any price. But seeing how a boat the size of Boris' yacht could easily get into the bay and tie up at the dock, I was beginning to understand why the place might be a very good investment.

I was pretty sure I was going to go through with the deal but wanted to hear what Boris had to say first. I had a feeling his interest in it had more to do with Tony Ducks and what he may have left behind than it did with the land itself.

I was about to find out I was right.

Chapter Fifteen

We watched as the man on deck, who I assumed was either the captain or chief steward, touch his earpiece. He spoke a few words then nodded in our direction. Abby nudged my shoulder. "Looks like he's ready to see you."

The captain smiled, unlatched the gate leading onto the deck, and beckoned in my direction. "Mr. Chesnokov invites you to join him in the lounge."

I turned to Abby. "I guess it's time. Ladies, first."

She shook her head. "No, I'm not going. He wants to talk to you. Alone. No one else. Just you. He made that clear when I spoke with him this morning."

I was surprised she hadn't mentioned speaking to Boris earlier. I was also surprised she wasn't going with me to hear what he had to say. She was the one who had gotten me involved by pretending to be my wife, so in my mind, she should be with me when I met with Boris.

But she wasn't going to be.

And she knew that before we even left the RV park.

No doubt there were a lot of other things about this deal she hadn't told me. But with Abby, I shouldn't have been surprised. It was just the way she was. She held things back. Sometimes, important details that might change the outcome of whatever it was she was trying to get me to do.

Like I said, I should have expected as much. But since I was already neck-deep in the deal, I couldn't bail without first hearing what Boris had to say.

"Okay, I'll go in by myself. But we need to have a talk

when I come back out. If you want me to trust you, you're going to have to change your ways."

I took a step intending to go up the gangplank, but Abby grabbed my shirt and whispered. "Take off your shoes. It's a yacht, you don't wear shoes on deck."

She was right. I'd been tromping through the woods and had dirt and mud and leaves on my shoes. If I didn't take them off, I'd leave a muddy trail of debris on the pristine decks of Boris' boat. He probably wouldn't like that.

I took them off and set them on the dock next to where Abby was standing. My socks were clean, having washed them the previous night.

I was happy about that.

Standing there in my stocking feet, I turned to her and said, "Anything else?"

I was being sarcastic and didn't really think I'd need to take anything else off, but I was wrong.

She pointed to my pants. "Your phone. Leave it with me."

She didn't have to explain why. Boris wouldn't want me carrying anything that could record our private meeting. More than a few of his brethren had ended up in prison when recorded conversations had been used as evidence against them. He wasn't going to risk it happening to him.

Pulling my phone out of my pocket, I handed it to Abby.

When she took it, she asked, "If any women call, you won't mind if I tell them I'm your wife, will you?"

She was joking.

At least I thought she was. But since I didn't think any women would be calling, I said, "No, not at all. Tell them whatever you want."

It might have been a mistake saying that.

Leaving my shoes on the dock and my phone in Abby's hand, I headed up the gangplank. When I reached the Captain, he smiled and said, "Welcome Aboard the Charon. Please follow me."

He led me to the center of the boat. From there we went down three steps to a room separated from the open deck by a wall of dark tinted glass. When he pressed a doorbell-sized button at the edge of the wall, the center panel slid to the right, creating a doorway into a room with a dramatic view over the bow to the open water beyond.

To say I was impressed, would be an understatement. It was truly a million-dollar view on a boat that likely cost at least that much.

The Captain waved me into the room. Hesitantly, I stepped in. Almost as soon as I did, the glass door behind me slid closed. The Captain remained outside, resuming his assigned duties, whatever they might have been.

After my eyes adjusted to the light, I saw that I wasn't alone. Boris was in there with me, sitting in a leather recliner strategically positioned to give him a view of anyone entering through the glass door without them immediately being able to see him.

When he saw I had finally noticed him, he stood, walked over, and reached out to shake my hand. "Walker, I'm glad you could join me."

I could have said something snarky like, "I didn't really have a choice," but knew better. And really, I liked Boris and was happy to see him again. And happy he had survived the virus. I shook his hand and said. "Good to see you. Nice boat."

He nodded. "It is. I've just acquired it from an associate who ran into some financial difficulties. I like to think I helped him out by taking it off his hands.

"He wasn't going to be in a position to use it for the next five to ten years and it would have been a shame to let such a fine vessel go to waste. We reached an agreement, and now the boat is mine.

"If you like, I'll give you a tour later on."

I nodded. "Yes, I'd like that."

He pointed to a fully stocked bar built into the wall. "Would you like a drink?"

I wasn't sure of the proper response when a mafia boss offers you a drink, but since I wasn't thirsty and wanted to hear what he had to say, I declined.

"No, I'm fine. Thanks anyway."

He nodded. "Maybe later."

He pointed to a leather chair that matched the one he had been sitting in. "Have a seat."

This time, I didn't hesitate. I sat.

After he took the chair across from me, he gazed out over the water and said, "It's beautiful here. I can see why Tony Ducks picked this place."

Then he turned and asked me what I considered to be an odd question. "Are you familiar with the TV show, The Curse of Oak Island?"

I didn't watch much TV, but I had seen a few episodes of the show and knew what it was about. "Yes, I've seen it."

"Good, then you know they are searching for buried treasure supposedly hidden centuries earlier in something they call the money pit."

I nodded. "Yes, the money pit. Not sure it really exists, but if it does, I hope they find it and it's filled with gold and valuable artifacts."

He smiled. "I'm glad to hear you say that. Because I think there's a money pit on this property. And I want you to find it."

He paused to let the words sink in. A money pit. On the property he wanted me to buy. If anyone else had suggested there was such a thing in this part of Florida, I would have laughed in their face. If you live in the area, you know that when digging, after you scrape away the first few feet of topsoil, you hit hardened coral mixed with limestone. Mother Nature's version of concrete.

Unless using heavy equipment and explosives, there was little chance of being able to dig an actual money pit on the property. At least not like the one on Oak Island which was supposedly hand dug to a depth of a hundred and sixty feet. There was no way anyone could dig that far down into the soil on the west coast of Florida. They'd be lucky to go six feet before hitting the limestone hard pack.

True, there were lots of stories about caches of gold being hidden along Florida's coasts. Mostly involving pirates. But in reality, pirates didn't bury treasure. They squandered their plunder on booze and booty.

Bury it instead of spending it? Never happened.

The only treasures actually found in Florida were those from Spanish shipwrecks. The Treasure Fleet of 1715 being the most famous. Thirteen ships laden down with gold and silver heading from Cuba to Spain were caught up in a fierce hurricane. Eleven were destroyed, scattering precious cargo along a hundred miles of the eastern shore of Florida.

Tons of gold coins and silver bars, along with gems and intricately carved jewelry sank with the ships. Over the years, shifting sands, tidal changes along with raging hurricanes brought some of the treasure ashore. Even today, gold and silver coins occasionally wash up on what is now known as the sands of the Treasure Coast.

But those treasure beaches are on the other side of Florida, a long way from the coast we were on. The hard ground here, the lack of verifiable stories about hidden treasure in the area, made a strong argument against the idea of a money pit being nearby.

I could have shared this with Boris, but didn't. I didn't want to tell him he was wrong; that there was no way there was a money pit nearby, so I kept my mouth shut.

My silence probably gave me away. He likely guessed what I was thinking because he smiled and said, "You must think I'm crazy. Talking about a money pit and buried treasure.

"And you'd be right. I'd be crazy to believe that someone has dug a deep hole and buried treasure around here. But there is a reason I call it a 'money pit.' I think you'll understand after I tell you more."

He pointed to the liquor cabinet. "You sure you don't want that drink?"

Chapter Sixteen

Boris got up from his chair, went to the bar, and poured us drinks. He handed me a glass filled with a golden liquid and said, "Taste this."

I'm not much of a drinker, especially of hard liquor. It's not that I have anything against drinking. It's just that if I drink too much, it makes me feel old the next morning.

I don't like feeling old.

But I figured it wouldn't hurt to try a little of what Boris was offering. I was thinking there was no way I could get drunk from just one glass. Even if I did, Abby was driving.

I thanked him for the drink but didn't dare take a sip until he sat back down. I didn't know much about drinking etiquette but figured a guest should wait for the host to tip his glass first.

I'm glad I waited.

As soon as Boris sat, he nodded in my direction, held out his glass to make a toast, and said, "To Duckville and the money pit."

That was the first time I heard the place had a name. Duckville. I guess it fit, being named after Tony Ducks.

I still didn't think there'd be a money pit, but I repeated the toast and we clinked glasses. Then we tasted our drinks.

My first impression was the liquid tasted like honey and went down smoothly. There was no after burn, no indication it contained alcohol. It could have been a health drink for all I knew.

After the first sip, Boris placed his glass on the table nearest his chair, then asked, "Have you ever heard of a booze cruise?"

I smiled, thinking back to the last time I was in Key West. While walking along the docks, I had picked up a brochure for one of the nightly booze cruises. The boats, mostly barges or wide catamarans, would take passengers out on the bay. They'd head out about an hour before sunset and stay out long enough to see the sun go down over the horizon.

While some of these cruises were geared to older clientele who preferred hor d'oeuvres and wine, the boats promising true booze cruises targeted the younger crowd by offering an open bar with unlimited free drinks.

The brochures for these usually included photos of bikini-clad girls with drinks in their hands and smiles on their faces. Had the photos been taken after the cruises ended, the smiles might not have been so broad. The makeup not so perfect. The combination of heavy drinking on a rocking boat likely induced severe cases of seasickness in many a landlubber.

I was still thinking about this when Boris said, "I can tell by your smile that you have heard of them. That's good, it will make it easier for you to understand what I tell you next.

"As a reward for services rendered, John Gotti made sure that Tony Ducks received a percentage of the profit from certain operations he had overseen while he was living up north. When Ducks retired to Florida, that cash flow continued.

"The problem was, Ducks couldn't spend the money freely unless he had a way to show the IRS it was legally obtained. That would have been difficult due to the nature of the businesses he was involved with.

"He needed a way to clean the money. The easiest way was to start an all-cash business. Like a laundromat, a bar, or a pawnshop. Then make it look like the cash flowing through it was legitimate.

"But Tony didn't want to go through the trouble of actually running a real business. He just wanted it to look like he had one that could generate the kind of cash he wanted to clean.

"He had visited Key West and seen the booze cruises and decided they would be perfect for what he needed. They were mostly all-cash, and his bookkeeper would have no problem laundering any amount of money through one.

"The way Tony figured it, if his booze cruise charged a hundred dollars a person, and he had a boat that could take out sixty people on each daily cruise, he could show six thousand cash income per day.

"If he ran his boat thirty days a month, he could show up to a hundred eighty thousand dollars of cash flow each month, which meant he could launder a lot of money. Maybe even do it for some of his friends from up north.

"So he had his accountant set everything up. They created a new company, got all the required permits and licenses, and everything else they needed. The only thing they didn't get was a boat. Because Tony didn't think he needed one. The business would exist only on paper. A boat and crew would just add unnecessary overhead and other problems he didn't want to deal with.

"He figured if the IRS ever sent someone down to Key West to look into his booze cruise business, he could tell them the boat was out of service or in for repairs. Worse case, he could buy a broken-down boat in one of the nearby boatyards and show it to the IRS. It wouldn't be unusual for it to be out of the water for annual maintenance or updates.

"To make it look more like a legitimate operation, Tony came up with a business name, printed up some flyers which he never handed out, and rented a mailbox with a Key West address. On paper, it looked like the real deal. His accountant immediately started showing daily income from the fictional cruises."

"As it turned out, it was a huge success, at least on paper. Being in Florida, he didn't have to worry about paying state income taxes on his imaginary profit, and his accountant was able to create enough fake boat expenses to minimize his federal tax burden.

"As a bonus, having a business in Key West, even a fake one, gave Tony an excuse to maintain an office there and to make frequent trips to the area. The only real problem was after he had legitimized his cash flow, he had lots of money he could freely spend.

"At the time, there were plenty of things to spend big money on in Key West. The most interesting, at least to Tony, were the salvage items being brought up by treasure divers.

"Most of these were small operators working with limited funds. They would take their boats out whenever they could afford fuel and search the nearby reefs for spoils of past shipwrecks.

"More often than not, they'd come home empty-handed. But once in a while, they'd get lucky. They find a few gold coins or one or two silver bars. Not enough to make them rich, but enough to refuel their boats and recharge their scuba gear.

"These were the people Tony sought out. He knew they needed cash to keep their operations going, and he had a feeling that buying gold and silver coins might be a way to protect his wealth should the IRS catch on to his booze cruise business."

Boris paused and took another sip from his glass. I did the same.

After he put his drink down, he continued his story.

Chapter Seventeen

"So Tony was down in Key West getting to know the people who ran the treasure salvage boats. He befriended them, by paying more than they asked for the gold coins and silver bars they found.

"Word got around he'd buy anything made of gold, no questions asked. Key West was pretty much an anything-goes place back then and Tony's willingness to buy gold and silver didn't seem to raise any eyebrows. There were a lot of strange people there at the time, and compared to them, Tony Ducks seemed to be a fairly normal guy.

"He did eventually buy a boat. But not for his booze cruise business. Each trip down from his estate in Casey Key meant he spent hours on the narrow roads getting to Key West. More often than not, they'd be jammed with slow-moving tourist traffic that made what should have been a four-hour drive an all-day affair.

"When he eventually got to Key West after the long drive, he would have to find a safe place to stay and run his gold buying business. During season, all the high-end hotels would be fully booked, and since buying gold meant he was always carrying a lot of cash, he had to be careful. He was vulnerable on the drive down as well as wherever he ended up staying.

"He knew that as word spread he was traveling with a lot of cash, someone would eventually try to take it from him. He always kept a gun nearby but worried if he had to use it, it would bring unwanted attention to what he was doing. He decided the best way to avoid being a target was to get a boat. One big enough to get him to Key West and give him a place to stay once he got there.

"With help from a broker, he found and bought a yacht. In fact, he bought the one we are on right now. The Charon. It was luxurious, could handle open water, and was fast enough to get him to Key West in half a day. Once there, he wouldn't have to worry about finding a hotel room. He could stay on the boat.

"He'd come into town every two or three weeks, usually on a Monday, and anchor out in the bay. His pal, Joey Guzik, who accompanied him, would take their skiff into town and let potential sellers know they were there to buy gold. If they had something of interest, Joey would pat them down to make sure they weren't carrying a weapon, and then take them out to meet Tony on his yacht.

"There, the seller would either make a deal and get paid or be sent away disappointed. Being offshore meant only those who Tony invited onto the boat, could get to him. It was definitely safer than going into town carrying a suitcase full of cash.

"In the years that he did this, he bought a lot of gold. From treasure salvors who had found it on the ocean floor. Or pawn shops needing to raise cash. Or from people who snuck into the homes of others at night and took their gold while they were sleeping."

Boris paused and looked out at the water. He took a breath and reached into his shirt pocket and pulled out an old photo. He looked at it for a moment, then said, "I was in Key West back then. Running my own business. I had a house in town. Not too far from the docks. I didn't know Tony at the time and didn't know about his gold buying business. Had I known, I wouldn't have cared.

"But now I do, because I've learned from an associate that the gold brooch that once belonged to my mother and was stolen from my home in Key West, was sold to Tony by the thief who took it.

"Even though it was twenty years ago, I still remember how much it hurt my mother when she discovered the brooch was gone. It had been given to her mother by her father back in Russia when they were married. Then it was handed down to her when she married my father.

"It was one of the few things she was able to keep when she left Russia behind. It meant a lot to her. And it means a lot to me still."

He showed me the photo he had been holding.

In it, there was an older woman with gray hair and a pleasant face. She was wearing a dark blue dress. Pinned to it, just below her neckline, a gold brooch in the shape of a sunflower. A nickel-sized blue gemstone in the center. The brooch looked to be about three inches across.

Boris tapped the photo. "I want it back."

I could understand why he would want it. It had been in his family a long time. Handed down by his grandmother to his mother. A family heirloom with deep sentimental value. If someone had taken something like that from me, I'd want to get it back as well.

According to Boris, it had been stolen twenty years earlier. The chances of finding it now were almost zero. It could have changed hands many times, the gem could have been removed, the brooch could have been melted down for the gold content.

If that were the case, it was gone forever. It would no longer exist. I probably didn't have to tell him this, but I did.

"Boris, if it's been twenty years since it was taken, there's almost no chance it will ever be found. I'm sorry for your loss, but you know that after so much time, it would be next to impossible to find it now."

He nodded. "I agree with your assessment. It would be impossible to find. Except for one thing. I know for a certainty that Tony Ducks never sold any of the gold he purchased. He didn't need the money. He kept it as a form of insurance in case his cash was seized and his bank accounts were frozen.

"In the business he was in, along with his reputation, he knew there was always the possibility the feds would come knocking. He'd seen it happen to others in his line of work. He knew that when they came, there would be no warning that they were seizing your bank accounts.

"The goal of the feds is to starve you of money. To make it difficult to pay for things, like expensive lawyers. Tony didn't want to be put in that position. He didn't want to be broke. So he bought gold and never sold any of it. He kept it hidden away. To be used just in case.

"I learned this from one of his close associates. I confirmed it by reviewing the fed's asset seizure records. They listed everything taken when his estate was raided. Every single item, including things of little to no value like knives and forks and spoons from the kitchen. The search was very thorough. They took everything, missing nothing. The asset seizure records also listed every item found in his home safe as well as his many safe deposit boxes.

"There were a few gold coins on the inventory list, but none of the older ones he had purchased from the salvage divers. No silver bars, and no women's jewelry.

"The fact that the feds searches did not find these items at his residence, in his vehicles or in his bank boxes, suggests that either he gave them to someone else for safekeeping or he hid them and they have yet to be found.

"It is my belief that he would never turn over the bulk of his gold holdings to an associate. He would never be that trusting. Instead, I believe he hid it somewhere. And I think that somewhere is on this property. Duckville.

"That's one of the reasons I want you to buy this place. So you can look for his treasure. And my mother's brooch that may be hidden with it.

"It is important to do this before Tony is released from prison. He will not want to leave this earth without recovering the treasures he believes rightly belong to him. Even if those treasures were stolen from others."

I nodded. I could understand why he wanted me to search the property. But why have me buy it? Why not buy it himself and hire someone to do the search.

I decided to ask him.

"Boris, why have me buy the property? Wouldn't it be easier for you to purchase it yourself? Then hire someone to do the search? Why involve me?"

He smiled. "Walker, I like you. I've come to believe you're an honorable man. You've helped me out in the past and asked nothing in return. You saved my daughter's life and helped my wife resolve a delicate situation. Again, asking nothing in return.

"It's true that I could buy Duckville myself. But that would create a paper trail which I prefer to avoid. For some reason, the feds still monitor my activities. If they see my name on a real estate transaction, they might decide to look into the history of the property.

"I would prefer that not happen. It would be better for all involved if there is nothing leading back to me. But that's not the only reason I want it to be you who buys Duckville."

He pointed to the view over the bow of the boat. "As you can see, this is an amazing place. A rarity in this part of Florida. A large piece of land on the water that hasn't been developed.

"I would prefer it stay that way. Perhaps forever."

He took a sip from his glass, finishing off the remaining liquid, then continued speaking.

"If it were possible, I'd like to see this land turned into a preserve. A place that would be forever protected from development. To do that would require turning it over to the state. Whoever owned it at the time, would lose whatever they had invested in it.

"If it were yours, you would not want to lose what you will have paid for it. Unless there was another option. And there is.

"Let me explain."

Chapter Eighteen

"I believe Tony Duck's treasure is buried somewhere here on this property. My source told me that on one occasion when Tony had had too much to drink, he mentioned something about a money pit. He used those exact words, 'money pit'.

"He never told anyone where it was. Or even if it actually existed. It may not.

"But the feds never found the gold and that likely means it's still hidden somewhere. Tony would have stashed it in a place they didn't know about. Somewhere it wouldn't be easily found and would withstand the elements.

"I'm betting it's on this property. Probably buried in the money pit he talked about.

"If the pit actually exists and if it's here, and if you find it, you can have everything in it, except the brooch that was stolen from my mother. That's all I want. The brooch. Nothing else. You can have the rest.

"If there is no money pit, no treasure to be found, you will have drained your bank account buying this place. You probably didn't plan on doing that. But if you were to list Duckville for sale, you could get your money back quickly and probably quite a bit more.

"I'd rather you not do that. I don't want you to sell. I want you to hold onto it for a few years. If you agree to do that, I'll make it worth your while.

"I'll start by offering to pay five thousand a month for five years for use of the dock. This will allow me or my associates to use it whenever we choose. It is a reasonable rate for a dock this size in this location.

"The lease will not be in my name. It will be in the name of a shell corporation with no ties to me or my family.

"In addition to the dock, I'd like to provide a place for Abby to live. She has left her previous rental and is currently living full time in her camper. I would feel more comfortable if she had a home base. A place where she could stay when she isn't on the road.

"I've offered to provide her the funds to buy her own place, but as you know, she is somewhat hardheaded and wouldn't allow me to do so. She says she isn't interested in my money.

"But she likes you and she likes Duckville, and I think you might be able to convince her to move into the Quonset hut and use it as her home. It's just weird enough for her to like it.

"So, I'll pay you three thousand a month on a five-year lease to rent the hut.

"Between the dock and the house, you will be paid eight thousand a month. Additionally, I will give you fifty thousand dollars for a five-year option to buy Duckville. The purchase price to be negotiated at the time the option is exercised. It also gives me the first right of refusal on any other offers you may receive.

"Should you still own Duckville upon my death, I will authorize my estate to purchase it from you for the sum of one million dollars or the current appraised value, whichever is higher. Upon purchase, the land will be turned over to the state of Florida with the condition that it will become a preserve in my mother's name."

He paused, letting me consider his offers.

On the face of it, they sounded pretty good. The dock and house lease would generate almost a hundred thousand dollars a year for five years. The additional fifty thousand for the purchase option would be an unexpected and immediate cash dividend just for buying the place.

The opportunity to sell the land back to Boris and have it made into a permanent preserve was definitely an added bonus.

While the odds of finding any treasure were remote, the hunt would give me something to do for the next few months.

And who knows? I might get lucky.

It didn't seem like there was any way I could lose out.

But instead of agreeing to it right away, I thought about the possible consequences of getting involved in a land deal with Boris. As he had said, the feds watched him closely and if my dealings with him came to light, they might look into me as well.

They wouldn't find anything, but it would be a nuisance to have them looking over my shoulder.

It felt like I was forgetting something. Something important. But since I couldn't come up with it and since Boris was waiting for my answer, I said, "It sounds like you've structured this so I can't lose. I very much appreciate it. If you want me to go ahead and purchase the property, I will. I'll sign the papers this afternoon."

He smiled. "Good. I was hoping you'd say that. I'll have my people draw up the lease papers along with the purchase option and get them to you within the week."

He hesitated, then said, "Be careful around Tony Ducks. If I'm right about the money pit, he'll probably pay you a visit. When he shows up, treat him with respect and don't do anything to make him angry. If you haven't found the treasure by then, and he wants to search for it, let him. But call me right away. Don't let him leave the property with my mother's brooch."

He started to say more but was interrupted by a soft chime that sounded a bit like a doorbell. He looked at his watch, something most people no longer wear, and said, "It seems my captain is telling me we need to be on our way if we are to get through Stump Pass before the tide goes out.

"I would prefer to spend the night here, but there are pressing matters I must attend to back home."

I smiled, "I understand."

I extended my hand to shake, but instead of meeting me with his, he reached into his pocket and came out with an envelope. "Give this to Abby. She will know what to do with it."

He led me out of the lounge and back onto the main deck where the Captain was waiting. After shaking my hand, he said, "We will talk again. Hopefully, you'll have good news for me."

He saluted which I took as a signal that our meeting was over. I thanked him for his hospitality and followed the Captain to the gangplank. He unlatched the gate, and I walked down to the dock, expecting to find Abby.

She wasn't there, but my shoes were. My cell phone was tucked into one of them. A flashing light told me there was a message waiting to be read. It said, "Meet me at the house."

Apparently, she had gotten tired of waiting and had gone back to the Quonset hut. I pulled on my shoes and as I did, I heard the diesel motors of Boris' yacht increase their speed. Looking over, I saw the mooring lines being reeled in, in preparation for leaving the bay.

Two minutes later, I watched the big boat as it moved away from the dock and head toward the Intracoastal waterway and Stump Pass. As it motored away, I again saw the boat's name emblazoned in gold on the stern. Charon.

Boris had said the boat once belonged to Tony Ducks. Maybe he was the one who named it. Perhaps after a woman? Maybe a variation of Sharon? I'd have to look it up.

With the boat gone and my shoes on, I headed back to the Quonset hut to meet up with Abby. I hoped she was still in a good mood. Women tend not to be if you make them wait too long.

Chapter Nineteen

I knew we needed to get back in town in time for the closing. Boris wouldn't be happy if we missed it and someone else stepped in and bought Duckville.

Abby was sitting on the low step in front of the Quonset hut when I got there. Instead of asking me how the meeting had gone, she pointed down the road we'd walked in on, and said, "We need to get going. Don't want to be late. It'll take us almost an hour to get there, and along the way, you'll have to stop at your bank and get a cashier's check. We'll be cutting it close."

She took off walking and I followed. When we reached the gate, we climbed over as we had before, and hurried to her van. Inside, she started it up and backed down the road until we reached a point where she could turn around. Once that was done, we headed back into town.

On the way, she asked, "So how was the meeting?"

"It went well. Boris was in a good mood."

"Is that all you're going to tell me? That it went well?"

I nodded. "That's pretty much it. We talked about the property, his boat, and a little about Tony Ducks. It's a nice boat. Have you ever been on it?"

"No, Not yet anyway. Are you sure you didn't talk about anything else? Did my name come up?"

Her question reminded me of the envelope Boris had given me. I figured now was a good time to tell her about it.

"Boris gave me an envelope. Said to give it to you. That you'd know what to do with it."

She looked over at me. "Did you open it?"

"No, I didn't. He didn't tell me to look inside it. He just said to give it to you."

"Good. Open it now. Tell me what's in it."

We were still thirty minutes out of Englewood and it looked like we would have no problem getting to the closing on time. If Abby wanted me to open the envelope and tell her what was inside, I could see no reason not to.

Opening it, I saw it contained a single sheet of paper. There was a list of type-written names on it. I showed the list to Abby.

She glanced at the page and said, "I can't read it while I'm driving. Read it for me. Out loud."

I read the names in the order they appeared.

"Joey Guzik, Vinny Pike, Thomas Vilotti, Angelo Ruggiero, Tick Tock Caridi, Pete Ciotti, Tommy Shots, Benny Eggs, Vito Manco."

After getting through the list, I paused long enough for Abby to ask, "Does it say anything else. Locations, phone numbers, anything like that?"

"No, it's just the names. That's it. Nothing more."

She frowned. "That's not good. It means it's going to take me longer than I thought."

I was intrigued. "What do you mean?"

She shook her head. "Nothing you need to worry about. In fact, it'd be best if you forget you ever heard those names."

After that, she stayed quiet until we pulled into the parking lot of the SunTrust bank. Leaving the van running, she reached into the console and pulled out a slip of paper. Handing it to me, she said, "Get a cashier's check in this amount. Have it made out to the name shown. I'll wait for you out here."

Inside the bank, it took me about twenty minutes of showing my ID and confirming it was me before they'd cut the check. After I explained I was buying a home, they called the title company to make sure everything was on the up and up. After hearing it was, they pulled the money from my account and printed the check.

The friendly teller gave me a slip of paper showing my remaining balance. It was a lot smaller than it had been when I walked in.

Back in the van, I showed Abby the check. She compared the amount and the payee to the slip of paper she had given me. Seeing that everything was correct, she put the van in gear and we headed over to the real estate office for the closing.

There, we learned that they were still following Covid protocols and we'd be doing what they called a touchless closing. We'd be in a room with a large computer screen where a title agent at another location went over the contract with us.

Because I was paying cash, there weren't any financing documents to sign, so the process went fairly quickly. The title agent explained that per Abby's instructions, the deed had been made out in my name only. Hers was not on it.

All I had to do was sign a few e-Docs using the room's computer and show the cashier's check. After signing, an aide wearing a mask walked into the room, handed me a stack of still-warm from the printer documents, and left with my check.

The title agent congratulated me on my purchase and said that our real estate agent would provide us with the keys to the property. She thanked us and disappeared from the screen.

A moment later, Anna walked into the room carrying a small satchel. It'd been more than a year since I'd last seen her in person and she looked great. I hesitated to tell her that, afraid Abby might not appreciate me hitting on another woman with her in the room.

Anna didn't seem to care. She walked over, hugged me, and said, "Walker, I'm glad you're back in town. I missed you."

She turned to Abby and smiled, but said nothing. Then turned back to me. "Well, it's all yours now. Not sure what you're going to do with it, but you'll need these to get in."

Reaching into her satchel she pulled out a key ring with several keys. "One of these fits the lock on the front gate. The others are for the Quonset huts along with two mystery keys. Don't know what they go to, but I'm sure you'll figure it out.

"You'll need to call Florida Power and Light and get the electricity put in your name. You don't have to worry about water or sewer. The place is on a well and has a septic tank.

"When you call the power company, they'll want to know the property address. It's on the deed. You might want to write it down and keep it in your wallet. You'll need it to get mail delivered out there."

She smiled again and asked, "Is Mango Bob still living with you?"

"Yeah, he is. Bigger and goofier than ever. If you ever get out our way, stop in, I'm sure he'd like to see you."

Instead of answering right away, she looked over at Abby, then back at me. "Are you thinking about living out there? In the hut? Really? Way out there?"

I shrugged. "Maybe. Maybe not. Depends on what it's like inside. In the meantime, I'll stay in the motorhome with Bob. There's plenty of room to park it there."

I had barely gotten the words out when Abby moved over and put her arm around my waist. She smiled and said, "What he means is we'll both stay in his motorhome until we get the house the way we want it. Then we'll move in. We'll invite you over after that."

Abby was marking her turf. Letting Anna know that I was off-limits. At least as long as our pretend marriage was in effect.

Anna took a step back, smiled, and said, "I guess you two are still on your honeymoon. Having this new place will be a great way to start out together."

She turned to me. "That woman you met last night? In the RV park? She came in this morning. Her and her husband. Did you get to meet him?"

"No, just her."

She smiled. "Why am I not surprised? You always seem to meet women in RV parks. That's how we met, remember?"

I remembered it well. But with Abby, my pretend bride, standing next to me, it wasn't something I wanted to talk about.

I changed the subject.

"So, she came in to see you this morning? And she brought her husband. Are you going to be able to help them?"

She nodded. "I hope so. They seem like nice people. You'd probably like the guy. He spent twenty years in the Marines. After he got out, he started a home repair business in Pensacola. They were doing great until the hurricane hit. They said it leveled their house and they lost their business.

"Fortunately, they had insurance. When they got the payout they decided to move down here.

"They'll be living in their fifth wheel until we find them a place to buy. It might take a while, but I'll find them something.

"In the meantime, enjoy your new place. I'll call you later to see how you're doing."

She turned to Abby. "It was nice seeing you again. I hope you and Walker enjoy your new home. If you ever want to get together for lunch, give me a call. I'm sure we'd have plenty to talk about."

She turned back to me and winked. Abby saw her do it and I knew it might mean trouble later on. Even if we were only in a pretend marriage, Abby wanted to protect her territory.

She took my hand, smiled at Anna, and said, "We need to be going. Lots of things to do before the day is over. I'm sure we'll talk again."

As she pulled me toward the door, I looked over my shoulder and saw Anna mouthing the words, "Call me."

Chapter Twenty

As soon as we got back in the van, Abby turned to me and said, "You and Anna have a history, right?"

I nodded. "Yeah, we know each other. But only as friends. It never went beyond that."

She wasn't buying it. "You sure about that? It seemed like there was more going on than the two of you being just friends."

I smiled. "Abigail, I assure you, you're the only one when it comes to pretend wives."

I tried my best not to chuckle when I said it, but couldn't help myself.

She reached over and punched me in the shoulder. "I told you to never call me Abigail. Next time, I'll punch harder."

She started the van, put it in gear, and said, "Call FP&L. You need to get the power put in your name. We don't want them turning it off."

I made the call and spent twenty minutes with a very helpful woman in accounts, who after asking all the right questions and getting acceptable answers, was able to get the power transferred into my name. I had the billing set up on auto-pay so I wouldn't have to worry about being out of town and missing a payment.

By the time I got off the phone, we had reached the other side of Venice, just a few miles south of Oscar Scherer where we'd be spending the night. We'd left both cats in my RV, and I hoped they'd stayed out of trouble while we were gone. We would soon find out.

When we reached the turn-off to the park, Abby didn't slow. She passed the entrance and kept going north. I was going to ask her why, but before I could, she said, "We're going to Walmart. There are a few things I need."

Four miles later, she pulled into Wally World's parking lot and found a spot on the far side, away from other shoppers. I'd parked in the same spot two years earlier, chasing down a repo man who had taken my RV by mistake.

It could have ended badly. But it hadn't.

After getting parked, Abby turned to me and said. "We're moving to Duckville tomorrow. If there is anything you need to stock up on, now's a good time to get it. I'll meet you back out here in thirty minutes."

She stepped out and walked away. Leaving me behind to wonder just how mad she really was.

I figured I'd find out later.

Since we were traveling in her van and since it was pretty much already full with everything she owned, I didn't think it would be wise of me to go into the store and load up a shopping cart and try to cram my things into her camper.

A better plan was to wait until the morning, come back to Walmart in my own RV, and buy whatever I needed then. It would be a lot easier and less stressful that way.

Still, since she'd said she'd be gone for about thirty minutes, I didn't want to sit out in her van waiting for her return. So I went into the store.

Inside, I headed straight for the outdoor section. I wanted to see if they carried chain saws. I would need one to clear the larger branches hanging over the road into Duckville. My RV was tall and a stray branch could tear up my roof or damage the air conditioner and I didn't want to take a chance on that happening.

As fortune would have it, Walmart had several chain saws in stock. The Black Max with the sixteen-inch bar for a hundred and twenty-five bucks looked like what I needed. I made a note to pick one up, along with a pint of two-cycle oil, and a plastic two-gallon gas tank when I came back the next morning.

In the hardware section, I found Private Property and No Trespassing signs. The gate to Duckville needed new ones. I'd get them and a new lock and chain when I returned to the store.

Fifteen minutes had passed and even though Abby had said to give her thirty, I wanted to get back to the van before she did. I didn't want her again having to wait for my return.

Out in the parking lot, I was happy to see the van was still there and Abby had yet to return. Four minutes later, she came across the lot pushing a heavily loaded shopping cart.

I got out to help. The cart was mostly filled with food. People food, cat food, and enough raw ingredients to make several quick meals – the kind that wouldn't require much prep. She'd also picked up a ready-to-eat rotisserie chicken and a Caesar salad – which I assumed would be our evening meal.

After we got her cart unloaded, she asked, "What'd you get?"

"Nothing. I figured it would be easier to come back in the morning. I didn't want to cram my things into your van. You've got everything nicely arranged in here, and I didn't want to mess it up."

She looked at me, nodding like she approved of my decision. Then she asked, "So you're coming back here in the morning?"

"Yeah, that's my plan."

"Good. I'll come with you. There's some things I wanted to get but was afraid I wouldn't have room for them. They'll fit in your RV. We'll get them in the morning."

It was just after dark when we got back to the campground.

The rangers had already closed and locked the front gate for the night. It keeps non-paying guests out after the park closes. Fortunately, Abby knew the gate code and was able to get us through.

Back at our campsites, we hooked her van up to shore power and went over to see what kind of trouble Buddy and Bob had gotten into while we were gone.

When we got to the door of my RV, I expected to hear Bob talking inside. He usually knows when I'm getting ready to come in and will start meowing to let me know he's waiting for me.

But this time, there were no meows. No sound at all.

I unlocked the door, opening it just enough to peek in. Making sure there wasn't a cat waiting on the other side planning to make a run for it. Escaping into the wilds of Oscar Scherer would not be a pleasant experience for a kitty. Signs all over the park warned visitors of the presence of alligators. A cat, even one as big as Bob, would be no match for one.

Fortunately, neither feline was near the door. I opened it fully and waved Abby in. I wanted her to go in first in case Buddy came running. She'd have a better chance of catching him than me.

Turned out, I didn't need to worry. Neither cat came out to see us. It was unexpected. Bob almost always comes up front to greet me when I return. Being a bit worried, I headed to the back to see what the two cats were up to.

Before I reached the bedroom, I found out.

The bathroom door, which I had left open so they could get to their food and litter box, was closed.

From the other side came a soft meow. One or both of the cats was locked inside. Opening the door, I was surprised to see Abby's cat, Buddy, was sitting on the toilet. The lid was down, so he wasn't using it. He was just sitting there, looking a little sad.

On the floor below him, the food and water bowls had been turned over. The dry cat food had mixed with the water and had turned to mush. Kitty footprints tracked the wet food through the room, as well as onto the vanity and sink.

If it had been someone else's bathroom, I would have thought it was funny.

But knowing I was the one who was going to have to clean it up, I didn't laugh.

Abby had a different take. She thought it was hilarious. She had a big grin on her face when she tiptoed in and picked up her cat. As she passed me on the way out, she said, "Sucks to be you."

Since Bob wasn't in the bathroom with Buddy, I figured he was back in his favorite place. My bed. That's where I found him. With his head on my pillow. He looked up at me, blinked, and yawned. Like he had no idea that little Buddy was locked in the bathroom.

But I knew better.

He had probably gotten tired of playing with him, and when he had the chance, locked him in there. I'd seen him close the bathroom door before, so I knew he could do it. I just didn't think he'd lock Buddy in with the food. That was something he probably regretted.

Both cats were okay and other than the mess in the bathroom, there didn't appear to be any other damage.

Up front, Abby had just finished drying Buddy's messy paws with a paper towel. She put him on the floor and he ran straight back to the bathroom and went in.

We couldn't help but laugh. Her Buddy was a real character.

Maybe not very smart, but plenty of fun to be around.

She got up from the couch, tossed the roll of paper towels to me, and said, "While you're cleaning the mess back there, I'll get dinner ready."

Later that evening, after our meal and a few glasses of wine, Abby raised her glass and said, "To a long and happy pretend marriage."

I shook my head. "Uh, no. How about we just toast to Duckville? That seems safer."

She nodded, "OK, if you say so."

After finishing off her wine, she put the glass down and said, "I was thinking about spending the night here with you tonight. But since you didn't want to toast the marriage, I've changed my mind. Me and Buddy are going next door. See you in the morning."

As she headed for the door, I didn't try to change her mind. Had she decided to stay and share my bed, it would have definitely complicated what was already a pretty weird situation.

And it was about to get a lot weirder.

Chapter Twenty-One

The next morning I got up early and headed to the campground bathhouse to grab a quick shower. I could have showered in the RV but didn't want to worry about running out of fresh water or filling up the holding tanks and having to dump them before leaving the park.

Plus, it's always a hassle to move Bob's litter box out of the shower stall. I keep it there because it gives him privacy when he needs to take care of his business. As a bonus, should his big behind hang over the back of the litter box, it's easy to wash his leavings down the drain.

In the campground bathhouse, I was happy to see I was the only one there, at least on the men's side. After showering, I headed back to the RV and dressed. Choosing what the wear was easy. Tan cargo shorts and a well-worn Columbia fishing shirt. Pretty much what I wear every day. Some people prefer wearing t-shirts, but I like fishing shirts because they have ventilation slats on the sides and deep pockets on the front which are a great place to keep your sunglasses.

After getting dressed, I set about getting the RV ready for the road. Stowing away anything that might shake free and cause damage while we were in motion. I had learned on earlier trips that even the smallest loose item can cause a problem when you take a sharp turn. When you're the one driving, you can't just get up and go see what made that crashing sound you just heard. For that reason, I put everything away that could possibly move while we're in motion.

I buttoned up all the cabinet doors, closed and locked the windows, and made sure the TV antenna was down and the MaxxAir vents on the roof were closed.

With the inside taken care of, I went out and unhooked from shore power and stowed the cord. Then I walked around the RV and checked that the basement doors were locked. As the last step, I checked that the tires were all still holding air.

They were.

It was a few minutes before eight and I had yet to see Abby come out of her camper. It was possible she had gotten up earlier and gone for a run. It was also possible she was sleeping in.

I decided to find out what was going on.

I walked over to her van and knocked on the door. "Abby, you up yet?"

There was no response. I knocked again, "Abby, you in there?"

Again no response. Just a soft meow from Buddy.

Her blinds were drawn and the foil-backed shades she had over her cab windows kept me from getting a clear look inside. Going around to the front, I could see there was a sliver of open space between the sunscreen and the edge of the windshield. Maybe just enough to peek in. Her van's front bumper had a step, designed by the manufacturer to make it easier to reach the windshield for cleaning. I used the step to get up off the ground to see if she was inside.

As I was about to press my face against the windshield, a woman's voice behind me said, "You need to get down from there. We don't like peeping Toms around here."

My first thought was one of the park rangers had walked up and saw me trying to look into the van's window. That would be bad. I didn't want to get a reputation as a peeper. I stepped down, ready to explain that I was trying to check on a friend.

As I turned to face the voice, I realized no explanation was necessary. Abby was standing behind me, holding a bar of soap and a bottle of shampoo. A towel wrapped around her head.

"What are you doing?" she asked.

"I was worried about you. You said for me to be ready by eight, and I was. But I couldn't find you. I was afraid you overslept."

She shook her head. "I've been up for hours. Decided to shower after my morning run. Now, if it's okay with you, I'm going to go inside and change. It'll probably take me a few minutes, so why don't you go on ahead to Walmart. Park where we were last night. I'll meet you there in a bit."

Using her remote, she unlocked her side door, stepped in, and locked it behind her.

I'd been given my orders for the day. Go to Walmart and wait for her.

I left the park, turned right onto US Forty One, and drove the four miles to Walmart. I pulled into the lot and parked in the same spot we had the night before.

Instead of waiting for her to catch up with me, I let Bob know I was going to be gone for a few minutes and headed into the store to do some shopping.

My plan was to make two trips. On the first, I'd get enough food for me and Bob to last at least a week and bring it back to the RV and stock the fridge. Then I'd go back in and get the chainsaw and other things I had seen the night before.

I had just gotten back with the chainsaw when Abby pulled up in her camper. She parked beside me, and after getting out, asked, "Do you have enough room in there for a picnic table?"

My immediate mental response was 'no'. There was no way a picnic table would fit inside my RV. At least not one that was fully assembled. But that's not what I told her. Instead, I said, "If it comes as a kit, I might be able to fit it in. It just depends on how big it is."

She smiled. "Let's go inside and check. Because it would be nice to have a place to sit outside on the deck at Duckville."

She took my hand and led me into the store. Apparently, she wasn't mad at me for letting her leave the night before. That was a good sign.

Eight minutes later, we were back out in the parking lot with me pushing a shopping cart with a picnic table kit in it. According to the box, it included ten pine two by fours and a box of wood screws. Along with directions on how to put it together.

My RV has a long outside storage compartment and after moving a few things around, I was able to get the picnic table kit to fit into it.

Before leaving Walmart, I headed back into their deli section and picked up a warm apple fritter and a Coke. Breakfast of champions. I figured Abby would make fun of my unhealthy food choice, but she didn't. She got the same thing.

Back in the parking lot, I showed her the chainsaw and told her I'd be using it to clear a path wide enough to get both of our campers safely to the Quonset hut at Duckville. I'd have to stop for gas and would be doing that before leaving the Walmart lot.

Since she didn't need to stop, we agreed she'd go on ahead and I'd meet her at Duckville's front gate. After she left, I headed to the Marathon station next to Walmart and topped off the fuel tanks in the RV. While there, I filled the plastic gas tank I'd gotten for the chainsaw, and stored it in the generator compartment.

Then I headed to Duckville to meet up with Abby.

Chapter Twenty-Two

As expected, Abby got to Duckville long before I did. She had gone first and was driving a fairly nimble Class B camper van that made getting through the traffic a lot easier.

I, on the other hand, was driving a big heavy thirty-foot long Class C motorhome that was slow to take off, slow to brake, and hard for cars behind to see around. It was a fact of life that nobody wanted to be stuck behind an RV, including mine. So when traffic allowed, cars would zip around me.

I couldn't blame them and for the most part, it didn't bother me. I'd probably be doing the same thing if I were in a car stuck behind a motorhome blocking my view in traffic.

But what I wouldn't do is speed around the RV, pull in front of it, then stomp on my brakes to make a right turn. It was crazy how many people thought this was safe. Maybe they didn't realize how much it'd hurt if they were hit from behind by what was essentially a rolling house.

Since I didn't want their carelessness to cause me to damage both our vehicles and perhaps kill someone, I had to keep falling back every time a car pulled in front of me. Far too often, I had to hit my brakes to create a safe distance between their back bumper and my front.

With so much heavy braking going on, I was worried the plastic tank of gas I'd gotten for the chain saw might not survive the trip. I didn't want to think about what might happen if it burst and started dripping raw gasoline on the RV's hot exhaust pipe.

For that reason, I was relieved when I left traffic behind

and pulled onto the narrow lane in Grove City that led to Duckville. Even though the RV shook with every bump, at least I didn't have to worry about anyone running into me.

I was about halfway to the front gate when I reached Abby's van. She had parked in the middle of the road and was sitting on the back bumper doing something with her phone. I figured she was waiting for me to get there with my chainsaw so I could clear a safe path.

I pulled up close behind her, killed the motor, and went out to see what was up.

She saw me coming and said, "Took you long enough."

I shrugged. "Lot of crazy drivers out there. All of them wanting to slow me down."

She put her phone away and pointed in front of her van. "Time to get the chain saw out. We've got some branches to clear."

I went back to the RV, and got the chainsaw. After filling it with gas, and adding two-cycle oil to the mixer tank, I gave the starter cord a quick pull.

The little motor coughed but didn't start. There were only three controls. A knob labeled 'run', a trigger to rev up the motor, and a knob labeled 'choke'. I'd already put it in 'run' mode, but hadn't adjusted the choke. I set it to 'start' and tried the starter again. This time, the saw fired right up.

I let it run for about a minute, then put the choke back to 'off' mode. This cleared the initial puff of smoke and the little motor continued to idle smoothly.

With the chainsaw ready for action, I headed to the front of Abby's camper. And for the next hour, we cut branches that blocked our path.

We started with the lower ones first, then after we had cut

all the ones we could reach from the ground, I climbed up on top of her van, and had her pull up close to the higher ones that needed cutting.

She was a bit nervous about me standing on her roof while holding a running chainsaw over my head. It was something that OSHA definitely wouldn't approve of. But I got the job done without hurting myself or scratching her van with the falling branches.

After we reached the front gate, I decided it was time to take a break. I was covered with sweat mixed with sawdust and probably lots of small unseeable insects and spiders that had been living on the branches I had cut. Fortunately, my RV had an outdoor shower and I used it to wash the dirt and insects off my arms and legs. I'd definitely have to strip off my pants and shirt before going back inside.

After a twenty-minute break, I unlocked the front gate and we went back to clearing away branches on the old driveway that led to the front of the Quonset hut. It took another two hours to finally get everything cleared. When we were done, Abby went back to get her van and brought it up to the house, parking it close to the front door.

I stayed behind – mainly because she said I was too dirty to ride with her. I didn't mind. It gave me a chance to rest.

After she pulled up to what was soon to be our home, she got out and walked over to me. Holding out her hand, she said, "Keys please."

The Quonset hut's front door was locked and she needed the key Anna had given me to unlock it. I would have happily handed it over, except all the keys were back in my RV, which was parked about a quarter-mile back down the road we had just cleared.

I told Abby where they were and asked, "You want to walk

back there with me to get them?"

She shook her head. "No. I'll stay here. But before you go, I've got something for you."

Reaching into her van, she came out with a bottle of cold water. "Drink this while you walk. You look like you need it. I'll wait for you here."

I took the bottle and headed back to my RV. I walked slowly, mostly because I was tired. My arms hurt from holding the chainsaw for three hours, and my legs hurt from climbing up and down the ladder on the back of Abby's van about a hundred times.

I was about halfway back when a stout woman wearing daisy dukes, a bikini top, and carrying a large machete stepped out of the brush. She stopped and we stared at each other. Both of us surprised to see someone else on the road.

She started to turn and walk away, but changed her mind, and headed in my direction.

Lowering her machete, she walked to the now cleared road, stopping about six feet in front of me, and asked, "Have you seen my monkey?"

Dressed the way she was, in the very revealing cut-off shorts, I might have been able to see it if I had been looking in that direction. But with her carrying a machete and me not knowing her intentions, I didn't dare look down. I maintained eye contact and said, "Uh . . ."

Chapter Twenty-Three

The woman was not impressed with my answer. She asked again, "Have you seen my monkey?"

This time, I came up with a better reply than just saying 'uh'. Still maintaining eye contact, I said, "Ma'am, I don't know what you're talking about or why you're on my property carrying a machete. You want to explain yourself?"

She looked at me and shook her head. "You one of them treasure hunters that's always digging holes around here? I don't like them and Clyde don't either. You better not be one of them."

The woman, who I figured to be in her mid-thirties, had just given me some valuable information. People had been on the property digging holes looking for something. Probably the same thing I would soon be looking for.

But she hadn't answered my question.

"Lady, I'm not a treasure hunter. I just bought this place and plan on living here. I don't know who you are or why you're trespassing. Or why you're carrying a machete. You here cutting down my trees?"

She looked at me with a question in her eyes. "You bought this place? And plan on living out here? Are you some kind of nut?"

I could have been insulted by her question. But I wasn't. I was more interested in finding out who she was and what else she might know about the people who had been on the property digging holes.

I smiled. "Yeah, I bought it. And yes, I plan to live out

here. And yeah, I might be some kind of nut. I've been called that a few times in my life. But before I answer any more of your questions, maybe you should answer mine. Who are you and what are you doing on my property?"

She raised her heavily tattooed arm and wiped sweat from her face. After taking a deep breath, she said, "I'm Trudy. Trudy Love. I live in the trailer in the next place over. Clyde got out this morning and I've been looking for him. I figured he heard somebody messing around over here and he came to check it out.

"He don't like treasure hunters or strangers around here. One of them took a shot at him. He didn't like it. Since then, he watches, staying hidden until he gets a chance to take them by surprise. When folks see him running at them with his big teeth, they usually skedaddle.

"So you haven't seen him? Really?"

Remembering her name, I said, "Trudy, I haven't seen your dog. Does he bite?"

She smiled, "Clyde ain't no dog. He's a chimp. Big one, too. And smart. He's been with me since he was a baby and thinks he's a human. Two things he don't like. Guns and fire. If he comes around, don't pull a gun on him, and don't have no open fires.

"Another thing he don't like is strangers. If you plan on living here, you need to make friends with him. And soon. When I catch up with him, I'll bring him over to introduce you. You going to be up at the big hut?"

I didn't answer right away. I wasn't sure I was up for visitors, especially the Trudy Love and Clyde the monkey kind. But if there was a chimp roaming the property, it might be a good idea to get to know him.

If she was really my neighbor, she might be able to tell me

what was going on in the area, so I said, "I'd like to meet Clyde. Bring him up to the big hut any time before dark. I'll be there."

I didn't mention that Abby would be there with me. At the time, I didn't think it was important.

After assuring Trudy that it was okay for her to look for Clyde on my property and that as long as he didn't cause trouble, he could visit anytime, we parted ways. She stepped back into the brush she had come out of, and I continued down the road to where I had parked my RV.

When I got there, Bob was waiting for me at the door. He meowed a couple of times and took a few steps toward the back bedroom. When he realized I wasn't following, he meowed again and gave me a look that said, "Follow me. I want to show you something."

I've learned when he wants to show you something, it's almost always in your best interest to go see what it is. It could be an empty food bowl or a full litter box. Or a broken pipe in the bathroom and a flooded floor. That had happened once and he had alerted me to it before it got too bad.

Occasionally he'll want me to see the remains of a lizard or a mouse that had somehow gotten into the RV. He'd finished them off, then get me to come see his handy work.

But this time, it was none of those things. This time, he took me to the back bedroom, jumped up on the pillow, and looked out the back window. He pawed the glass and meowed as to say, "look over there."

I looked and saw a large chimpanzee sitting in the middle of the road behind the motorhome drinking from a can of Bud Lite.

Apparently, I had found Clyde. Or more precisely, Bob had found him.

Chapter Twenty-Four

It was odd to see a chimpanzee sitting in the road behind my motorhome drinking a beer. But it wasn't anywhere near the top of the list as far as weird things you might see in Florida. Still, it was worth getting my phone out and shooting a few photos to prove that it actually happened.

After getting the photos, I put the phone away and let Bob know that we were going to drive a few hundred yards to where we'd be spending the night. The ground in front of the Quonset hut was flat and at some time in the past, a layer of gravel had been put down as a parking area. Most likely by the previous tenants so they could safely park without fear of getting stuck in the mud after a heavy downpour.

My plan was to park the RV on the gravel, and assuming the power company hadn't turned off the electricity, I would run an extension cord from the house to give me shore power. That way, Bob and I could stay in it and be able to run the air should we need it. If the house power was off, I could still run the AC using the RV's solar-powered battery bank. As long as the sun shined a few hours every few days, the batteries would stay charged.

I didn't know what Abby's plans were, but she had her own camper and could stay in it if the house had no power. What I did know was I wanted to be around when Clyde the chimp and Trudy Love came to visit us. It was hard to surprise Abby with anything, but I figured an Amazon woman walking out of the woods accompanied by a chimpanzee might do the trick.

I took it slow driving the RV to the house. Even though

I'd done a pretty good job of clearing away the overhanging branches, there was always the chance that I might have missed one. There was also the chance that a chimpanzee might run out of the road in front of me. I was pretty sure if I hit him, Trudy Love wouldn't be happy.

Fortunately, there weren't any branches that caused any damage and no further chimp sightings.

Abby was sitting on the small deck at the front of the Quonset hut when I pulled into what would eventually be our front yard. I parked on the gravel, grabbed the keys for the house, and headed over to her.

Her first words were, "You've been gone a while. Was there a problem?"

I was tempted to tell her about Trudy Love and Clyde, but didn't. I wanted it to be a surprise when they met. So instead, I said, "There were a few branches I had to cut and clear away. Took longer than I thought. But I got the keys."

I handed her the key ring. "I don't know which of these will unlock the door, but it's supposed to be one of them."

She touched each key, then said, "It's probably this one."

Stepping up to the front door, she put it in and turned it to the right. The lock clicked. The first one she'd chosen worked. It was one of the mysteries of Abby. She could do things like that. Pick out the right key on the first try.

Instead of opening the now unlocked door, she turned to me and said, "We're supposed to be newlyweds. Aren't you going to carry me over the threshold?"

We weren't newlyweds and I had never signed on to the fake marriage. It was her idea from the very beginning, and I didn't want to encourage it. On the other hand, what could it hurt to play along, at least when no one was looking.

I walked up behind her, put one arm under her knees and my other around her back, and picked her up. I shoved the door open with my foot, and we walked in.

Neither of us was expecting what we saw when I flipped on the overhead lights.

Abby immediately said, "Put me down."

She didn't have to ask twice. She was a small woman. Maybe five foot one and weighing not a pound over a hundred. It was no problem picking her up and I could have carried her a mile or more without getting tired. But when we saw what was in the room, we both wanted to be free to roam.

The first surprise, and a pleasant one at that, was the power was actually on. When I flipped the light switch, the overhead lights came on. That was a big deal. Being in this part of Florida without electricity would make life very difficult. No way to cook, cool, or power the well pump.

But with electricity, we didn't have to worry about any of that. Life was good.

The second piece of good news, also a surprise, was the interior of the Quonset hut was not only quite clean but was well furnished and nicely laid out. To the left of the front door, was a galley kitchen with a frig, stove, and microwave. The Formica countertops had a double stainless steel sink cut in, and above, several solid wood cabinets. At the back of the kitchen, there was a door leading to what I suspected was a small pantry.

On the other side of the room, directly across from the kitchen, was a farm-style dining table with four matching chairs.

Further in, a living room of sorts, with a couch, two recliners, and an older TV against the wall. There were side tables with lamps on each end of the couch and a coffee table in front of it. Everything was dated, but was clean and looked serviceable.

Off to each side of the living area, there were doors leading to other rooms. I suspected these were the two bedrooms that had been mentioned in the listing.

Abby spoke first. "Anna said that the bank kept this place up after it was repossessed but I never thought it would be this nice. I expected it to be a mess, with years of dust. Maybe even mold.

"But this? I never imagined it would be like this. I can't wait to see what it'll be like when we get the hurricane panels off all the windows and get some sunlight in here."

She went into the kitchen and opened the fridge. Clearly surprised, she said, "This thing is on and it works. We could put our food in it right away."

While I was happy that the fridge worked, I was more interested in finding a bathroom. I had worked up quite a sweat clearing branches and wondered if the place had a shower.

I hoped it did.

Abby came out of the kitchen and pointed to the door on the right side of the living room. "You check out that room, I'll check the one on the other side."

She opened her door and went in. From where I was standing I heard her say, "It's a bedroom. And it has a bath!"

Almost immediately, I heard running water. "The sinks work. We have water."

While she explored the bedroom on her side, I went through the door on mine. It too opened into a small bedroom. With a single twin bed in the center. A small closet at the back, and a second door leading to what I hoped was the bathroom.

Opening the door, I was glad to see that it indeed led to a

washroom. It was small, with just a toilet, sink, and shower, but had everything a bathroom should.

Back out in the bedroom, I opened the door to what I assumed was a small closet. There was a clothes bar inside with an empty shelf above it, and nothing else.

When I left the bedroom, I found Abby in the kitchen. She had opened the door to the narrow pantry and called out to me. "Walker, come check this out."

I went over and saw that the pantry had four rows of shelves against the wall, and at the very back, a small upright freezer. The door was open, and the power cord was laying on top. The freezer was clean and looked almost new. Having one when living this far from the nearest grocery store would be a big plus.

I got the feeling that Abby was already putting together a shopping list in her head of things to pick up the next time she went into town.

Leaving the pantry, I went back into the living room and looked around. The far wall was covered by a heavy blackout curtain. Wanting to know what was behind it, I walked over, pulled the center of the curtain aside, and found that the wall was actually four panels of sliding glass doors. On the other side of the panels, heavy hurricane shutters were closed, protecting the glass. They also blocked any light from coming in. I'd have to open them to see what the outside view looked like.

Abby walked up beside me, stood on her tiptoes, and kissed me on the cheek. Surprised, I said, "What's that for?"

Smiling, she said, "I can't believe you bought this for us. It's so much nicer than I expected. I thought for sure we'd be spending weeks trying to get this place cleaned up and livable. But now we don't have to. I could move in today and be happy."

I was glad she was happy. Of course, I didn't really buy the place for her. But that didn't matter. Boris wanted her to live in it and was paying me rent to make it happen. If she was happy, I was happy, figuring that Boris would be happy too.

After the kiss, Abby said, "I know you want to shower, but I wondered if you could get the storm panels off the windows first. It won't take long and while you're doing it, I could make us lunch."

It was an offer I couldn't refuse. Mainly because I was hungry and I too wanted to see what the place looked like without the storm panels covering the windows.

Chapter Twenty-Five

I was relieved to discover all the storm panels were the roll-away kind, that once unlocked could be rolled to the side. On the sliding doors, the panels slid along a track on the floor and stowed in compartments on the end of each wall.

All that was needed was a key to unlock them. Fortunately, one of the mystery keys on the key ring fit.

What could have been a four-hour job if the panels had to be individually removed and stowed away, only took fifteen minutes. I was done before Abby was finished making lunch.

After washing up in the newly found bathroom, I walked into the kitchen to find her making chicken tacos, using white meat from the rotisserie chicken we had the night before. She had filled stand-up taco shells with chicken, shredded cheese, avocado, peach pineapple salsa, and topped them off with sour cream. The shells had been heated in the oven and the chicken in the microwave. Both appliances apparently worked.

How she was able to keep all the ingredients for a meal like this in her little van while living on the road was a mystery. But I was glad she somehow had figured it out.

We ate at the dining table near the front door, looking out toward where we'd parked our two campers. Beyond them, we could see the road leading into the property. It was a good place for the table because if we had visitors, we could see them coming long before they got to our door.

As tempted as I was, I still didn't tell her about Trudy Love and Clyde. I wanted their visit to be a complete surprise. To make sure that happened, I needed to get her away from the dining table so she wouldn't see them when they came walking up.

To do that, after I helped her clean up the kitchen, I led her into the living room so I could show her what was behind the wall-to-wall blackout curtains.

I had already rolled away the outside shutters but had yet to open the inside curtains to reveal the view. To make the most of it, I had Abby sit in one of the recliners facing the curtain. Then I went to the corner and after making a drum-roll sound, pulled the curtain cord, opening them slowly.

I watched her eyes as the outside view was revealed, expecting to see her smile. But that didn't happen. With the curtain halfway open, she jumped up, pointed outside, and yelled, "What the hell is that?"

I looked where she was pointing. At first, I wasn't sure what I was seeing, then I understood. Just outside the door, Clyde was standing with his face pressed up against the glass, trying to look in.

If you've ever seen a human face pressed up against a glass door, you know how strange it can look. Now imagine what it would look like if a five-foot-tall very hairy chimp with huge teeth, surprised you with his face pressed up against the door leading into your home.

Abby, who is rarely afraid of anything, had taken three steps back and had hidden behind the recliner. She was peeking over the top, trying to figure out what she was seeing.

I knew it was Clyde but didn't know if he was alone or not, or if he was going to cause trouble. Wanting to look brave, I didn't join Abby behind the recliner. Instead, I pulled the cord to fully open the curtain and was relieved to see that Trudy was standing next to the chimp.

In her hand, a six-pack of Bud Light.

I turned to Abby, who was still hiding behind the chair. "Abby, get up, I want you to meet our neighbor."

She looked at me. "Neighbor? That's Big Foot. Not a neighbor."

"Abby, please get up. I want you to meet Trudy Love. Our neighbor. And Clyde, her chimp."

She stood slowly, and when she did, Trudy Love waved in her direction. Abby shyly waved back. She looked at me and said, "You've already met her, right? You knew she was coming."

I nodded. "Yes, on both accounts."

She shook her head. "I'll get you back. You know I will. You'll see."

She walked over to the door, and after I slid it open, she smiled at Trudy and said, "Walker tells me you're our neighbor. Pleased to meet you. I'm Abby."

Trudy smiled. "I didn't mean to scare you. But Clyde here, he sometimes likes to check things out when we visit our neighbors. We came in across the fence, not the driveway. Clyde headed for your patio doors. The people who were here years before, used to give him a treat when he showed up at the door. I guess he was hoping there'd be something for him today."

Trudy turned to the monkey. "Clyde, shake the lady's hand."

He grunted, then stuck out his hairy arm with an open palm, ready to shake. Abby smiled at me and took his hand. They shook, but he didn't let go. Instead, he grinned widely, showing a row of large teeth. The kind that would be terrifying if they were to rip into you.

After Abby got her hand back from the monkey, Trudy

turned to me and told Clyde to shake with me. Expecting him to put his hand out as he had done with Abby, I extended mine to meet his. Instead of him taking it, he stepped in through the door and wrapped both his arms around my chest and squeezed. He looked over at Abby, grinned with his big teeth, and made a cooing sound. He squeezed me again, and then let me go.

When he stepped back, Trudy handed him a beer. He pulled the tab and took a long drink.

She smiled. "When he grabs you like that, it means he likes you. Or is about to tear your head off. He's very strong. He could do it if he wanted to. But I think he likes you. Both of you."

She held up the six-pack, or what was left of it. "Either of you want a beer?"

Chapter Twenty-Six

The picnic table we'd bought was still in the box. I hadn't had time to put it together yet. If I had assembled it, we could have it out on the front deck and it would have been a great spot to sit and drink beer with Trudy Love and Clyde.

As it was, the only comfortable place to sit was inside the Quonset hut on the couch or in the recliners. While I don't want to be accused of being anti-primate, I really didn't want to bring Clyde inside and let him sit on our furniture. He might have had fleas or whatever it is that chimps get when they spend time outdoors.

Instead of offering to go inside, I suggested we sit on the steps of the front deck and finish our drinks.

When Trudy offered us a beer, Abby took one, but I passed. I needed water, not alcohol. I'd sweated out a lot of fluid while trimming branches and I didn't need to replace it with the devil's drink. I grabbed a bottle of H2O from the fridge and I was sticking with that.

It was probably a good thing I passed on the beer. Clyde finished his quickly and wanted another. There was only one left and had I taken it, there wouldn't have been any. Clyde might have marked me off his friend's list if I had taken the last beer, leaving him without one. I didn't want that to happen.

My feeling was if there was a chimp living next to us, I wanted to be on his good side, not his arch enemy. So while Abby, Trudy, and Clyde drank beer, I sipped water and asked questions.

"Trudy, you mentioned treasure hunters earlier. Do you know what they were looking for?"

"Yeah, shark's teeth and fossils."

"Really? Here? I thought Venice was the place for shark's teeth."

She nodded. "It is. But some fool posted a video on YouTube showing a six-inch tooth that he claimed was found around here. According to him, when the Corp of Engineers dredged the Intracoastal they dumped a lot of bottom sand on the shoreline of Grove City. Some of it is on your property.

"The guy on the video said that the sand was full of shark's teeth and fossils. The kind that can bring a lot of money. So people are coming out here and digging.

"Just recently, two men with picks and shovels were on your land digging holes. In the middle of the day. They weren't even trying to hide.

"A few weeks earlier, same thing. Three people were out here with shovels. In broad daylight."

I was stunned. People were trespassing and digging on the property. I asked the only question I could think of. "Did they find anything?"

She shrugged. "No way to know. The most recent guys dug for a couple of hours, set some flags, and left."

"They set flags? Could they have been surveyors?"

"Maybe. I didn't see their truck."

I nodded. "Any chance you could show me where they put the flags?"

"Yeah, I can do that. But not today. Me and the little guy have already taken up too much of your time."

She started to get up but stopped when Abby said, "Tell me

about Clyde. How did you end up with him?"

Trudy sat back down, reached over, and rubbed the back of the chimp's head. He grunted his appreciation. "He's been with me since the day he was born. We're circus people. Most everyone around here is. Back when Ringling used to come to Venice for the winter, management and artists would stay there or in Sarasota, while the lower-paid riggers, roustabouts, and animal handlers couldn't afford to. Even if they could, they didn't want to live around non-circus types.

"They wanted cheap land and privacy. That's what they found out here in Grove City.

"My father worked with the chimps. He was their caretaker, their trainer, and the one responsible for keeping them happy and healthy. He trained a lot of different ones over the years. All of them were smart, but there was one that stood out above the rest. Her name was Bubbles. She was super smart and he said she learned quicker than any other animal he'd worked with. He said she was smarter than many of the humans he knew.

"So when the circus decided not to have as many animals around, they started offloading the chimps to carnivals, zoos, and any place that would take them in.

"Pop saw the writing on the wall, he knew without the chimps, they wouldn't need him. So he retired and took Bubbles with him. They moved out here and settled in.

"He didn't know it at the time, but Bubbles was pregnant. I had been living up north with my mother, Pop's ex-wife, but when she got a new boyfriend, I was shuffled out the door. Being sixteen and underage, I didn't have many options, so I came down here to live with him.

"Imagine my surprise when I walked in the door and was greeted by Bubbles the chimp. She walked right up to me, grinned, and gave me a hug. She acted like I was her long-lost sister. In some ways, I guess I was.

"About six months later, Clyde was born. He and Bubbles lived with us just like they were family. They ate with us, played with us, and when we slept, they were in the room with us. As Clyde grew, we could see that he was smart like Bubbles. He'd learn things just by watching. Then he'd surprise us by doing what he had learned, by himself. One time, he watched as Pop built a shed.

"A few days later, we woke to the sound of a hammer, and when we went outside, Clyde was building a little lean-to shed for himself, using the same tools Pop had been using."

Trudy turned to Clyde. "You want another beer?"

He grinned big, handed her his empty can and she handed him the last one from the pack. He quickly pulled the tab, opened the beer, and took a long swallow. Pulling the can away from his lips, he said "Ahhhhhh."

Trudy shook her head. "He learned that from TV. Those damn beer commercials."

She looked out at the yard in front of us, pausing for a moment to catch up with her story. "Bubbles lived a good life. She passed on Christmas day eight years back. Died of old age.

"Pop passed a month later."

She paused again, took a deep breath, and smiled. Probably thinking about the good times she had with her father and Bubbles.

Finally, she said, "I've been here watching over the place ever since. It's the only home Clyde ever had, and no one's ever going to be taking him away from here."

She turned and rubbed the chimp's head, stood, and said, "We need to get back to the house. There's chores that need to be taken care of.

"If you want me to come over tomorrow and show you where those guys were digging holes, honk your car horn three times. That's our signal around here. When we hear a neighbor honk three times, we know something's up. Do it, and I'll come over. But not too early. Clyde likes to sleep in."

They said their goodbyes and headed out across the property going north, to the adjoining piece of land. I hadn't seen a road to their place when I drove in, but I'd be looking for it next time I went out.

Chapter Twenty-Seven

After Trudy and Clyde left, Abby stood, stretched, and said, "That was interesting."

I smiled. "You think?"

"Yeah, mostly because there's a pretty good chance Clyde might be smarter than you. He learned how to use hand tools and built a shed. Think you could do that? Build a shed?"

I shook my head, "Probably not as good as he could."

She grinned. "That's what I thought."

It was obvious she was in a good mood. Either from the beer or from being around me. My money was on the beer.

Both our RVs were parked out in the yard. Bob was in mine and Buddy in hers. I knew Bob would sleep most of the day and be perfectly happy where he was. I suspected Abby's cat, Buddy, would feel the same way. But we couldn't leave them in the campers forever. Especially if we weren't going to be there with them.

It was time to talk about our living arrangements. I figured it was up to me to start the conversation. But before I could get the words out, Abby asked, "So what's the plan? Who's living where?"

I smiled, only because once again, she knew what I was going to say before I said it. It was scary, but part of her charm.

Or at least, that's what she'd claim.

Rather than wait for her to tell me what I was about to

say next, I said, "Boris wants me to stay here and look for the supposed money pit. You probably already know that. So I'm going to be here for a while.

"He wants you to help. Which means you'll be here for a while too. Unless you have somewhere else you need to be.

"Assuming you're staying, we can both move into the house. There's really no need for either of us to live in our RVs. The house has two bedrooms, and plenty of room for both of us.

"Will that work for you?"

I paused, waiting for her answer.

She was shaking her head when she said, "If you think I'm moving in here with you to be your sex slave, you're wrong. It's not going to happen."

I didn't know whether she was joking or not but opted to think she was. I sighed, making sure she saw me do it. Then I said, "That's such a relief. I was afraid you'd expected the same of me. For me to be your boy toy, ready to service you whenever you wanted. I'm glad we both agree that's not going to happen."

She smiled. "Yeah, right. You just wish you were my boy toy. I know how you are."

She went inside and I followed her to the living room. Stopping there, she looked around, and said, "I'll take the bedroom on the left. You can have the other one. We'll each have our own bathroom. Don't use mine for any reason. And don't come into my bedroom unless I ask you to. Don't get your hopes up though, it's not going to happen."

She took a breath, then continued "We'll put the litter boxes in your bathroom. You'll be responsible for keeping them clean. We'll put their bowls in the pantry."

She turned and walked into the kitchen. "We'll need to stock up on food. Enough to last for at least a week. We don't want to have to go into town every time we want to eat."

She was on a roll, so I didn't stop her. After opening the fridge, she said, "We have enough food for tonight, no problem. I'll make dinner, you'll clean up. Then in the morning, we'll take my van and go grocery shopping. On the way in, we'll stop by Mango Bay so you can pick up your Jeep. It'll come in handy out here. Then we'll buy food on the way out of town."

She opened the kitchen cabinet above the sink. "We definitely need to get a few things. I'll make a list."

She went out to her camper, grabbed a pen and notepad, and came back in carrying Buddy. He was probably waiting for her when she opened the door and there was no way she was going to leave him out there alone, knowing she'd be bringing him in any way.

She put him on the floor, told him to explore, and then started working on her shopping list. Since I didn't want to get in her way, I went out and got Bob and brought him in. Then I went back out, got his food and litter box, and set things up for him in my bathroom. He was smart enough to find the box when he needed it.

I wasn't sure about Buddy, though. Someone might have to show him where it was.

I spent the next hour bringing things from my RV and putting them in the bedroom where I'd be staying for the next few weeks while looking for treasure.

That evening, we had tacos and chips for dinner. After eating, I went outside and spent an hour putting the picnic table together. I was pretty proud of myself when I showed the finished piece to Abby. She said it looked good, but she was pretty sure Clyde could have gotten it together quicker.

She was probably right.

Chapter Twenty-Eight

The next morning, after sleeping in our separate bedrooms, we were both woken by Bob and Buddy playing a rough game of chase. The way Buddy was screaming, it sounded like Bob was killing him. I jumped out of bed and ran into the living room to break them up. When I got there, I found little Buddy laying on top of Bob, nipping at his tail.

Bob was on his back, rabbit footing Buddy's belly. It didn't look like either one was in pain. In fact, it looked like they were having fun.

When Abby came bounding out of her bedroom, the fun was over. Wearing only panties and an oversized white tee shirt; her hair a ratty mess, she looked down at the two cats, and with gritted teeth said, "You two keep quiet! I'm trying to sleep!"

Then she looked up at me with evil in her eyes and said, "You put them up to this, didn't you?"

I did my best not to smile. I knew it wouldn't go over well if I did. But I couldn't help myself. Seeing her standing there, in her skivvies, her hair a mess, and a frown on her face, I just couldn't keep from laughing.

As soon as I did, I knew I was in trouble.

She squinted and said, "What are you laughing at boxer boy?"

It took me a few seconds to get the reference. Then I remembered all I had on were my Popeye imprinted boxer shorts. Nothing else. I'd bought the cartoon boxers along with several other pair when I found them on sale at Beall's.

They were supposed to be made out of some new space-age material that wouldn't chaff in Florida's humidity. The tag said wearing them was like cradling your private parts in silk.

That was enough to win me over. I bought eight pair. Each with a different cartoon on them. It made it easy to keep up with which ones to wear on which days. Yesterday had been Popeye day. Today was Sponge Bob.

The cats took off when Abby growled at them, leaving just the two of us standing in the living room in our undies, facing each other. I was still smiling. As far as I was concerned it was a good day. The sun was up, the cats were happy, and I'd gotten to see Abby nearly naked before breakfast.

Seeing me grinning in her direction, she shook her head, pointed a finger at me, and said, "Don't you get any ideas. This is not a peep show for your entertainment."

She turned and headed back into her bedroom, slamming the door behind her. From inside, I could hear her talking to herself. It didn't sound like a happy conversation.

I went back into my room, changed clothes, and got ready for the day. Thirty minutes later, Abby joined me in the kitchen, all smiles as if nothing had happened. I played along. It was the safest option.

"Morning Walker. You ready to go into town today?"

"Yeah, whenever you are."

"Good, let's go now. We'll pick up breakfast on the way."

She grabbed the small backpack she usually carries and headed out the door. I followed. Outside, she stopped on the deck and turned to face me. "Make sure it's locked. We don't want the kitties getting out. Or Clyde getting in."

I'd already locked the door, but since she wanted me to check it, I did. I grabbed the doorknob and gave it a twist. It didn't budge. It was locked. She nodded her approval, and we hopped into her camper and headed into town. After pulling past our gate, she stopped and I got out, closed, and locked it.

Twenty minutes later we pulled into the McDonalds at the corner of Beach Road and 776. Abby got a breakfast burrito and a small orange juice. I went for a sausage egg biscuit and a medium Coke. We left McDonald's and made the short drive to Englewood beach parking lot where we ate our breakfast watching the morning tide roll in.

After eating, we got back onto Beach Road and drove north to the Sarasota county line. There, the name of the road changed to Manasota Key Road. A narrow strip of two-lane blacktop running up the center of the key. White beaches and the Gulf of Mexico on one side, the waters of Lemon Bay on the other.

When we reached the north end of the key, we crossed over the draw bridge and got back onto the mainland. From there, I expected Abby to turn right on 776 and head toward the Publix grocery store at the corner of Dearborn. But she didn't. Instead, she made a U-turn at the light and headed back in the direction we had just come from.

"You forget something?"

She nodded. "Yeah. I forgot I don't like shopping for groceries with you. In the store, you're like a little kid. Always putting junk food in the cart. Complaining when I make you take it out. I'm not going through that again.

"I'm taking you to Mango Bay so you can pick up your Jeep. Then you can go wherever you want and I won't have to tote you around in my van anymore."

Mango Bay was a small RV resort nestled on Lemon Bay in the heart of Englewood. Two years earlier I had helped the owners buy the place, and in return, they had offered me a site

153

in the park, rent-free for as long as I wanted it. It was the kind of deal I couldn't turn down.

Soon after moving my motorhome into the park, I realized I needed a way to get around when I went to town without having to unhook my big RV and drive it through the narrow village streets.

So I bought a Jeep.

I figured it was the perfect get-around rig, especially since the one I bought was already set up to tow behind the motorhome. I used it every day for about three months, but when it came to towing, it turned out to be more trouble than it was worth. It was another set of wheels I had to worry about, another set of potential problems, and frankly, I quickly grew tired of hooking and unhooking the Jeep at every stop.

After that first trip, whenever I went out on the road, I left the Jeep back at Mango Bay. I'd left it there when I headed out on my latest trip, and it would have still been at my assigned site, had the management of Mango Bay not changed after the deaths of the two owners.

It had been more than six months since I had used the site, and the new management decided it made sense to rent it to a paying customer. When they did, they moved my Jeep to their storage lot.

Abby had called a few days earlier and told them I'd be picking it up. They said no problem. They'd park it outside the entry gate and the keys would be above the visor.

With most cars, you wouldn't want to leave it unlocked in a public place with the keys barely hidden. But with Jeeps, it didn't really matter. Several models, including the one I had, could be started and driven away without a key. Fortunately, car theft in Englewood, especially near Mango Bay, wasn't much of a problem.

When Abby pulled up to the front gate, my Jeep was parked where they said it would be. The windows intact, tires and wheels still attached, and nary a dent.

I did a quick walk-around, looking for obvious problems, but found none. The old girl looked pretty good. Especially considering she had sat unused for much of the previous year. I opened the driver's door, found the key over the visor, and sat behind the wheel. After clearing dust off the gauges, I put the key in the ignition, pumped the clutch, and tried the starter. Surprisingly, the motor fired right up. Even after sitting for six months, it still ran.

Abby was in her van, waiting to see if the Jeep would start. If it wouldn't, she'd have to take me to find tools and parts to get it running. I was pretty sure she wasn't looking forward to doing that. That's probably why she smiled and gave me a thumbs up when the Jeep roared to life.

She figured, and rightly so, that she was off the hook. She wouldn't have to carry me around wasting a good part of the morning when she'd rather be doing something else.

With the Jeep's motor still humming, I returned her thumbs up with one of my own, letting her know all was good.

Instead of her asking me, "Are you sure?" or "Don't you want me to stay just in case," she put her van in gear and drove off, probably wanting to get out of sight before the Jeep had a chance to break down.

It was a smart move on her part.

She hadn't been gone more than a minute when the Jeep's motor coughed. It kept running, but not nearly as smooth as it had on the initial startup. I was beginning to get worried, especially when the motor coughed two more times.

I knew if the Jeep broke down at Mango Bay, it'd be a long walk to where I could find the tools and parts to get the problem fixed. With that in mind, I put it in gear and headed to the nearest gas station, the motor stumbling all the way. Twice it died on me. Both times I was able to restart it, but each time took longer.

I knew that sooner or later, it wouldn't start. It'd leave me stranded. But to my surprise, it didn't. Even though it coughed and kicked most of the way, it got me to the big Shell station on 776 next to Burger King. The little motor was sick but had made it.

Rolling up to the pumps, I started to diagnose the problem. Gasoline motors require three things to run well. Fuel, air, and spark. Since the motor had started right up, it had all three. But when it started stumbling, it meant that at least one of the elements was a weak link. My gut told me it was fuel. The Jeep had sat unused for the most part of a year. If the gas in it had gone bad, it would explain the coughing and sputtering. Water in the fuel tank would do the same thing.

The fix was easy. I filled the tank with fresh gas from the pump. Then went into the station and bought two cans of SeaFoam. I emptied both into the gas tank, then started the Jeep and pulled over to the side of the lot, out of the way of others. I let the motor run for five minutes to get the fresh fuel and Seafoam into the system.

Just like that, the problem was solved.

With a win under my belt, I headed to Babe's Hardware, the store I had stopped at two days earlier to buy hedge clippers and gloves. When I got there, I decided that even though I was pretty sure the Jeep would start, it would be a good idea to park it so the nose was facing the slight downhill slope to the road. That way, I could try to roll start it if the key didn't work.

Inside Babes, I resisted the urge to browse every aisle.

Instead, I focused on the two things I needed back at Duckville. A shovel and a wide brim straw hat. I quickly found both, paid, and headed out to the Jeep.

I was happy to see it was still where I parked it and hadn't rolled away. I jumped in, put the key in the ignition, and gave it a turn. It started right up. It was my lucky day.

Or at least, that's what I thought.

Chapter Twenty-Nine

Back on the road heading to Duckville, I mentally went through the list of things I needed to do when I got there. The most important was to start the search for the supposed hidden treasure.

I didn't think it existed, and even if it did, I doubted it would be hidden anywhere in Duckville. But I'd promised Boris I would look for it, and I would.

Before that though, I wanted to get with Trudy and have her show me where the men had been digging holes on the property. That might give me a clue as to where the treasure was buried, if it existed.

Thinking about Trudy naturally led me to think about Clyde and his fondness for Bud Lite. We didn't have any beer at Duckville and it would be a good idea to get some, to have it around when Trudy and Clyde came to visit.

I had already turned onto Placida Road off Seven Seven Six and was heading to Grove City when I remembered the beer. Winn-Dixie and Publix were three miles behind me and I didn't really want to turn around and go back. Traffic was always tight around the two stores, with a lot of people trying to get in and out at the same time. It was okay if you hit them early in the morning, but I'd burned a good part of the day getting the Jeep squared away. The early morning hours were long gone. The stores would be crowded and it'd be a pain getting into either one. Especially if all I was going to get was a twelve-pack of cold beer.

I was pretty sure I remembered seeing a sign advertising beer, lotto tickets, and bait in front of a small shack just outside Grove City.

I'd stop there.

Four minutes later, I rolled up to the tiny store. The parking lot was gravel, centered around two ancient gas pumps in front of a small cinder block building. It had once been white, but the exterior color had faded to a dingy brown.

The front door was flanked on both sides by large picture windows. Each one was plastered with ads for various brands of beer, smokes, and bait. Off to the side, an older window air conditioner was working hard, trying to keep the inside of the place cool.

After walking through the door, I was greeted by an older man behind the checkout counter. He looked up at me from his newspaper, nodded, and grunted out the words, 'Need something?'

I looked around, saw the beer coolers in the back, and pointed in their direction. The man nodded and went back to his paper. It could have been a racing form.

In the back, I grabbed two twelve packs of Bud Lite. One cold, and one room temperature. The cold one I'd put in the fridge right away. The other one would go into the pantry until it was needed. I figured with Trudy and Clyde doing most of the drinking, the beer would last at least a week. When it ran out, I'd come back for more.

While the guy at the counter was ringing me up, I noticed a collection of small photos taped on the back of his cash register. They were printed on real photo paper, the kind with a white border. You rarely see those these days.

They looked to be from a family album. In each one, an animal was front and center. But not the typical family pet. The animals included a bear dancing with a young woman, a man leading a prancing horse, and another young woman petting a leopard.

I was still looking at them when the man behind the register asked, "Anything else?"

I pointed to the photos. "You take those?"

"Yeah, some of them. Back in the day."

"You were with the circus?"

"Yeah, a long time ago."

I decided to introduce myself. "My name's Walker. I just bought the place next door to Trudy. Trudy Love. You know her?"

He looked up at me and growled. "You a developer?"

I could see the disgust in his eyes. It was clear that people in these parts didn't hold with those that came in with bulldozers intent on ripping up green spaces just to replace them with concrete slabs and condos.

"No, I'm not. In fact, I bought the place so developers couldn't get their hands on it."

He shook his head. "Yeah, that's what they all say. Then next thing you know, they clear cut the land, stake it out, and start selling lots. We don't need any more of that around here."

He tapped the two twelve-packs I had paid for. "They're going to get warm. You best be going."

I took the hint.

I grabbed the beers and headed for the door. When I opened it, I could see his reflection in the glass. He had picked up his phone and was making a call. Maybe to Trudy to check out my story. Or maybe not.

Outside, I put the beer behind the Jeep's front seat and continued on to Duckville. The gate was still locked. I'd gotten back before Abby, which was a good thing since I'd be taking up some of her fridge space with the beer. Hopefully, she wouldn't notice.

Back at the house, everything was as we had left it. The door was still locked, and inside the cats had moved onto the couch for their afternoon naps. Bob heard me moving around and opened one eye to make sure it was me and not an intruder. Satisfied that he was safe, he went back to sleep.

I put the cold beer in the fridge trying my best to spread out the cans so as not to take up so much space. I knew Abby would have something to say about it otherwise.

With the brewskies taken care of, I sat in one of the recliners and thought about the treasure. More specifically, I thought about where Tony Ducks would hide a suitcase full of gold.

He would want it hidden where others wouldn't easily find it. But it needed to be somewhere he could get to quickly without being seen and without needing help to dig it up.

Since it seemed like Tony's plan was to be able to grab the gold when the feds were hot on his heels and he needed to get out of town quickly, he would want it somewhere close to his escape vehicle, whatever that might be.

As I thought about it, I wondered about his boat. The Charon. The one that Boris had recently acquired.

The boat seemed like a logical place to stash the treasure. It had many advantages, including being a way to quickly get offshore and away from the long arm of the law. Tony surely understood this and he may have in fact, hidden his treasure within the bowels of his yacht.

If he had, and if the treasure was still there, my job would be over.

I picked up my phone and called Boris' private number. He answered almost immediately.

"Walker, what have you got for me."

There were no pleasantries. Just 'what have you got for me.'

Since I didn't have anything other than a thought, I jumped right in. "Have you searched the boat? The Charon? That's the most logical place for Tony to hide the gold. On the boat."

He didn't answer right away. Maybe because he wasn't alone. I could hear voices of other men in the room with him. It may have been for that reason that he answered as he did. "Yes, we have considered that option and have taken steps to confirm that it is not the situation. Please continue your effort."

He ended the call, clearly telling me that they had searched the boat and not found any treasure.

Disappointed that my idea hadn't panned out, I decided to try something else.

I grabbed four cold beers from the fridge, went outside, and tapped the horn on the Jeep three times.

Chapter Thirty

Ten minutes later, Trudy Love, in all her tattooed glory, minus the machete she had been carrying when I first met her, stepped out of the woods. She was wearing the same Daisy Duke shorts she had the day before, cut high and showing a lot of skin. There was no way I couldn't notice how nice her legs were. Tanned, toned, and long.

Instead of a bikini top, she was wearing a button-up fishing shirt much like the one I had on. Hers was mint green. Mine was faded wheat. Her top three buttons were undone revealing much more skin than I was. No nonsense dark sunglasses hid her eyes. A leather retaining strap hung over her ample bosom, presumably to keep the glasses from falling away when she removed them.

If she walked into any bar in the world dressed as she was, there would be a lot of men wanting to buy her drinks.

Including me.

Clyde followed a few steps behind. Moving slowly, sniffing the air as he walked. When he saw me, he stopped, stared in my direction for a few seconds, then bared his teeth. He held the pose long enough for me to understand the message he was sending. Trudy was his. Leave her alone. Or else.

As quickly as he struck the pose, he relaxed. He let out a whoop, a war cry of sorts, and came galloping toward me. It took him less than four seconds to cover the fifty yards that had been separating us. A lesser man might have turned and run. I didn't. I stood my ground. Mainly because Clyde reached me before I could get out of the way. All I could do was close my eyes and brace for the hit I was sure to take when his body slammed into me.

But it never happened.

He slid to a stop three feet in front of me, chattering away like a child. It almost sounded like he was laughing about the trick he had played. At that moment, it dawned on me that he had a sense of humor. Instead of being a wild animal or a circus curiosity, he was intelligent, playful, and more human than a lot of people I've met.

By the time Trudy joined us, Clyde and I were both grinning at each other. He'd picked up a small purple flower and handed it to me. It seemed like a gesture of friendship, so I accepted it, sniffed it, and gave him a thumbs up. He responded with a grin and a whoop.

Trudy translated. "He's trying to bribe you. He wants a beer. He gave you something and in return, he gets a beer. In his mind, that's how it works."

I nodded. "Well, I guess it's good that I've got cold beer inside. You mind if I give him one?"

"No, it won't hurt him. As long as it's lite."

"That's what it is. Bud Lite. You want one?"

She shook her head. "Not now. Not until after we go out and look for those holes. By the way, where's Abby?"

I pointed to the gate. "She's in town stocking up on food. She'll be back before long."

I went inside and grabbed a beer for Clyde, and for me, the straw hat and shovel I picked up at Babe's.

As soon as Clyde saw me come out with a beer in hand, he started bouncing up and down and chirping like an over-excited kid seeing the ice cream truck. But instead of running up and taking it from me, he was very polite. He stayed where he was and let me walk to him.

When I held out the beer, he looked over at Trudy to make sure it was okay. After she nodded her approval, he took the can, quickly pulled the pop-top, and took a long swallow. After which he burped loudly and grinned.

He was a happy monkey.

Five minutes later, Trudy was leading me along the fence line that separated her property from mine. Based on what I had seen on the satellite photos, I had assumed that Duckville was heavily wooded and it would be difficult to walk the boundary lines. But as it turned out, the satellite photos were old. The property had been cleared after they had been taken, the grounds replanted with palms, and most of the underbrush cleared. It had grown back since then, but it wasn't too bad to walk through. At least in the daylight.

With Trudy leading, we followed the fence line to the edge of the property where it bordered the Intracoastal. There, she pointed to a hole that had been dug at the corner, just a foot off the old seawall that had been built when the waterway was dug.

"See, the men I saw came out here and dug that. Looks like they put something in it."

I stepped over to the hole, which was about the width of a coffee can. Looking in, I could see that whoever had dug it, had planted some kind of battery-powered device. It looked like a plastic box with a very small antenna on top.

Looking closer, I could see there was writing on the antenna. In order to read it, I had to get down on my hands and knees. I hoped that Clyde didn't see my bent-over butt as some kind of invitation. Or think it was his chance to play another trick by shoving me over the seawall into the water.

Fortunately, Trudy stepped behind me. Presumably to keep Clyde away. Or maybe to look at my butt.

Whatever the reason, I bent over and focused on the words etched on the antenna. I read them out loud so she could hear.

"Property of the Corp of Engineers. Do not disturb."

After seeing that it had been put there by the COE, I stood up, dusted off my knees, and said, "I think it's some kind of monitoring device. Probably to track water levels or something else that the Corp monitors. Did you say there was another one?"

Trudy pointed along the seawall. "Yeah, down there, maybe a hundred feet."

We walked to where she pointed and found another hole. It looked pretty much like the first, but without the monitoring device. Maybe the Corp wasn't satisfied with the location. Or maybe someone else had dug it.

Continuing our walk, we found four more holes. Each one a different size. Only the last one, the one at the corner where the bay flows out into the Intracoastal, had the same kind of electronic device as the first.

Clearly, two of the holes had been dug by the Corp of Engineers. We weren't so sure about the other ones. They were bigger, random sizes and locations, with no attempt to cover them up.

"Trudy, what do you think?"

She shook her head, "Don't know for sure, but they look like what you get when you dig for sharks' teeth. And they look recent."

I didn't want people coming onto my property digging holes for any reason. It had to stop.

"Trudy, what about that video on YouTube? Is it still up there?"

"No, they pulled it down after a few months. Got

complaints from other landowners around here. Unfortunately, a lot of people saw the video before it was deleted. It had six thousand views at last count."

The good news was the video was gone. The bad was lots of people had seen it and at least a few of them had decided to come out and dig for shark's teeth on my property.

I needed to put a few no trespassing signs up along the water's edge. And maybe get a big dog. Or a watch monkey.

We'd been out almost an hour and it looked like Clyde was ready for another beer. At least that was the excuse I used to convince Trudy that it was time to go back. It wasn't that I was tired, it was just that I had other things I wanted to look into and questions that needed to be answered.

I figured that once we got back to the house, I could break out the beers, and maybe after one or two, Trudy would be able to tell me what she remembered when Tony Ducks lived on the property.

As it turned out, two beers wasn't enough.

Chapter Thirty-One

Abby was waiting for us when we got back to the house. She was outside sitting at the picnic table I'd put together the night before. The fact that it was still standing was a good sign. Abby probably weighed less than a hundred pounds, so it wasn't a real test, but still, it did bode well.

She had her laptop open and was using the keyboard to enter text. When she looked up and saw the three of us heading her way, she quickly closed the cover and slid the device into a tote bag under her seat. She stood and came off the deck to greet us.

"Did you find anything?"

"Yeah, we did. Trudy showed me where the people were digging. Right at the corners of the property. Two of the holes had sensors in them. From the Corp of Engineers. Probably to monitor water levels or boat traffic."

"So, no treasure hunters?"

I shook my head. "We found other holes that could have been dug by people looking for sharks' teeth. No way to know for sure, but they didn't look like the Corp of Engineers holes. The only good thing about them was they were right at the water's edge. The diggers hadn't come onto our property. At least as far as we could tell."

Abby shook her head. "We'll have to keep checking. And figure out a way to keep people away."

She turned her attention to Trudy, but before she could say anything, Clyde picked up one of the little purple flowers that seemed to blanket the ground and offered it to her.

Abby smiled and said, "Why thank you, Clyde. That's very nice of you."

She sniffed the flower, then tucked it into the top buttonhole of the shirt she was wearing.

Clyde was waiting. Trudy and I both knew what he wanted but Abby didn't, so I told her.

"Abby, when he gives you a gift, it's only polite to give him something in return. That's what he's waiting for."

She frowned. "I don't have anything to give him. What do you suggest?"

I knew the answer. "A beer. If it's okay with Trudy."

Abby turned and asked her. "Would you like a beer?"

"Sure, I'll take one. And if you have enough, get one for Clyde. But we don't want to impose."

"You're not imposing, not at all. We really appreciate you coming over and helping us get settled in. I don't know how we can return the favor, but we've got plenty of beer."

While Abby was inside getting the brewskies, which I assumed she'd discovered when she put groceries away, I suggested we move over to the picnic table and sit. It'd be more comfortable, plus I wanted to see if it could hold the weight of three adults and a chimp, assuming Clyde would be joining us at the table.

When Abby returned, she had three beers. One for Trudy, one for Clyde, and one for herself. She knew I wouldn't be drinking one so she brought me water instead.

Clyde hooted when he saw what she had and he loped over to where Abby was standing. He stopped in front of her and grinned a chimp-sized smile. Abby couldn't help but smile back. She said, "Clyde, would you like a beer?"

He hooted in excitement and she rewarded him by

handing him the cold brew. He popped the top and took a long swallow. When he pulled the can away from his mouth, he grinned and nodded in Abby's direction, seemingly thanking her. Then he walked over to the edge of the steps and sat.

The three of us sat at the picnic table. We talked about how human Clyde seemed, and how he had better manners than most of the people we see out in public. Trudy told us that it was her father who had taught him manners and how to act around people.

I used the mention of her father as an excuse to ask her a question. "Did your dad know any of the people who lived here before we bought it?

She nodded, "He knew the woman who owned it and sold to the developer. He didn't know her well, just that she had inherited it from her own father. He was the guy who supposedly put the Quonset huts in. They say he got them from the Army. I don't know if it's true or not. Pop never talked to him. He had moved away before he got here."

After taking a sip of beer, she continued. "The people who were here when Pop moved in pretty much kept to themselves. Some kind of men's club I think. They'd show up every once in a while to play cards or fish. They had a couple of boats and would go offshore every now and then.

"According to Pop, they never caused any trouble. They stayed on their side of the fence and we stayed on ours.

"Then one day, they were gone and never came back. They just left, leaving everything behind. A few years later, the daughter showed up and listed the place for sale. Pop would have bought it, but the price was more than he could afford. He made her a couple of offers, but we weren't in the ballpark.

"The place eventually sold. A young guy bought it. He showed up here in his fancy car, wearing expensive shoes and a silk shirt. He came out with an architect and showed us the plans they had drawn up. They were going to put up condos. Wanted to know if we wanted to invest.

"Pop didn't want to have anything to do with him. He said there was no way the guy could get permission from the state to build condos on this land. There were too many issues to overcome. Not the least was the lack of a water and sewer system.

"But the guy went ahead and put up survey stakes showing where the condos would be. He had brochures printed up showing what the buildings would look like. He even had a big sign at the gate saying 'future home of Grove Landing', along with an artist rendition of the condo towers.

"He brought in a series of potential investors trying to convince them to help fund the project. Not sure if any of them did or not, but Pop was right. The whole thing was a scam. About a year into it, the guy folded up shop and disappeared. He left the investors holding the bag.

"The bank had no choice but to take the property back. They were pretty good about it, at least from our point of view. They kept the place up, made sure no vagrants moved in, and apparently, over the years, cleared away all the legal issues. I guess that's why you were able to buy it."

I nodded. "So after the men's club left, no one really lived here, right?"

"As far as I know, no one's lived on the property since then. The developer used the big hut as an office of a sort, and his crew moved a lot of dirt around, mostly near the dock and out at the seawall. But they never lived here."

"Moved dirt? What do you mean?"

She smiled and set her now empty beer can on the table. Abby quickly asked, "Would you like another?"

"Sure. Why not?"

Abby went inside and came back out with three more beers. She put one in front of Trudy and one where she'd been sitting. She held the third up so Clyde could see it.

"Clyde, you want another?"

She didn't have to ask twice. He plucked a small flower from the ground and brought it over to Abby. After handing it to her she handed him a beer in return. Between them, they had worked out a rate of exchange. One flower for one beer.

After Trudy opened her can, I repeated my question, "You say they moved dirt? What do you mean?"

She pointed over her shoulder toward the Intracoastal. "They brought out the smallest front-end loader you've ever seen and used it to clear away brush and scrape up a few piles of dirt. Pop said they wanted potential developers to think work on the project was already underway.

"But that little tractor was a joke. It wasn't big enough to dig and not heavy enough to move much. It was mostly for show."

She paused for a moment, tilted her head like she was trying to remember something, then said, "I think that they left it. The tractor. I think it's still out in the tool shed. The one with the garage door."

Abby had said there were three huts on the property. So far, I'd only seen the main one. The one we had moved into. I definitely needed to check out the other two. And soon.

"Trudy, have you been in them? The other huts?"

She nodded toward Clyde. "He's been in both of them. A few years back in early spring, he was out exploring. He didn't come home for lunch and didn't make it back for dinner either.

"I was worried he was hurt, so I went out looking for him. Nobody was living here then, so I climbed the fence and came over here.

"It took me almost an hour to find him. I was calling his name over and over as I walked. I was up close to the workshop when I first heard him. A whimper. Like he knew he was in trouble.

"I looked around and when I got closer to the building, I could hear him inside. I don't know how he got in there, but he couldn't get back out. He had somehow locked himself in.

"He was moaning and I knew I needed to get him out before he panicked. He's strong and can do a lot of damage if he gets out of control.

"The overhead door was locked. I couldn't budge it. But the walk-in door was easy to get through. All I had to do was give it a good kick and it gave. I went in, found Clyde, and led him outside.

"I did look around while I was in there. There were tools and some old farm equipment. And a row of metal lockers, the kind you find in a high school gym.

"Lot of acorns and palm nuts on the floor. Like maybe squirrels or rats had moved in and stashed them there. I didn't stay long enough to find out.

"Clyde explored the other hut too. It's open-air, just a roof, no end walls. There's a broken-down boat in that one. An old cabin cruiser. It was probably nice back in the day, but not any more. Things are living in it now."

Trudy finished off her beer and stood. "I guess it's time for me and Clyde to head back home. He likes the new weather girl on Wink News and he gets upset if we miss her four o'clock show.

She turned to him. "Clyde, you want to watch Wink News?"

He hooted. It was clear he understood the question. He wanted to go home and watch the weather girl. I could understand why. She was a looker.

Trudy thanked us for the beer and after she stacked their empty cans on the picnic table, they walked back toward their place, holding hands.

When they were out of earshot, Abby asked, "Is there something going on between you and her?"

"No, why do you ask?"

"It may be nothing, but I noticed she was wearing makeup. Women usually don't go to the trouble unless they have a reason."

I acted surprised. "Really? You think I'm the reason?"

"No, that's not what I think. But when a woman puts on makeup, it usually means there's someone special around."

I made a fake frowny face. "What about you? You put on makeup before you went into town today. Does that means there's someone special there I need to worry about?"

She smiled. "Maybe there is. Or maybe I put it on for you. It's something you'll have to figure out on your own."

Chapter Thirty-Two

While Clyde and Trudy were watching the weather girl on Wink News, Abby and I decided we should check out the other two Quonset huts. Abby referred to them as number two and number three. The one we were living in, was number one.

I hadn't seen the other huts and knew I'd have to eventually search both for Tony's hidden gold. Before I could, I'd have to find out where they were.

Abby said she'd show me.

I grabbed the key ring with the last unknown key and we headed out, following the same general path that led to the boat dock. About halfway there, we veered west and followed a trail that led to the huts. The curved walls on both were painted a camouflage green and brown pattern. They blended in well with the nearby palms and palmettos dotting the landscape. Had I not been looking for the buildings, I could have easily missed them.

Of the two, number three was in the worst shape. It looked to have been originally designed as a shelter for small aircraft. Just a metal hoop structure wide enough to keep an airplane out of the elements. There was no wall on either end, making it easy for a quick entry or exit when needed.

The lack of backing walls was its undoing. The wide-open expanse on both ends made for an easy entry for animals, wind, rain, and whatever else mother nature threw at it.

Apparently, a lot had been thrown.

The remains of an old cabin cruiser sat forlornly under

the shelter. Sitting on a sagging two-axle trailer, the fiberglass hull was a spider's web of hairline cracks, any one of which could split the boat in half in heavy waves. The rubber gaskets around the windows and portholes were long gone. Either devoured by vermin or dry rotted by relentless Florida heat. The glass that had once held firm was nowhere to be seen.

The once-proud flybridge had collapsed into the cabin, creating a jumbled mess of fiberglass and plexiglass shards.

The bow was facing us, and the maker's name, while faded, was still visible in gold script. Chris Craft. From where I was standing, the boat looked to be about thirty-two feet long. A manageable size for cruising the Intracoastal.

I couldn't tell whether it still had its motors or not. They were at the back and to get to them, I'd have to cut a path through the weeds that surrounded the boat. It wasn't something I wanted to do anytime soon. No telling what kind of vermin had taken up residence under the hull.

In its current condition, the boat was nothing more than an environmental hazard. A pile of broken fiberglass filled with shards of glass posing a danger to all that came near. It needed to be put down. A sorry ending for what had once been a fine vessel.

From behind me, Abby said, "It's a shame, isn't it?"

I nodded. "It is. Somebody should have rescued it."

The truth was, go anywhere in Florida where people have boats and you'll find lots of them in a similar condition. Some will have gotten that way after having been caught out in a storm, but most will be a simple case of long-term neglect.

Knowing there was nothing I could do about it, I decided that the best thing would be to hire someone to take it to the crusher. But that would have to wait until the treasure hunt was over.

Abby led me over to hut number two. Unlike number three, it had end walls in place and was totally enclosed. The front walk-in door and the two windows were intact, as was the large roll-up garage-type door.

Trudy had said that when Clyde locked himself in, she was able to get in through the front door. She made it sound like it was unlocked at the time. But when I tried it, it wasn't. Maybe someone from the bank had secured it when they took over the property.

Fortunately, the last key on the key ring unlocked it. I opened the door slowly, thinking it was likely that a raccoon or possum might have taken up residence inside. I didn't want to surprise or corner the critter and force it into attack mode.

Abby didn't share my concern. She stepped around me, kicked the door open, and yelled, "We're coming in. If you want out, leave now."

If there were animals inside they may not have understood her words, but they would have gotten her meaning. She was coming in and they needed to be gone.

The only way out would be through the same door where we were standing. The critters would have to get past us. Fortunately, none tried. We didn't hear any scurrying around, but we did smell the distinct odor of animals nesting in the area.

Once inside, Abby looked around, then pointed up at the ceiling. "There's lights. See if you can find the switch."

I didn't know whether the electricity would be on or not, but it didn't take me long to find a switch near the door. I flipped it on, and to my amazement, the overhead fluorescents buzzed to life. In a matter of seconds, the inside of the building had gone from darkness to full-on light.

We were finally able to see what was around us.

As Trudy had said, there were a few tools and some

equipment, as well as a workbench and a row of metal lockers. All but one of the lockers was open and empty. The one that was closed had a padlock keeping us from seeing what was in it. I'd have to come back with bolt cutters to check it out.

The workbench on the far wall was devoid of tools, except for a heavy-duty angle grinder. There were cardboard boxes under it, sagging from age. We hadn't thought to bring gloves, so I didn't bother digging through them.

Off to the side, directly in front of the garage door, was the small tractor Trudy had said the developer had brought in to move dirt. Three tires were flat and the front bucket was sitting on the cement floor. Other than that, it looked to be in decent condition. If I could get it started, it might be handy to have on the property. I could use it to grade the road leading in from the gate and maybe even clear walking paths to the dock and seawall.

Before I fooled with the tractor though, I'd need to come back and do a thorough search of the building. It seemed to be an ideal place to hide something of value. It was weather-tight, easy to get to from the house or the dock, and had electricity.

After checking out both buildings, we headed back home. It was a short hike, and we got there quickly. Bob met us at the door. His younger companion, Buddy was nowhere to be seen. Abby called his name, expecting him to come running. But he didn't. He was a no-show.

Seemingly not worried, she said, "He's probably sleeping. When he hears us moving around, he'll show up."

She headed to her bedroom and I, to mine. I washed up and after changing shirts, met her back in the kitchen. I offered to help her with dinner, but she said, "No, you'll only be in the way. Go do something else."

There wasn't much else to do so I went into the living room

and turned on the TV. We didn't have cable and the old TV couldn't stream from the internet. But it was connected to an outdoor antenna and using that, I was able to pick up local stations from Fort Myers, Sarasota, and Tampa.

One of the stations was Wink News, and when I turned to it, the weather girl that Clyde liked, was telling us about an impending cold front. I figured Abby would want to check her out so I said, "Abby, it's the weather girl. The one Clyde likes. Come see."

She looked over her shoulder at the TV, watched the girl point at the map for a few seconds, then turned away shaking her head.

Apparently, she wasn't impressed.

Ten minutes later we ate dinner. We had the same thing that we had the day before. Chicken tacos.

I didn't dare complain though. Mainly because I liked the way she made them and I didn't want to give her a reason to put me in charge of preparing meals in the future.

Chapter Thirty-Three

Buddy showed up just as we were clearing away our plates. He was blinky-eyed and had a spider web hanging from his whiskers. Abby went over, gave him a pet, and asked him where he'd been.

He meowed a response, but neither of us understood what he was saying. After getting two more pets, he trotted over to his food bowl. He was apparently hungry after a hard day of sleeping.

While he ate, Abby and I filled our wine glasses and moved over to the couch in the living room. So far we hadn't talked about our involvement in Boris's treasure hunt and I decided it was time to do so.

"Abby, if you were Tony Ducks and were worried about the Feds coming in and seizing your assets, and you had a suitcase of gold coins, where would you hide them? More specifically, where would you hide them here, on this property, assuming that's what Tony did?"

She didn't answer right away, which was a good sign. It meant she was thinking about it. After about ten seconds she said, "Grab a pencil. I want you to make a list."

It would have been easier to jot down notes on my computer, but since she said she wanted a pencil, that's what I was going to get her. If I could find one.

I went to the kitchen and looked for a junk drawer. Just about every house has one, and you can usually find a pencil or pen in it. The Quonset hut's kitchen was no different. It came fully stocked with dishes and silverware, and as expected, a junk drawer filled with things the previous occupants didn't really need but didn't want to throw away. Including a pencil and notepad.

I grabbed both and went back to the couch where Abby was waiting. Seeing me holding the pencil, she said, "Write this down.

"Size of container. We are looking for something probably no bigger than a suitcase. We don't know how many gold coins there are, but let's assume two hundred along with a few pieces of jewelry. That would weigh less than twenty pounds and would fit in a small briefcase.

"Container construction. The container needs to be waterproof and able to withstand the elements. It also needs to be light enough for Tony to lift and carry, and small enough to fit into whatever vehicle he is traveling in. A military ammo box or a waterproof pelican case would be a good choice.

"Where to hide it. This is where it gets tricky. His yacht would have been my first guess. But Boris says it's been searched and it's not there.

"If it's not on his yacht, then my second guess would be somewhere here at Duckville. The feds didn't know about this place, so Tony would feel safe hiding his gold here. He wouldn't want any of his people knowing about it because he wouldn't want them looking for it when he wasn't around. He'd want to hide it in a place they would never think to look in or accidentally find.

"I don't think he'd put it in this house. With its rounded walls, there aren't too many places to hide things. There's no room for a wall safe and no way to put in a floor safe without jack-hammering up the concrete floor. I haven't seen any evidence of that.

"He could have hidden it in a big piece of furniture, but

that's not likely. It'd be too easy to find and there's a chance that the furniture could get sold or taken away."

She checked to make sure I was taking notes. To her, it probably looked like I was. I was moving the pencil on the paper, but in reality, I was only writing the first couple of words of each point. I didn't think I needed to take down everything she was saying.

The important thing was the direction she was going. Hopefully, she'd end up with the answer to the question I had asked, which was, 'Where did she think Tony Ducks would have hidden the gold on the property?'

I wanted to keep her train of thought on track, but also wanted to cover the bases, so I said, "I agree with you so far. About the size, the construction, the weight, and whether or not it would be in this house. But I think we still need to search in here, just in case."

She nodded, "You're right. This place needs to be searched. You should plan to do that tomorrow."

"Me? By myself? Aren't you going to help?"

"No, I'm not. I won't be here. I'm leaving for a couple of days."

"You're leaving? Where are you going?"

She hesitated with her answer, then said, "Miami. To see if I can talk to some of Tony's old crew. Their names were in that envelope you gave me. Three of them live there. I'm going to go see if they know about the money pit.

"I know it's a long shot. They probably won't even talk to me. Even if they do, they may not know much. But it's worth trying."

I nodded. "You want me to go with you?"

"No, I don't. I think I'll have better luck going alone. I'll tart myself up and hope they'll want to spend an afternoon with me talking about the old days."

"Tart yourself up? How do you plan on doing that?"

She smiled. "I'll put on some makeup, wear a short skirt, and show a bit of cleavage. That almost always works."

"It does?"

She smiled. "Yeah, it does. It worked on you."

She was right. It had worked on me. Back when we first met. It would probably work on me again.

If she only tried.

Chapter Thirty-Four

"While you're off in Miami flirting with old men, I'll search the house. Including your bedroom. If you have anything in there you don't want me to see, you better take it with you."

"Don't worry, I will. You mind taking care of Buddy while I'm gone?"

"No, I'll cover for you. You driving your van?"

"Yeah, it has everything I need. My food, my clothes, and a bed if I feel like a nap."

That was one of the advantages of traveling in an RV. Even a small one like Abby's. You could take off at a moment's notice and have everything you needed. Food, clothing, a bathroom, and a bed. You didn't have to worry about getting a motel room and wondering who slept in it the night before or what germs they could have left in it.

Traveling in an RV, you didn't have to stop at rest areas and use public bathrooms where toilet seats were still warm from the person who used it before you. Or eat at places where food safety was low on the list of priorities.

The more I thought about her trip to Miami, the more I wanted to go with her. "You sure you don't want me to tag along? I could help you drive, give you someone to talk to on the way. It'd be fun."

She smiled and patted my leg. "No Walker, not this time. I'm going alone. And anyway, there are things you need to take care of around here. Like searching this place and making sure Buddy and Bob have plenty of food and water."

She was right.

My time would be better spent looking for the treasure. But that didn't change the fact that I wanted to get back on the road. And soon.

"You'll call me if anything comes up, right?"

"I will. Don't worry, it'll be an easy trip."

I hoped she was right. But you never knew what to expect in Miami. It's a crazy town with lots of crazy people. Including more than a few retired Mafia henchmen.

I didn't want to think about the risks she might be taking, so I changed the subject. "Let's get back to your list. You said you didn't think Tony would have hidden the gold here in the house. I think you're right about that. So if not in here, where?"

She thought for a moment, then said, "There's a lot of ground outside where he could bury something as small as a briefcase. He could get down a couple of feet with a shovel before he hit hard pack. That would be deep enough to cover it up.

"But if he buried something, he'd have to worry about heavy rains exposing it, or hurricanes washing it away, or someone using a front-end loader finding it.

"So while I think burying is probably what he would do, he'd have to find the right place. It'd have to be out of the way, somewhere it wouldn't accidentally be dug up. It'd need to be away from ditches and away from where water could wash the soil away. He'd want it far from any place that someone might consider planting a garden or flowers or running plumbing or water lines.

"He'd want it easy to get to when he needed it. If he buried it too deep or stored it in something too heavy to lift, he'd need help and I'm sure he'd want to avoid that.

"Ideally, he'd want to be able to show up in his car, drive to where the gold was hidden, grab it and get away without anyone seeing what he was doing.

"In that case, he might want it near the road. At a spot with enough room to quickly turn his car around and get away – regardless of the time of day or weather.

"But for starters, I think you search the house first, then the two other Quonset huts. After that, start searching along the driveway. Look for a turn-around spot with maybe a rise or a pile of rocks nearby. Try to imagine what the place looked like twenty years ago. Before the developer came in with his dirt mover.

"I'll be back in two days. If you haven't found anything by then, I'll help."

We spent the rest of the evening talking about Tony Ducks and the places he could have hidden his treasure. My feeling was it was hidden somewhere on his yacht. He conducted most of his gold buying on the boat and that's was where he kept his money and purchases during his trips to the Keys. It seemed reasonable that his treasure would be stashed either on the boat or close to it.

Abby agreed, at least partly. "The problem with his yacht is the weather. You can't predict it. A squall or a hurricane could be the end of it. Even a boat moored in a safe harbor can be blown out to sea during foul weather. If it got lost or sunk, the gold would be gone forever. Plus the feds may have known about his yacht. If they did, they would have seized and searched it.

"So Tony probably wouldn't want to keep the bulk of his gold on it. He wouldn't want to risk it being seized by the feds or lost in a storm."

Her points were valid. Plus the yacht had been searched by

Boris's people and they hadn't found the gold.

But I still had a question about the boat.

"The boat's name. Any idea what it means?"

She nodded. "Yeah, I know exactly what it means. But I'm not going to tell you. Look it up. See for yourself."

It would have been easier if she'd just told me, but since she wanted me to look it up, I did.

I pulled out my phone, brought up Google, and searched for 'Charon'.

The results were surprising.

According to Wikipedia, Charon was the name of the boatman of the underworld. He carried souls of the newly deceased from the world of the living to the world of the dead.

It was definitely a strange choice for the name for a boat – unless the boat was owned by a mafia hitman who made his living moving people to the world of the dead.

Choosing that for the name, told me a lot about Tony Ducks. Instead of someone trying to hide what he did for a living, he wanted people to know. Naming his boat Charon told the world he was proud to be the ferryman of the dead. He was the one who brought death to the living.

The name was a clear warning for those that might cross him.

I wondered if that warning applied to me. Especially since I was living on what he likely still considered his property, and I was searching for gold that he believed belonged to him.

Would he be the boatman that took me to the land of the dead?

I would soon find out.

Chapter Thirty-Five

The next morning, Abby got up early and headed out. I was still in bed when she left. She tiptoed into my room, kissed me on my forehead, and said she'd see me in two days.

Had I been a better man, I would have gotten up earlier and had breakfast ready for her. I would have helped her load her van and made sure it was ready for the road.

Instead, I stayed in bed and slept.

After she left, Bob joined me. He snuggled up between my legs and quickly dozed off. Not long after, Buddy joined the party. He wanted to squeeze in next to Bob, but that wasn't going to happen. Bob wasn't going to share his space. He didn't want Buddy sleeping too close to him. A quick swat across the nose convinced the younger cat to find another spot.

He moved to the bottom of the bed and settled in close to my feet.

The three of us slept fairly peacefully for the next two hours. Bob was the first to get up. He always had his morning snack around nine, and he wasn't going to miss out, no matter how much he enjoyed his sleep.

Five minutes later, Buddy heard Bob chowing down and decided it was time for him to get up and have a snack as well. He rolled out of bed and headed to the pantry where we kept their food and water. I expected to hear a fight as the two cats battled over who would be King of the food bowl.

But it was all quiet on the western front. Apparently, Bob had had his fill before Buddy showed up. Or maybe they decided to share. Either way, it was a non-event.

Five minutes later, I climbed out of bed and took care of my morning bathroom chores. I headed to the kitchen, made a quick breakfast of eggs and toast, and planned out my day.

My first priority was to search the house. I didn't think I'd find the treasure, but since I owned the place, I figured I might as well know what was in it.

I started in my bedroom, checking behind and under the few pieces of furniture. I followed up in the bathroom, doing the same thing, checking everywhere, even in the toilet tank. The only thing I found was a few stray ear swabs in one of the vanity drawers.

Back out in the bedroom, I checked the closet and only found my clothes.

Not finding anything of interest in my bedroom, I moved my search into Abby's. Hers was a lot nicer than mine. A bit larger and it had a rug on the floor. It smelled better too. She'd made her bed before she left and put all her things away. She probably knew I'd be in there and didn't want me to think she was a slob. I already knew she wasn't, but it was still nice of her to make it presentable.

I checked everything in the room, including inside all the drawers, under the bed, and under the rug. I didn't find anything except for a few errant dust bunnies. Her closet was mostly empty. Two shirts and three pairs of shoes.

Her bathroom, like her bedroom, was larger than mine. The vanity had more drawers, the toilet looked to be newer and larger. Instead of just a shower, she had a tub, one that I could easily fit in. I was thinking I should give it a try while she was away.

Not finding anything in the search of her room, I checked the rest of the house. The kitchen, the pantry, the utility closet, and the living room. I found lots of interesting things, mostly cooking-related in the kitchen but no gold.

I carefully checked all the walls and floors, and under the rugs, looking for any sign of a safe, but found nothing. After searching for two hours, I was pretty much convinced there was no gold hidden anywhere inside the Quonset hut.

I had just finished my search when my phone chimed with an incoming call from Abby. I answered on the third ring.

"Hey Abby, how's it going?"

"Not too bad. I made good time and just pulled into Miami. I'm meeting with Biscuit Gravano in about an hour. He was one of the guys who worked with Tony. When I called him, he said he'd be happy to talk about the old days, but I have to meet him at his place because he doesn't drive. I'm heading in that direction now. How are things going there?"

I decided not to tell her about me sleeping in. She might not appreciate it, especially since she had to get up so early. Instead, I made it sound like I'd been real busy. "I searched the whole house. Every room including yours. I checked everywhere, opened all the drawers, even moved all the furniture, and rugs. It was a lot of work, but it had to be done. Unfortunately, I didn't find anything. Just some dust bunnies and a pair of girlie undies in your bedroom. They were nice. I'd like to see what they look like on you."

She laughed, "Walker, that's not going to happen. You can put that thought out of your mind. And don't be playing with my undies while I'm gone. You're supposed to be searching for treasure. Where are you searching next?"

"Well, after I put your undies back, I'm going to go outside and look around the foundation. Maybe I'll find something there. If I don't, I'll start in one of the other huts. But don't worry, I'm leaving the one with the boat in it until you get back."

She laughed. "You don't have to do that. Go ahead and search both of them. If you get all the dirty work done before I get back, I might bring you something."

"Really? You're going to bring me something? Like what?"

She paused, and in the background, I heard her GPS giving her directions. When it finished, she said, "Sorry Walker, I've got to go. I'll call you later and let you know if I learn anything."

She ended the call before I could tell her to stay safe.

Chapter Thirty-Six

It had taken me most of the morning to search the inside of the house. It wasn't a whole lot of work since the curved walls made it hard to hide anything. Most of the space was wide open, and other than the kitchen cabinets, there just weren't a lot of places to stash a treasure.

Because I told Abby I would, I needed to go outside and check around the foundation. The building had a concrete footer around it, and it would have been possible to bury something just under or next to it. There was a water line running from the well and a shallow ditch with a sewer pipe going to the septic tank. The soft dirt around the lines could be a way to bury a treasure that no one would notice. I would be sure to check the area.

But before going outside, I decided it was time for lunch. Abby had bought plenty of food a day earlier, including everything I needed for a turkey sandwich. I put one together with bread, lettuce, and three slices of turkey.

After opening a bag of chips and pulling the tab on a cold coke from the fridge, I had assembled what I considered, the perfect lunchtime meal.

While I ate, I thought about what I needed to take with me when I went to search the other two Quonset huts. Definitely gloves, boots, long pants, a shovel, and maybe my metal detector.

I had it in my RV and had gotten pretty good at using it to find things. I could put it in gold mode, and it would search down to about eighteen inches below the surface. If gold were found, it would beep wildly to let me know.

The only problem with using the detector around a structure is it would alert on every metal object nearby. Nails, beer cans, aluminum scraps, and whatever else people had left behind. If I didn't adjust the settings just right, it would continually sound off and I'd spend a lot of time digging junk.

If I didn't find anything with the detector, I could fire up my DJI drone and fly it up over Duckville, looking for old roads and places where treasure might be hidden. Plus, it would help me get a better lay of the land.

After finishing my lunch, I let Bob and Buddy know I was going to be outside for a while. Neither seemed too concerned. They had food, water, and their afternoon naps to keep them busy until I came back in.

I went to the RV and grabbed the detector along with my special treasure digging shovel. It had a serrated edge, which made digging in hard dirt a bit easier.

I had just grabbed it when I heard what was clearly a shotgun blast, close enough that I could feel it in my chest. It was followed by a man's voice yelling 'stop!', then 'get away from me!'. Followed by screams of terror. I wasn't sure what was going on, but whatever it was, it was close.

It sounded like it was coming from Trudy's. I'd never been there, but knew the path she used when she came visiting. I figured if I took it, it would lead me to her home. I was still deciding whether I should go or not when I heard a car horn beep three times.

Trudy had said that three beeps meant to come running. Not having any other weapons nearby, I held on to my serrated shovel and took off toward her place.

Chapter Thirty-Seven

The path leading to Trudy's was well-worn and easy to follow. There was only one fence to cross. It was low enough that I could get over it without any effort. I stayed on the trail until it opened into a clearing. In the center, an older mobile home with a seventies model Chevy truck parked off to the side. The truck had two flat tires.

Next to it, an old travel trailer covered with circus artwork. Probably belonged to her father. To the right of it, a chicken coop. Inside the coop, a man wearing a suit cowering under the roosting nests.

He was covered in chicken poop and feathers.

Just outside the wire cage, Clyde was pointing what looked to be a twelve-gauge shotgun at the man. He was jumping up and down and screaming in rage. I could understand why the man in the coop would be scared, but couldn't figure out why he was in there and why Clyde was pointing a gun at him.

Since I didn't want the monkey to swing the gun around toward me, in my calmest voice, I said, "Clyde, it's me, Walker. What's going on?"

He looked over at me, then back at the man in the coop. He screamed at the man, then turned back toward me and shook his fist. It looked like he was telling me the man in the coop had done him wrong and Clyde was getting his revenge.

I looked around, expecting to see Trudy, but didn't see her. The door to her trailer was wide open. I wondered if she'd left it that way, or if someone had tried to break in. Maybe that's what set Clyde off.

Or maybe Trudy was inside and hurt.

I had to find out.

Walking over to the door of the trailer, I leaned in and called out her name. There was no response.

I called her name again. Still no response.

I didn't want to go into a private home without an invitation. That's rarely a good idea. Especially in Florida where almost every homeowner has a gun and knows how to use it. But this was different. There was an unknown man being held at gunpoint by an oversized monkey in the woman's yard. Her door looked like it had been jimmied and her condition and whereabouts were unknown.

Thinking that maybe she was hurt, I stepped inside and looked around. The place had been trashed. Furniture had been turned over, bookshelves pulled down, holes punched into the walls. Someone had been looking for something.

My guess was it had been the man Clyde was holding at gunpoint,

I didn't care about that. I wanted to find Trudy. To make sure she was okay. I called out her name again.

As before, no response.

This time, I didn't wait, I quickly went through her trailer, checking all the rooms, making sure she wasn't laying on the floor, hurt, or worse. It didn't take me long to see that she wasn't anywhere inside.

Feeling weird about invading her private space, I went outside to check on Clyde and the man in the chicken coop.

I had just stepped out the door when a late model Toyota Tundra pulled into the yard. Trudy was driving. She saw me and waved like everything was normal. But then she saw Clyde holding the gun, and things changed.

Before her truck stopped rolling, she was out and running over to Clyde. Yelling his name over and over, repeating the words, 'Clyde, no!', 'Clyde, no! Not again!'.

He heard her but kept the gun aimed at the man. It wasn't until she got close enough to touch him that Clyde lowered the weapon. When he did, she took it from him, and after clearing the chamber, laid it on the ground behind her.

Clyde was still riled, screaming and pointing at the man. His body language and facial expressions reminded me of the Planet of the Apes when the animals went on a rampage. Like them, he was in attack mode. It seemed like he wanted to go into the coop and tear the man apart.

Trudy tried to calm him.

She put her arm around his shoulder. "It's alright Clyde. Everything's alright. I'm home now. You did good."

Like a child seeing his mother for the first time after a long absence, the monkey wrapped his arms around Trudy and pressed his face into her chest. He made sounds much like that of a child sobbing in relief. Trudy held him tight while watching the man in the chicken coop.

Thinking the situation had calmed down enough for me to walk over, I announced myself by saying, "Trudy, it's Walker, your neighbor. I'm behind you."

She turned to me. "Tell me what happened."

I shook my head. "I don't know. I heard a blast, a scream, then a car horn beep three times. I came running. When I got here I saw Clyde holding a gun on that guy.

"I was afraid you were hurt, so I checked your trailer. The door was open. I went in. The place has been tossed. I'm thinking the guy in the coop had something to do with it."

"You went into my trailer?"

"Yes, I was afraid you were hurt."

"Did you take anything?"

Her question caught me by surprise. It was strange of her to ask.

"No, I didn't take anything. I was checking on you. I was afraid you were hurt."

She nodded as if my answer was acceptable, then she turned to Clyde and asked. "What's going on?"

As she said those words, she used what looked like sign language to reinforce her question.

Clyde watched her hands move, and after a moment, he replied with hand movements of his own. When he was done, he pointed to the man in the coop, who, so far had said nothing.

Trudy stood, took Clyde's hand, and walked him to the trailer. She led him inside, and after a moment, returned without him.

She walked over to the feather-covered man in the coop and asked, "Who sent you?"

Instead of answering her question, he said, "I'm going to sue you for everything you have. I'm going to make sure they put that monkey of yours down. He's a menace. He could have killed me. You better let me out of here right now!"

Trudy turned to me. "Walker, did it sound like he answered my question?"

I shook my head. "No. All I heard were threats."

She nodded. "Maybe I should ask him again. Give him one more chance before I let Clyde decide what to do with him."

She turned to the man. "Okay, last chance. Tell me what you are doing on my property and how Clyde ended up with a gun that apparently belongs to you."

The man, still angry, said, "Your damn monkey tried to kill me. I only got the gun after he attacked me. It was self-defense. Anyone would have done the same."

Trudy nodded. "Self defense, huh? Interesting. What were you doing trespassing on my property in the first place?"

The man, getting bolder by the minute, said, "Let me out of here. You can't keep me prisoner. Let me go now and maybe I won't call the sheriff."

Trudy picked up the man's shotgun and pumped the slide to clear all the remaining shells. She then took it over to her truck and laid the barrel lengthwise in front of the driver's side front tire. After getting in her truck, she pulled forward over the gun, bending the barrel and crushing the pump mechanism.

After she got out, she picked up the gun and brought it over to where I was standing, and laid it on the ground beside me.

Looking at the man in the coop, she said, "Clyde doesn't like guns. Someone tried to kill him once. With a gun. Unfortunately, that person never got a chance to tell us why he took a shot at him. He was found dead in the woods soon after.

"The same thing could happen to you. Unless you tell me why you trespassed on my property carrying a loaded weapon. Tell me why you broke into my place. Last chance to talk before I call in a few of my friends. They won't be nearly as nice as I've been."

The man looked around, then said, "Look, it's just a misunderstanding. I was told you were interested in buying some life insurance. I came here to sell you a policy. I parked out on the road and walked in. I knocked on your door. No one answered. It was unlocked, so I opened it to leave my card.

"That's when that ape of yours charged me. He came running, arms up in the air, screaming and showing his teeth. I thought he was going to kill me. I ran all the way back to my car and he followed. I was afraid he was going to tear my face off, so I got out my gun and fired a warning shot. Over his head.

"I wasn't trying to kill him. I just wanted to scare him off.

"But it didn't work. He jumped me and took the gun. Then chased me back to your place. I ran into the chicken coop to get away."

When he stopped talking, Trudy turned to me and asked, "So, why would somebody go back to the safety of their car, get a gun and then come back on my property to shoot at Clyde?

"Why wouldn't they just drive away?"

Before I could answer, she said, "I'll tell you what I think happened. This guy came onto my property carrying a shotgun planning to rob me. When he found out I wasn't home, he broke into my trailer and started looking for something to steal.

"Clyde was probably out in his tree house. When he heard the ruckus in the trailer, he went over to see what was going on. When he went in the door, Chicken Man saw a big hairy ape coming in after him. He probably got scared and took a shot.

"Clyde don't like guns and don't like people shooting at him. So when the first shot missed, he went after the guy and took the gun away from him. Then he chased him out of the trailer into the hen house. Clyde locked the gate so the guy couldn't get out. Then remembered to honk the car horn to call for help.

"Does that sound reasonable to you?"

It did. I nodded.

She took a deep breath, then continued. "I could be wrong about the whole thing. Maybe the guy is telling the truth. Maybe it was just an innocent mistake. Maybe he really didn't break into my trailer. Maybe he didn't shoot at Clyde."

She paused for a moment, then pointed to the chicken coop. "Several years back, we had a problem with a varmint getting our chickens at night. We weren't sure what it was, but it would get in there, kill a hen and drag it off."

"Pop didn't like losing birds and wanted to set up a trap to catch the thief. We set out several, but never got anything. Whatever it was, it was smart enough not to get caught."

"Then one day I saw this TV ad from a company called Ring. They had these wireless security cameras and supposedly you could set them up around your place and they'd start recording whenever anything moved. Even at night.

"So I ordered three of them and put them up. Two on the front of the trailer, and one pointing out toward the road.

"And you know what? They work. They record everything.

"Any time something goes on around here, I can check my phone and watch video from those cameras. I can see what happened. They are still active and I'm going to be checking the video in a few minutes.

"But first, I'm going to invite some friends over."

She pulled out her phone and punched in a number. When the call connected, she said, "Tiny, I've got someone over here I'd like you to come talk to. Bring some of the other boys if you can."

She ended the call and turned to me. "Walker, thanks for coming over and checking on me and Clyde. I really appreciate it. It shows you care. But you can go back to your place now. I've got this covered."

It felt like she was sending me away, which was strange. I figured whoever was coming over would want to talk to me, to find out what I had seen when I first showed up. But maybe since she had it on video, they wouldn't need me.

Still, I wanted to know what was going on. Why the man in the chicken coop had decided to break into her house. And whether break-ins were common in the area or not. More importantly, I wanted to know why Trudy had called her friend Tiny instead of calling the Sheriff.

I kept these questions to myself. Trudy had made it clear she wanted me to leave. I got the feeling she was doing me a favor by telling me to go. Apparently, she didn't want me around to see how Tiny and the boys would be taking care of business.

I said goodbye and walked back to Duckville. When I got there, I went to the RV, unlocked the door, and walked to the back bedroom. There, I threw the covers off the bed and lifted the mattress to get to the hidden storage underneath.

It was there that I kept my Smith & Wesson three fifty-seven revolver.

I grabbed it along with a box of hollow-point shells and after locking up the RV, went to the house.

I had no plans to use the pistol any time soon but wanted it close at hand, just in case.

Chapter Thirty-Eight

The two cats were sleeping on the couch. As far as they were concerned, everything was right with the world. Their food was where it was supposed to be, their water bowls were full, and their litter boxes clean.

They didn't have to worry about the man in the chicken coop or about Tiny and his friends. They didn't have to wonder about how someone armed with a shotgun could shoot at and miss a monkey in close quarters, or how that monkey could end up with the gun. They didn't have to wonder why Trudy had asked me if I had taken anything while I was in her trailer checking on her safety.

Bob and Buddy didn't have to concern themselves with any of these things. But I did. I knew I'd be thinking about what had happened next door for a good long while.

In the meantime, I decided it would be a good idea to start locking the front gate to make sure no one came on the property without my permission.

If I was away from the main house, searching the other Quonset huts or out by the dock and the front gate was unlocked, it might seem like an open invitation to unwanted guests.

I didn't want that. Unlike Trudy, I didn't have a monkey that could chase visitors away when I wasn't around, and I didn't have a chicken coop to pen them up in until I returned.

So I'd be locking the front gate. Always. Even when I was on the property. I might even order some security cameras like the ones she had. I might even put up a sign at the front gate telling visitors we were a guard dog training facility, and trespassers would definitely get bit.

It might sound like I was a little paranoid. Maybe even going overboard on the security setup. But having someone armed with a shotgun breaking into the house next door will do that to a fellow. Make him want to armor up his own place.

It was a shame that the world had come to this. That even in a place as remote as Duckville, I needed to lock things up and keep a pistol close by.

But hey, that's the world we live in.

I didn't know if Abby had left the front gate open when she headed out to Miami that morning, so my first order of business was to go check. If it were open, I would close and lock it.

Leaving the house, I grabbed my pistol and locked the front door behind me. I walked the three hundred yards to the front gate and saw that it was open. Abby hadn't closed it when she left. There was no reason for her to think she should.

As far as she was concerned, we were as safe as we could be in Duckville. Our place was way off an unmarked, unpaved road, the kind that most people would go out of their way to avoid. Even the brave ones that ventured down the road, wouldn't get far before seeing 'no trespassing' signs.

A little further on, they'd reach the front gate, which from now on, would be closed and locked. Anyone with any sense would turn around and never come back.

Unfortunately, there are a lot of people on the planet who don't have enough sense to get out of their own way.

The guy being held in the chicken coop next door was proof of that.

After closing and locking the gate, I headed back to the house.

I still had things to do before the day was over.

Chapter Thirty-Nine

Earlier that morning, my plan for the day was to thoroughly search the inside of the house, then use my metal detector to search around the outside. I'd finished the inside without finding anything and on the outside search, had gotten as far as getting my detector out of my RV.

But then I was interrupted by the ruckus over at Trudy's place.

I spent about an hour over there before she sent me home, telling me that she had it under control. When I left, the intruder was still locked in the chicken coop and his fate was unknown. I suspected his bad day was going to get much worse before it was over.

Secure knowing that my front gate was closed and locked, I decided it was time to get back to searching around the outside of the house.

My metal detector was still where I left it at the back of the RV. Unfortunately, my special metal detecting shovel, the one with the serrated edges, wasn't with it. I had taken it over to Trudy's after hearing the shotgun blast, thinking I might need a weapon to deal with whatever was going on over there.

At some point, I must have set it down. Probably before I went into her trailer. The shovel was likely sitting outside her door on her deck, leaning against the wall.

Some day, I would go over and ask her about it. But not today. I didn't want to walk in on Tiny and his friends while they dealt with the man in the chicken coop.

Since I didn't have my special digging shovel, I'd use the smaller one I'd picked up at Babe's Hardware the day before. It was on the front porch, where I'd left it when Trudy and I got back from looking at the holes dug by the Corp of Engineers.

I got the shovel, put my detector in jewelry mode, and after hearing the start-up beeps, began my treasure hunt.

Almost immediately, the detector sounded off, telling me that there was nonferrous metal right below my feet. The beeping didn't mean it had found gold or silver, just that whatever it had found, wasn't iron, which was good. Finding iron usually means it's trash not worth digging. The jewelry mode automatically filters out iron and zeros in on better metals.

Unfortunately, even in jewelry mode you still find a lot of trash. Especially around man-made structures, where the ground is often littered with nails, washers, screws, and other materials discarded while the structure was being built.

In the case of a Quonset hut, where just about every joint was held together with either rivets or screws, there was plenty of metal in the ground. Every time I swung the detector, it beeped telling me there was a nonferrous object a few inches below the surface.

Even knowing that most of these would be screws or nails, I couldn't ignore them. I had to dig each one, because the detector can't tell the difference between a stainless steel screw and a gold ring.

The ground around the Quonset's foundation had been packed down. Digging into it with the small shovel from Babes took a bit of effort. It would have been a lot easier with my serrated shovel, but I wasn't going to go get it from Trudy.

Not until things settled down over there.

It took me almost three hours to work my way around the

foundation. Along the way, I found hundreds of screws, a few pennies, and a number of thirty-eight caliber shell casings.

No gold or silver.

I wasn't too disappointed. I hadn't expected to find gold buried so close to the house. Tony Ducks wouldn't have risked putting it there. It would have been too easy to find. Still, I had to look to eliminate the location as a possible treasure site.

I put the detector back in the RV and went to the house. I'd worked up a pretty good sweat digging a hundred small holes around the foundation and decided a shower was in order.

I went to my bathroom, stripped off my clothes, and turned on the water. Without waiting for it to warm up, I stepped under the showerhead, and let the cool spray wash the dirt and sweat away. After soaping up and getting good and clean, I got out and dried off.

With no one else in the house to worry about, I didn't bother getting dressed. Instead, I grabbed a pair of Sponge Bob boxer shorts and pulled them on. They were part of the 'like cradling your privates in silk' collection I'd picked up at Bealls. After working outside, I figured my privates needed all the cradling they could get.

Barefoot and bare-chested, I went to the kitchen and checked the fridge to see what I could put together for dinner. Most everything Abby had bought at the store would require me to mix ingredients and fire up the stove if I wanted to eat.

Since I didn't feel like cooking, I decided to heat up one of the microwave dinners I had brought over from my RV.

I had just taken it out of the box when I heard a knock on the door. To say I was surprised, would be an understatement. I wasn't expecting company, especially since the front gate was locked and no one other than Abby and I had a key.

Still wary from the earlier encounter at Trudy's, I put the

frozen dinner down and picked up my pistol. I didn't know who would be at the door when I opened it, but I wanted to be ready, just in case.

With gun in hand, I walked to the door and looked out.

There, standing with a smile on her face and a monkey at her side, was Trudy. In her left hand, a beer, and in her right, my metal detecting shovel.

Without thinking about what I was wearing, I put the gun down, opened the door, and said, "You brought my shovel!"

She smiled, looked down at my shorts then back up at my face. "Sponge Bob, huh? You a fan?"

I laughed, "No, not really. It's just that these shorts are really comfortable. Give me a minute and I'll put something else on."

Still smiling, she said, "No need for that. I like the way Sponge Bob looks on you. You say they're comfortable?"

"Yeah, they are. Kind of like silk."

"Really, silk? Mind if I feel?"

Before I could answer, she reached out and touched my boxers, putting her fingers way too close to my private parts. I stepped back, shaking my head. "Nope, don't do that. No touching."

She laughed. "Don't worry, I wasn't trying to cop a feel. You're married and I don't usually fool around with married men."

She pointed behind her to the picnic table. "Why don't you put some clothes on and come out here and sit with me. I want to talk to you about what happened today."

Chapter Forty

I closed the door, went to my bedroom, and quickly pulled on a pair of pants and a shirt. I stopped in the kitchen and put my TV dinner back in the freezer. Grabbing two beers from the fridge, I headed outside.

Trudy and Clyde were waiting for me at the picnic table, sitting side by side. I took a seat on the bench across from them and showed them the cold beers. Trudy nodded which I took to mean she was ready for another. I put the beer in front of her and turned to Clyde to see if he was ready for his. When I showed him the can, he grinned and held out his hand.

He didn't snatch it away from me. He was polite and waited for me to hand it to him, which I did.

He took the beer and in a single fluid motion, pulled the tab to open it. I was again amazed at how he was able to do it so quickly. He could open a beer faster than most of the humans I'd been around.

After taking a drink, Trudy started by saying, "First, I want to thank you again for coming over to help Clyde this morning. He was pretty stressed. I'm not sure what he might have done had you not come over and calmed him down.

"I also want to apologize for anything I might have said when I first got there. Everything was a little crazy. I might have misspoken. If I did, I'm sorry."

I held up my hand. "No need to apologize. You didn't do anything wrong."

"Good. I don't want there to be any problems between

215

us."

She took another drink, then continued. "We don't have much crime in these parts. Not many people know there are houses back here, and those that do, know better than to try to break into them. Most of us have guns and we aren't afraid to use them.

"That's why I was so surprised the guy came to my place planning to break in. He had to be crazy. If I'd been home, he'd be dead right now."

I didn't know how to respond so I said nothing. I wanted her to keep talking.

She took another sip and continued.

"You're probably wondering what happened after you left, and maybe why I didn't call the sheriff right away."

Again I nodded but didn't say anything. She was on a roll and I didn't want to stop her.

"We like to take care of our own around here. Most of us are circus folk and we tend to stick together. We have our own rules and when there's a problem, we try not to get the law involved. The few times we've called them, it didn't work out in our favor. So now we handle things ourselves.

"When there's a problem like there was today, we call Tiny. He's the head of our . . . uh, uh, neighborhood watch. You'll get to meet him one of these days. He's a little rough around the edges, but he knows how to solve problems without involving the law.

"That's why as soon as I saw my place had been broken into, I called him. I think you were gone when he showed up."

I nodded. She was right, I was gone, but only because she had sent me away. I didn't mention this. I just let her talk.

"So when Tiny got there, I told him the guy in the chicken

216

coop had broken into my house and had taken a shot at Clyde. I pulled up the videos on my phone and we watched them together. They showed the guy walking up my driveway carrying the shotgun. The second camera showed him kicking in the front door of my trailer. A few minutes later, it showed Clyde going in, then the guy running out with Clyde close behind with the shotgun.

"The third camera showed the guy running into the chicken coop and closing the gate behind him."

"After watching the videos, Tiny and I both knew what had happened. Of course, the big question was why? Why did the guy come onto my property with a shotgun planning to rob me?

"It's not like any of us drive fancy cars or live in big houses. We're all poor, living in shacks down dirt roads and driving dusty old pickups.

"It just doesn't make sense for someone to come out here and try to rob one of us. There are a lot of other people closer to town who'd be easier pickings.

"Tiny went over to talk to the guy. He asked him to tell us why he came with a gun and broke into my house. It was a simple question. He just wanted to know why the guy did it.

"But chicken-coop man stuck to the story that he was selling life insurance. Following up a list of leads he'd bought on the internet. He claimed someone had already broken into the trailer when he arrived. He only went back to get his gun when he thought the perp was still on the property.

"Of course, Tiny and I knew better. The videos showed us everything. Still, we wanted to be sure we weren't making a mistake. Tiny went out and found the guy's car. An older Tahoe. It was unlocked, so he searched it.

"There wasn't anything in it related to selling insurance. No business cards, no insurance forms, no brochures or flyers. But there was a box of shotgun shells and a hand-drawn map leading to my place.

"When he showed the guy the map, he kept to his story. He said he was trying to sell insurance. He said he was new at the job and hadn't gotten his business cards or policy forms yet.

"Of course, we didn't believe him. Everything he was telling us was a lie.

"When we checked his wallet, we found an expired Mississippi driver's license and a Bureau of Prisons ID card from Raiford. Both with his photo. The name on both cards was Daniel Griggs.

"When Tiny asked Danny boy about the prison card, he said it wasn't his. He said he'd found it and was planning to give it back to the owner. In the meantime, he was just trying to sell insurance. He begged us to let him out of the chicken coop so he could go home. He said his wife and kids would be waiting for him.

"Tiny didn't believe him. Everything he'd told us had been a lie. There was no reason to think he had a wife or kids. Even if he did, it didn't give him a pass for breaking into my house and shooting at Clyde.

"Since he wouldn't come clean, Tiny decided it was time to get him out of the chicken coop and off my property. He'd been there long enough and needed to be somewhere else. Tiny was going to take him to a place where the guy might be more motivated to tell the truth.

"He got a rope out of his truck and tied the guy up good and tight, then threw him in the bed. He covered him with a tarp and drove off.

"Two hours later, Tiny called me and said he finally found

out what was going on. Danny Boy had just gotten out of prison after serving a ten-year hitch for second-degree murder.

"While behind bars, his cellmate told him a story about a drug dealer who had delivered twenty kilos of coke to a buyer in Tampa. Trying to avoid the cops, the dealer made the trip in his go-fast boat up the Intracoastal. After delivering the product, he headed back to Naples with almost two million dollars in cash, stashed in a waterproof suitcase under the passenger seat.

"It was late and the weather was getting bad and the dealer was in a hurry to get back home. He was high on cocaine and going way too fast for the conditions. When he got to Stump Pass, he should have turned right and followed it out to the gulf, but he didn't. He kept going straight, directly into a field of broken tree trunks just below the water's surface.

"There was no way he could make it through, especially at low tide. At forty miles an hour, the boat was riding high, but not high enough. The stump he hit ripped the bottom out of the boat. The impact and sudden stop threw the dealer a hundred and fifty feet over the bow, breaking his back when he hit the water.

"The wrecked remains of the boat somehow stayed afloat and drifted to shore. The dealer was dead. It wasn't until the next morning that his boat and his body were found. There was never any mention of the suitcase of money.

"According to Griggs's prison buddy, the suitcase had been found floating near the shore by a young girl whose family lived in Grove City. When she took the suitcase home to show her father, they found stacks and stacks of bundled hundred-dollar bills inside. The father assumed it was drug money. He decided the best thing to do was to tell no one what they had found.

"He knew if he suddenly started spending a lot of cash, people would talk. And that could lead to the kind of questions he wouldn't want to answer. It might even attract the attention of those that would kill to get their hands on the loot.

"With that in mind, the father pulled out just one stack of hundreds, which he planned to spend slowly over time. He hid the rest. Supposedly somewhere in the trailer he and his daughter lived in.

"Griggs's cellmate claimed he knew where the money was. He offered to sell him a map leading to it. Griggs couldn't resist the lure of easy money, so he bought the map. That's what brought him to my house."

Trudy paused and took another sip of beer. She smiled before continuing, then said, "Griggs was scammed by his cellmate. According to Tiny, there's no record of a drug dealer wrecking his go-fast boat near Stump Pass. Tiny and his family have been living in these parts for more than fifty years. They would know if something like that happened.

"The whole story stinks. No drug dealer is going to use a boat to get to Tampa from Naples. The trip would take about four times longer than it would by car. In a boat, too many things could go wrong. Foul weather, motor problems, Coast guard spot checks.

"No drug dealer would risk it. A car would be the way to go.

"On so many levels, the story of the lost drug money just doesn't hold up. It was a fairy tale made up by Griggs's cellmate to scam him out of money."

She paused, finished her beer, and held up her can, signaling she was ready for another one.

I had a feeling there was still more to the story and if I got beers for her and Clyde, she might tell me the rest.

I pushed back from the table. "Let me get you another one.

I'll be right back."

After returning with two cold ones and giving one to Trudy and the other to Clyde, I settled back down on my seat, ready to hear the rest of the story.

Trudy didn't disappoint.

Chapter Forty-One

Trudy opened her fresh beer, took a sip, and continued with her story.

"After Tiny took off with chicken man, I started wondering who would draw a map to my place and claim there was money hidden in my trailer. It had to be someone who knew the area and knew I lived in a mobile home. That narrowed it down a bit.

"Danny got the map from his cellmate which meant the guy who drew it was in prison with him. The maps' detail suggested he had spent time in Grove city and knew the back roads. Because he did, it was probably someone I knew.

"I started thinking about it and it didn't take long to figure out who it was. One of my boyfriends, Randy Boggs, was sent to prison five years ago for armed robbery. He grew up in this area and we dated some. It didn't work out. He liked me more than I liked him, and that caused a problem after I broke it off.

"He kept coming around unannounced, telling me we were destined to be together forever. He said I was his one and only true love, and he'd do whatever it took to win me over.

"Of course I knew it was a load of BS, him trying to get into my pants.

"I kept telling him not to come around, but he kept coming. Usually drunk, wanting to party. He'd even come when I wasn't home. Sometimes he'd steal stuff, thinking I wouldn't notice. But I did, and I told him in no uncertain terms to never come back.

"Still, he kept coming. It got so bad I finally had to tell him if he ever came back, Clyde would mess him up. I made sure Clyde knew the guy was bad news.

"The next time he came, he was carrying a gun. Planning to kill Clyde. I wasn't home at the time, but I got it on video and saw what happened.

"Randy walked onto the property like he owned the place. Carrying a loaded shotgun, like the one the guy had today. He was sure he wouldn't have any problem taking Clyde out.

"But he figured wrong. Clyde was up in the big oak tree at the front gate that day. He saw Randy coming and the gun he was carrying. He knew that guns meant trouble, so he stayed out of sight. But he kept up with Randy, tracking him while staying hidden in the bushes.

"When Randy got to my trailer and saw I wasn't home, he put the gun down and tried to kick the door open. That was his second mistake, putting the gun down. The first was coming onto my property when I told him not to.

"When Clyde saw him put the gun down, he sprinted across the yard and was on Randy before he knew what happened. Clyde hauled him off the porch and got him in a bear hug. He squeezed until Randy nearly passed out.

"Then he dropped him on the ground and stomped on his back with his full body weight. He flipped him over and gave him several hard kicks to the ribs. He picked him up like a rag doll and threw him at least ten feet. It was like watching a professional wrestling match. The good guy winning against the bad. And it was all on video.

"Randy struggled to get up, but could hardly stand. Clyde had bruised him up pretty bad. Each time he tried to move, Clyde would bare his teeth, beat his chest, and yell like he was in a Tarzan movie.

"Randy finally got the strength to crawl back to the front gate, leaving his shotgun behind. Clyde stayed with him all the way, kicking at Randy's feet to keep him moving. At the gate, Clyde stood full height, beat on his chest, and let out a war cry, making sure Randy got the message not to come back.

"He never did after that. It wasn't long after, that he was arrested for armed robbery. He tried to hold up a liquor store in Tampa. He ran in waving a gun, never even noticing the armed guard in the back. The guard drew down on him and Randy gave up. The whole thing was captured on the store's video cameras.

"When he went to trial, he claimed it wasn't him in the video. But no one, not even his own attorney, could deny it. He was carrying a wallet with his driver's license when they caught him. It left no doubt that it was him who tried to rob the place.

"It didn't take long for the jury to convict him and send him off to Raiford. That's how he ended up in the cell with the guy who broke in yesterday."

I nodded. It was quite a story. It answered the first of my two unasked questions. Why had the guy targeted her place?

I was hoping she'd keep talking and answer my second one. But she said nothing for about two minutes. Just sitting there, smiling at me, while sipping her beer. I got the feeling she was waiting for me to ask before she'd tell me what I wanted to know.

I eventually gave in.

"So Trudy, I guess the mystery is solved. You know why he broke in, and who drew the map he was carrying. But what if the guy in prison does it again? What if he tells the same story and sells the map to someone else? What then?"

She smiled knowingly. "Tiny has already taken care of that.

Randy won't be telling the story or selling maps any time soon. He won't be saying much to anyone for a while."

I waited for her to tell me why, but she just smiled and said nothing. I wanted to know more but thought it might be better not to ask how Tiny had taken care of it. It might be one of those things a person shouldn't know.

I still had one more question and decided to ask it.

"What about chicken man? Did you call the sheriff and let him know about the break-in?"

She didn't answer right away. She looked over at Clyde and winked. He opened his mouth and showed his teeth in what might have passed for a smile. Then he winked back.

She turned to me. "Danny Griggs, the guy who broke into my place is a convicted felon. Armed robbery. Twice over. If we called the sheriff, he'd pick him up, charge him, and put him in jail.

"With the video, along with our testimony, there's no doubt he'd be convicted of home invasion. It'd be his third strike. He'd get at least twenty years. That's a long time to spend behind bars. Especially for a relatively young guy like him.

"But that's not the issue. The problem with getting the sheriff involved is, all of us, including you, will have to go down to the station and give sworn statements as to what happened. When it goes to trial, we'll have to appear in court and testify under oath. Once we're on the witness stand, the defense lawyer can ask us anything.

"That could be a big problem. Especially if he finds out that I have an unregistered chimpanzee living with me. He'll say that Clyde assaulted Danny while he was on my property. The video proves it. It shows Clyde with the gun.

"Once it comes out about Clyde, animal control will get

involved. In the end, they'll take him from me. They might even put him down.

"I can't risk that. Clyde depends on me and I can't let anyone take him away. So no, we didn't call the sheriff. Tiny came up with a better way to handle it."

Chapter Forty-Two

"Tiny offered Griggs a choice. Go back to jail for at least twenty years, or leave the country and never come back. He knew when he offered it, what the guy would choose. Not prison. Anything would be better than that.

"Danny boy said he'd leave the country. But Tiny isn't a fool. He knew even if Griggs left, he wouldn't stay away for long. He'd try to come back across the border.

"Tiny showed him the video of him carrying a gun and breaking into my trailer. He explained that as a convicted felon, he wasn't supposed to have a gun. Having it during the commission of a crime, guaranteed a long prison sentence.

"He told him should he ever come back to the US, screenshots from the video would be given to state and federal prosecutors along with Griggs's name and copies of his driver's license.

"That pretty much sealed the deal. Griggs knew if images got out showing him with a gun, there would be warrants for his arrest. If they picked him up, he would end up in prison. So he agreed to leave, probably figuring he'd have a few days before Tiny could get him across the border.

"What he didn't know, was Tiny had already arranged his departure. He'd called a friend who ships cars from the US to Haiti and was able to book passage for Griggs on the next transport ship. He'll be on it in the morning. One of Tiny's associates is making sure it happens.

"When the ship gets to Haiti, Griggs will be put ashore without a passport or driver's license. If he wants to come back to the US, he'll have to figure out how to do it without them. Unless he's a good swimmer, he won't be coming back to our shores anytime soon."

She didn't have to tell me why. To get to the US from Haiti, you have to cross a thousand miles of open ocean – either by plane or boat. No one walked or swam in from there.

She finished the last of her beer, set the bottle down on the table, and said, "You can't repeat any of this. In fact, it would be best if you forgot about everything that happened today. Tiny and I would really appreciate it if you did."

She paused, waiting for me to say something.

I knew there was only one right answer. "It's been a boring day. Nothing happened around here, right?"

"That's right. Nothing happened."

She stood. "Thanks for the beer. Clyde and I need to get back home. You take care. Say hi to the missus."

As they walked away, I got the feeling it wouldn't be a good idea to get on the wrong side of my neighbors.

Chapter Forty-Three

Both cats were waiting for me at the door when I went back inside. Bob got to me first. He came over, twined his body between my legs, meowed once, and then trotted off in the direction of his food bowl. Halfway there, he looked over his shoulder to make sure I was following.

I knew the drill. Go with him to the bowl, fill it with food, give him a pet, and walk away. It'd been our daily routine in the RV and he expected me to follow it now that we were staying in the house.

I did. He had taught me well.

After filling his bowls, I headed to the kitchen to cook the TV dinner I had planned on eating before Trudy showed up. The meal was long overdue, and it was time to get some food inside me.

When I got to the fridge, I saw that I had left my phone on the counter. The 'missed call' light was blinking. I don't get many calls, but the ones I do get are usually important. I checked the phone and saw that Abby had called three times, and had left a text message.

She hadn't left a voicemail, but the text said it all. "You better not be hurt. Call me."

I could have waited until after I ate to make the call, but I knew that wouldn't sit well with her. It didn't matter if I was hungry. She was across the state meeting with ex-mafioso and something bad could have happened. Or maybe she learned something important.

Or maybe she just missed me.

Whatever it was, I needed to call her back.

I hit the redial button and listened as the phone tried to make the connection. There were a few clicks and pops, and then the familiar sound of the phone ringing at her end. She answered immediately. "Walker, where are you?"

"At the house. Why?"

"Because you haven't been answering your phone. I called and called and you didn't pick up. I started to get worried. I was afraid you got hurt or maybe tangled up with an alligator. Are you sure you're okay?"

"Yeah, I'm okay. I was outside talking to Trudy. I didn't have my phone with me."

"Trudy? She came over?"

"Yeah, I had just gotten out of the shower and heard someone at the door. I went to check and it was her. I went back inside to put on some clothes, and I guess I forgot to get my phone."

"You were naked when you opened the door?"

"No, not naked. I was wearing underwear."

"But you did put clothes on before you talked to her, right?"

"Yeah, I dressed. Then we went outside and talked."

"You talked? About what? What was so important that she came over to see you when I wasn't there?"

I paused, thinking about the best way to answer her question. If I went with the truth and told her about the break-in and everything that happened after, it would explain it. But Trudy had said not to tell anyone and even though I wasn't sure whether that meant I couldn't tell Abby or not, I knew for certain not to mention it on the phone. People are always listening. All the time. The government. Federal agencies. Google.

They didn't need to know what happened.

So, instead of going with the truth, I said, "She came over to tell me she had chickens and if we wanted fresh eggs she'd be happy to share. She also said her tomatoes and zucchini were coming in and we could have all we wanted."

I quickly changed the subject. "So how are things going with you? Did you learn anything?"

Instead of answering my question, she said, "You and I are supposed to be married. Even if it's only pretend, I don't know how I feel about you answering the door buck naked and spending the evening with the neighbor lady when I'm not there. It's something we're going to talk about when I get back."

From the tone of her voice, I knew I was in trouble. But I'd learned the best way to deal with it was not to be defensive. Instead, act like you looked forward to whatever was going to happen. "Abby, I miss you. I really do. And when you get back, we can talk about anything you want. In fact, we can talk about it right now if you like."

I heard her chuckle. Then, "Walker, you are so full of it. That line might work on other women, but not on me. I know your tricks. And yes, we're still going to have that talk when I get back."

Instead of keeping quiet, which would have been the smart thing, I said, "Abby, after our talk, will we kiss and make up?"

Again, a chuckle. Then, "You wish. In the meantime, stay away from Trudy when I'm not there."

I nodded, even though she couldn't see me do it. "Yes, dear."

Apparently, our little spat was over. She started to tell me what she had learned. "First thing to know is the Mafia doesn't have much of a retirement plan. There's no pension or health care or anything like that. When people age out, they are on their own. Of course, it doesn't matter much because most of them never live to see retirement.

"But the guy I saw today, Biscuit Gravano, somehow made it through. He's almost eighty and still pretty sharp. Back when things weren't so expensive, he bought a small condo near the beach and has been living in it ever since. It's in a low-rise three-story building; not too impressive. But it's walking distance to all the places he needs to go, which is important since he no longer drives.

"He says he could sell the place and get more than ten times what he paid, but then he'd have to move. With real estate prices what they are in Miami, he doesn't think he'd be able to afford anything better than what he has. He said his dog likes it where they are. A little bug-eyed chihuahua that barks at everything that moves.

"Biscuit was happy to have someone to talk to. He told me about his dog, his girlfriends, and the pills he has to take every day. He even told me how he liked to go down to the beach and watch the topless girls on the sand. He said all he could do was look, but it didn't cost anything and was way better than what he could see on TV.

"Like I said, he was happy to talk, and I was happy to listen. But that changed when I brought up Tony Ducks. He got defensive and wanted to know why I was asking about him. He said he knew Tony was getting out of prison soon and if I was trying to dig up dirt, I could just get up and leave.

"I assured him I wasn't interested in doing anything that would hurt Tony. I told him it was the other way around. I was wondering how, after twenty years in prison, he would be able to afford to live on the outside.

"Biscuit didn't answer my question and didn't want to talk

much after that. I asked him to dinner, but he said 'no'. He was too tired to go out. Said he was all talked out and needed to rest.

"I thanked him for his time and left. After grabbing a bite to eat, I called the other two guys I was supposed to talk to and they both told me the same thing. They'd changed their mind. They weren't going to talk. When I asked 'why', they said they didn't want to help anyone trying to dig up dirt on Tony.

"I think Biscuit called and warned them off. I tried to convince them otherwise but had no luck. They weren't going to see me.

"So it looks like my work over here is done. I'll be heading back in the morning."

I was glad to hear that. The sooner she got away from Miami the better. I should have told her that, but I didn't. Instead, I asked, "So where are you staying tonight?"

She didn't answer right away.

It sounded like she took a sip of something from a bottle. Probably water. After she swallowed, she said, "All the RV parks in Miami are full. Same with most of the motels. So it looks like I'll be spending the night in the parking lot of the Miccosukee Casino. I've got everything I need in the van, so it'll be fine.

"I'll leave early in the morning and should be back by noon. Anything you need from this side of the state?"

I'd spent the night in the Miccosukee lot before. They have a section for RV parking and allow overnight stays. I had stayed there a couple of days, then driven back to Englewood on the same road she'd be taking.

Remembering that drive, the only thing I could think that she could get for me would be a ball cap from the Skunk Ape Headquarters. It was just a few miles west of the casino.

I'd had one of their caps before and really liked the look. It was black and had an ape's head in gold with the words, 'Skunk Ape Headquarters' above the bill.

It had burned up in the car accident that almost took my life. I wanted to replace it but was hesitant to ask Abby to get me another. There was no need for her to make an extra stop unless she wanted to. Then again, it was the kind of place she might find interesting. I mean how many times in your life do you get to visit the Official Skunk Ape Headquarters in Florida?

So I said, "Abby, you're going to be passing by the Skunk Ape Headquarters. If you stop there, get me one of their hats. A black one if they still have them. But don't go out of your way. It's not that big a deal."

She took another sip from whatever she was drinking, then said, "A hat, huh? That's all you want? Nothing else?"

I knew what she wanted me to say, so I went ahead and said it.

"Abby, what I really want is for you to come home. I don't need a hat, I just need you."

Of course, as soon as I said it, I knew I'd laid it on too thick.

"Walker, that's so sweet of you to say. If you ever get a real girlfriend, try it on her, see if it works. It's wasted on me. I'm not falling for it."

Before I could think of a snappy reply, she said, "It's been a long day. I'm going to bed. See you tomorrow."

She ended the call.

Chapter Forty-Four

Three hours after first taking the TV dinner out of the freezer, I finally got it in the microwave. Still frozen, because I'd put it back in the freezer when Trudy knocked on my door.

I was beyond hungry and when the bell beeped telling me the dinner was ready, I pulled it out, took it over to the table, and dug in.

I couldn't tell you if it was good or not. I was too hungry to notice. But it was filling, and at my late stage of hunger, that's all that really mattered.

After eating, I got out my computer and checked the internet. I wanted to see if there were any updates on Tony Ducks' prison stay. I did a quick search on Google and nothing new came up. Then I searched the Sarasota Herald-Tribune website, using the keywords 'Tony Ducks'.

Old articles about the houses he used to own on Casey Key turned up. But nothing current.

Not finding anything useful, I started thinking about the story Trudy had told me about the drug dealer's boat crash near Stump Pass. For something that supposedly never happened, the story had a lot of detail. About the dealer, the boat, and the location of the wreck.

These were the kinds of things usually missing from fabricated yarns. I wondered if it were possible the story was actually true. Since I was already on the internet, I decided to find out.

Going back to Google, I searched using the keywords

'boat crash, Stump Pass, Florida'. I expected to see a number of results, but nothing came up.

I changed the keywords to 'boat accident, Stump Pass Florida'. I figured most news sites would use the word 'accident' instead of 'crash'.

I was right.

This time Google returned links to several articles. Including one with the headline, 'Deputies investigate body found near Stump Pass.'

I clicked the link and it took me to an eight-year-old story from the Herald-Tribune. The details were eerily similar to the boat crash Trudy told me about.

According to the Herald-Tribune ...

"Early Friday morning, a fisherman discovered the body of a man who had washed up on the shore just south of Stump Pass. A partially sunken thirty-two-foot Baja Outlaw speed boat was found nearby. According to Sarasota County Deputies, the man had no identification and the boat's registration numbers were missing.

It was speculated the boat had been traveling at a high rate of speed the previous evening when it encountered a partially submerged stump. The impact ripped open the hull and the sole occupant was ejected. A search of the area didn't turn up any evidence that anyone else was on the boat.

An autopsy will be conducted to determine if drugs or alcohol were involved."

The story pretty much matched up with what Danny

Griggs had been told by his cellmate. There had been a boat wreck on the Intracoastal Waterway at Stump Pass late at night involving a go-fast boat that resulted in the death of the boat operator.

That part of the story was spot on. The only thing missing was any suggestion the deceased was a drug dealer. That was understandable since at the time the article was written, the police hadn't yet identified the body.

I wondered if the paper ran a follow-up with more details. Since I was already on the Herald Tribune site, I entered the keywords 'Stump Pass body identified' and pressed 'enter'.

This time, nothing came up. No new articles matched the keywords. Not wanting to give up so easily, I tried a combination of similar words, including the byline from the first article.

Again, nothing came up.

After spending twenty minutes trying every search combination I could think of and not finding anything new, I came to the conclusion there was no follow-up. Either the body had never been identified, or if it had, it wasn't newsworthy enough to be reported on in the newspaper.

Without the name of the man who died, I wouldn't be able to dig any deeper. Anyone else who researched the story would be in the same boat. Including Danny Griggs.

Trudy's jailbird ex could have read the story while in prison and decided to use it as the foundation for a scam. He could have embellished it by saying the body belonged to a drug dealer carrying two million dollars. He could claim that all a person would need to find the money is a map – which he could provide.

Hearing the story and seeing the map, his gullible cellmate would have plenty of reasons to head to Trudy's place. In doing so, her ex would have the satisfaction of getting a little revenge on Trudy and her monkey.

That scenario made a lot of sense. The pieces fit together nicely and explained why Danny Griggs had broken into her trailer.

But Trudy had said Tiny told her there never had been a boat wreck late at night on the Intracoastal at Stump Pass. He said it never happened. It was fiction.

According to the Herald-Tribune, it had happened. Almost exactly as described by Danny Griggs's cellmate, Randy Boggs.

So why would Tiny lie to Trudy about it?

I could only think of one reason.

Chapter Forty-Five

From what I could tell during my short visit to Trudy's place, she didn't have a lot of money. She was living in an older trailer, driving a ten-year-old truck, and didn't have any expensive toys that I knew about.

It was just her and her monkey.

The land her trailer was sitting on was probably worth quite a bit, nearly as much as I paid for mine. But according to her, it was purchased by her father, long before she showed up. She hadn't paid for it out of her own pocket.

So outwardly, it didn't look like she was sitting on a pile of money. Money that she might have found in a suitcase along the Intracoastal one early morning after a drug dealer met his demise.

The question was, if she hadn't found the money, why had she told me the wreck never happened?

It could be, she didn't know better. Maybe she believed Tiny when he told her it never happened. Or maybe Tiny told her nothing, and she just didn't want me thinking the story was true.

Of course, I was making a big assumption. That there was actually a suitcase full of money to be found. I was basing it on a story told by a con artist sitting in prison with vengeance on his mind.

It could have been I too was being conned by his scam. It was very likely, even probable, the suitcase of money never existed.

It was equally likely Trudy really didn't know about the

boat accident. There was only a small blurb in the Herald-Tribune and it wasn't likely they delivered the paper out to Grove City.

Unless she happened to go into town the day the wreck was reported and bought a paper and read the story, she wouldn't necessarily know about it. Unless someone told her.

She had said Tiny was the one who told her the wreck never happened. Maybe he was the one who had a reason to hide the truth. Maybe there really was a suitcase full of cash and he didn't want anyone talking about it.

It was then that I decided I had already spent too much time trying to fact-check a story told by a con artist. I only had a few scant details to go on and I didn't really have an end game. If Tiny or Trudy were hiding something, it wasn't any of my business.

I needed to focus my efforts on looking for the gold supposedly hidden somewhere in Duckville. The treasure hunt was the only reason I was on the property and not out on the road in my RV.

I powered down my computer, locked the front doors, and headed to bed. The two cats trotted along behind me, planning to take their positions on top of the covers as soon as I fell asleep.

The next morning, I woke early, thanks to Buddy. Apparently, he was bored and decided it would be fun to wake Bob by scooting up close and rabbit footing his belly.

Bob didn't appreciate being woken that way. When Buddy started kicking him, he jumped up and chased him off the bed into the living room. It sounded like a battle royal was going down when he caught up with him.

Bob outweighs Buddy by at least ten pounds. It wasn't going to be a fair fight even though Buddy was younger and presumably quicker. Bob was smarter and had the weight advantage.

From the bed, I listened for as long as I could stand it, but when Buddy's howls started sounding like he was in pain, I got up to see what was going on.

In the living room, I saw that Bob was sitting on Buddy's back riding him like a bucking bronco. The younger cat was trying to shake him off, but Bob held tight. He was going to make Buddy pay for waking him up.

I sighed, walked over to Bob, tapped him on the back, and said, "Don't do that. You're going to hurt him. Abby won't like it if you do."

I knew he heard me because he looked up and blinked. But he didn't care. He stayed on Buddy's back, pinning him to the ground. Buddy didn't like it.

I knew better than to try to pick up a cat in the middle of a fight. There were too many claws and teeth thrashing about. I decided to go old school. I walked over to their food bowls and filled each with kibble. Then I picked one up and shook it to get their attention.

That's all it took. Bob was off Buddy's back in a flash. He raced into the kitchen and started chowing down. Buddy joined him at his own bowl and they stood side-by-side, eating, seemingly forgetting they were in a death match just moments earlier.

After getting his fill, Bob went to the couch and worked on grooming. Buddy headed to his litter box and made his morning deposit.

The cats were doing what cats have been doing ever since they decided to live with humans. Play, eat, poop, and sleep.

Knowing that Abby was coming back from Miami and would probably show up around lunch, I decided it might win me a few points if I cleaned the house up a bit.

Not wanting to mess up the kitchen, I passed on making eggs and bacon and instead warmed up two strawberry Pop-Tarts. I slathered them with lots of butter and washed them down with orange juice. After eating, I washed and put away the dishes, wiped down the counters, and swept the kitchen floor.

Living with two cats and their litter boxes meant there were always fur balls and bits of litter everywhere. When the cats play rough as they had earlier, clumps of kitty hair were usually added into the mix.

The house didn't come with a vacuum cleaner which meant sweeping with a broom was my only option. As I swept, I could see kitty hairs floating in the air and settling back down onto the floor I had just cleaned.

As anyone who lives with a cat knows, trying to keep up with all the hair is a losing battle.

After doing my best to clean the house, I emptied both litter boxes and took out the trash. Living as far out as we were, there wasn't a regular garbage pickup. Whatever trash we had, we either took it into town and dropped it off at the waste collection site or incinerated it in the burn barrel in the back yard.

We'd only been in the place a couple of days and didn't have a lot of trash. Just food wrappers and two days of cat litter. Eventually though, it would start to pile up and we'd have to figure something out. I was pretty sure Abby would put a hard veto on using a burn barrel.

She'd think the smoke was toxic.

That meant I'd be taking bags of trash into town every few days until I could find a pick-up service. I'd have to ask Trudy if she knew of one.

I'd showered the previous evening and didn't think I needed to do it again. But I'd worked up a sweat cleaning, and since I figured at the very least, I'd get a hug when Abby got back, it might work in my favor to shower again. No telling where that hug might lead to.

I was heading toward the bathroom when my phone chimed letting me know I was getting a call. I answered without looking at the ID, thinking that it was probably Abby.

Unfortunately, it wasn't.

The male with the Russian accent on the other end of the line didn't bother to say hello or ask how I was doing. Instead, he asked, "Have you found anything yet?"

I knew instantly who it was and why he was calling. Boris was wondering if we'd found his mother's brooch.

I didn't want to disappoint him but knew it was a lot easier to simply tell him the truth.

"No, we haven't found it yet. I've searched the inside and outside of the main house and will be searching the other two buildings later today. Abby is getting back from Miami and we'll be using my drone to search from the air."

There was a pause on the line, then, "I hear Tony Ducks will be in Florida next week. He may pay you a visit. It would be good for all involved if you could find his money pit and retrieve the brooch before he arrives.

"But if that's not possible, you will want to be careful when dealing with him. Treat him with respect. Do not give him a reason to be angry with you. He may be old, but he still knows how to inflict pain.

"If he shows up wanting to take his treasure, don't get in his way. Offer to help him. Then do whatever you have to to get my mother's brooch back. If it helps, tell him you are doing it for me.

"No matter what, don't let him leave the property with it. You have to get it from him."

I started to tell him I'd do my best, but before I could, he said, "Don't let anything happen to Abby. Keep her safe. And don't get yourself killed."

He ended the call before I could assure him my top priority in life was not getting killed. Especially over a piece of jewelry.

Chapter Forty-Six

After the call with Boris, I hit the shower. I had just gotten out and dried off when my phone chimed with another call. I answered, hoping it wasn't Boris with more instructions.

Fortunately, it wasn't him. It was Abby.

"Hey Walker, I thought I'd check in with you. I slept in this morning and got a late start, but I'm on my way now. It looks like I'll get there around one as long as traffic doesn't get backed up."

She paused giving me a chance to say something. "Abby, the kitties and I will be glad when you get here. Buddy especially. I think he misses you."

She laughed. "I doubt that. I've only been gone a day. He probably hasn't even noticed I've been gone, unless you forgot to feed him."

"You know I wouldn't do that. Food is at the top of their 'you better do it' list. If I were to forget, they'd let me know."

She laughed again, then said, "You know that little store on the right just before you turn off to Duckville? The one that sells beer?"

"Yeah, I know the place. What about it?"

"There are a few things I need to get and I don't feel like stopping. So I was wondering if maybe you could get them for me. You won't need to go all the way into town; I'm pretty sure the little store has everything I need. If I text you the list, would you mind getting the things on it for me?"

It was rare that Abby asked me to do something like that

for her, especially when it involved shopping. If she was so tired from her trip to make the request, there was no way I would turn her down.

"Abby, no problem. You want me to go now or wait until you get back?"

She didn't hesitate with her answer.

"Go now if you can. That way, you'll be back by the time I get there and neither one of us will have to go out again. You sure you don't mind?"

"No, not at all. In fact, it'll give me a chance to pick up some more beer. Trudy and Clyde pretty much finished off what we had in the fridge. I think it's a good idea to always have some on hand when they come around."

She laughed. "Yeah, wouldn't want to disappoint a beer-drinking monkey. Or Trudy. I need to talk to her when I get back. It'll go easier after she's had a couple of beers."

I started to ask what she needed to talk to her about but thought better of it. Her answer might be one of those things I'd rather not discuss on the phone.

I changed the subject.

"You're going to text me your shopping list, right?"

"I will. There's a rest area up ahead and I'll send it from there. It'll be my last stop before I get home. I'll call you if anything comes up. See you in a couple of hours."

She was off the phone before I could tell her to be careful. There are a lot of crazy people on the road in South Florida and a young woman traveling alone in an RV would be high on their list.

Then again, she had proven she could take care of herself. She wasn't afraid to fight back, even use deadly force if needed.

I hoped it would never come to that.

A few minutes after the call, her text message with the shopping list came through. Just eight items. Toilet paper, paper towels, tissue, a six-pack of ginger ale, four bananas, a quart of vanilla ice cream, and two packages of Hostess chocolate cupcakes.

I could understand why she wanted me to get the paper products. We needed them in the house. They were the kinds of things you never wanted to run out of. But ice cream, bananas, and cupcakes? It sounded like she was planning a party.

If she was, I was all in.

I quickly dressed, got my wallet and phone, and after locking up the house, jumped into the Jeep and headed out. When I got to the gate, it was still closed and locked from the night before. There was no sign that anyone had tried to mess with it.

After unlocking it, I drove through and closed it behind me. Since I was coming right back, I didn't bother to lock it. If Abby got back before I did, I didn't want her to be locked out. I'd given her a key but didn't know if she had it with her.

It took me less than five minutes to get to the store. There was only one other car in the lot and it was leaving when I pulled in. I parked off to the side, making sure not to block the ice machine or bait tanks near the front door. I didn't want to do anything that might give the storekeeper another reason not to like me.

The last time I was in, he didn't seem too friendly. When he learned I had bought the place next to Trudy's, he figured I was a developer with plans to build condos. I assured him I wasn't, but I don't think it took.

In this part of the world, a land developer is about the lowest thing a person could be. Even lower than a lawyer. Developers would come in, buy up a tract of rural land, and bribe county commissioners to change the zoning from farm to multi-family housing. Then without regard for the people living nearby, they'd build high-rise condos, transforming a previously tranquil community into a nightmare of crowded roads, higher crime, filled with newcomers whose values didn't mesh with the locals.

It was no wonder developers were held in such low esteem and why the man behind the counter was wary of my intentions. If I were him, I'd be worried too. I was an outsider and he had no idea who I was or what I planned to do.

Still, he hadn't kicked me out the last time I visited. I figured he wouldn't this time either.

I grabbed Abby's list and went inside. The same man was at the register. He had the local paper in front of him and it looked like he was working the crossword. He looked up at me, nodded, and went back to his puzzle.

The first three items on the list were easy to find. Toilet paper, paper towels, and tissues. The prices in the little store were a bit higher than Walmart, but I didn't care. I was willing to pay extra not to have to drive all the way into town just to pick up a few things.

I could have saved a few pennies by going with the cheap single-ply rolls, but I didn't. Abby wouldn't hold with that. I went with the good stuff, the kind that didn't tear when you used it. I did the same with the paper towels and tissues, paying extra for brand names.

There were no shopping carts and the eight-pack of toilet paper and four-pack of paper towels along with the four boxes of tissues was about all I could carry. I took them to the counter, told the man I had more on my list, and went back to see if I could find the rest.

The ginger ale was easy. It was back with the stacks of soft drinks near the coolers. The bananas were a little harder to find. The store didn't have a fruits and vegetable section so I had to ask the counterman if they had any. Instead of answering, he pointed to the candy aisle. I wasn't sure he had heard me say bananas, but I went over to the candy aisle to check.

To my surprise, there were a few ripe bananas laying on the top shelf between the Little Debby donuts and single-serve boxes of breakfast cereal. I picked up four.

On my way back to the checkout counter, I found the cupcakes and grabbed two packages.

The last thing on my list was vanilla ice cream. I figured it was a key ingredient in whatever Abby was planning, and I wasn't going to forget it. I had saved it for last; I didn't want it melting while I shopped for everything else.

There was a six-foot-long top-loaded freezer near the front of the store where I figured I'd find the ice cream. When I looked, I wasn't disappointed. It was filled with popsicles, fudge bars, nut-covered drumsticks, ice cream sandwiches, and, lucky for me, a few quarts of vanilla and chocolate ice cream.

I grabbed the vanilla and added it to my collection at the counter. Checking my list, I saw I had gotten everything. Except beer.

Going to the back, I grabbed two twelve packs of Bud Lite and brought those to the register. I put the cases on the counter and said. "I think this is it."

The counterman stood and started ringing the items up. First, the paper products, which he didn't bother bagging. The same with the ginger ale and beer. No reason to bag them. I'd be carrying them out as is. He did bag the bananas, cupcakes, and ice cream. Looking up, he smiled and asked, "You planning a party?"

It was the only words he had spoken since I'd entered the store, and the first time I'd seen him smile. Wanting to keep him smiling, I said, "My wife. She made the list. I'm hoping it means she's going to be in a good mood tonight if you know what I mean."

He nodded knowingly, then pressed the button on the register to total up my purchase. The bill came to just under fifty dollars. Not surprising considering the cost of the beer and paper products.

I pulled out my wallet and paid with cash. Three twenties.

He put the money in the register and counted out the change. When he handed it to me, he said, "You're the one who bought that place next to Trudy, right?"

"Yeah, that's me."

He looked at the front door as if he were checking to see if anyone else was about to come in. When he didn't see anyone, he turned back to me and said, "I hear there was some excitement at her place yesterday."

His words surprised me. The man in the chicken coop was supposed to be a secret. No one was supposed to know. But somehow, the guy working the register at the local convenience store did.

Maybe that's the way it worked in the small community. The guy behind the counter at the bait and beer shop would hear stories from his customers and the news would spread from there. Even when the news was supposed to be kept secret.

Trudy had told me not to tell anyone. In fact, she had said it would be best to forget about the whole thing. So when the counter guy mentioned it, I shrugged and said, "I guess I missed it. I was working inside all day. Didn't hear a thing."

He looked at me, squinted, and asked, "You sure you didn't hear anything?"

I shook my head. "No, nothing at all. Far as I know, nothing happened."

He asked again. "You sure?"

I didn't know why he was pushing so hard to get me to talk, but I wasn't going to play along. I wasn't going to tell him anything. "Sorry, if something happened, I don't know about it."

I pointed to the bag with the ice cream. "I need to get this back home and in the freezer."

I grabbed the bag along with the ginger ale and took it out to the Jeep. After, putting it on the floor under the dash out of the sun, I went back in to get a second load, this time, the paper products. On my third trip back in, the man who had rung me up had come out from behind the counter and was waiting for me.

He smiled, held out his hand, and said, "I'm Tiny. You need anything around here, you let me know."

We shook hands and I left the store carrying the beer, thinking I may have just passed an important test. One that might benefit me in the future.

Chapter Forty-Seven

With the ice cream melting by the minute, I didn't waste time getting back home. All was good until I got to the gate. It was open and I was pretty sure I had closed it when I left.

Either Abby had gotten home early, or someone else was on the property. I hoped it was Abby, but it was unlikely. She'd said she was at least three hours away. Unless she was actually a lot closer and planning to surprise me, there was no way she could have made it in time.

It had to be someone else and I needed to find out who.

I pulled through, jumped out of the jeep, and closed and locked the gate behind me. If whoever had gone through was still on the property, they wouldn't be leaving without me knowing about it.

Back in the Jeep, I headed to the house. I didn't have my gun with me and I hoped I wouldn't need it. But a stranger bold enough to go through a closed gate, might not have good intentions. They could be like the guy who hit Trudy's the day before. Armed and dangerous.

She was lucky. She had Clyde on her side. He had disarmed the intruder and put him in a cage. Unfortunately, I didn't have a Clyde. There were no monkeys at Duckville – at least none that I knew of.

I was going to be on my own.

The only thing in the Jeep I could use as a weapon was a tire iron. It was heavy and pointed and would be useful in close combat. But if my opponent had a gun, close combat wouldn't be an option. I'd be shot dead before I could get near enough to use the tire-changing tool.

Still, going in with the tire iron would be better than going in empty-handed. It was stored behind the passenger seat and when I stopped, I'd get it out.

As I made the last turn toward the house, I saw a late model Lexus SUV parked near the front. A woman, presumable its driver, had gotten out and was sitting at my picnic table with a phone up to her ear. Her back was to me and I couldn't see her face.

I'd killed the motor and was letting the Jeep coast, trying to keep the element of surprise on my side. I'd almost reached her car when my phone rang.

Fearing it would alert the stranger of my presence, I quickly pressed the answer button and put the device to my ear. Before I could say anything, a familiar voice said, "Walker, I'm at your house. Where are you?"

It took me a few seconds to place the voice. Then it came to me. Anna, the real estate agent. She had come through my gate and was now sitting on the deck outside my door.

I wouldn't be needing the tire iron.

With phone in hand, I said, "Anna, I'm pulling up behind you. Turn around."

She looked over her shoulder and saw me in the Jeep. After waving, she stepped off the deck and started walking in my direction. Before she reached me, I brought the coasting Jeep to a stop and climbed out to greet her.

When we were a few steps apart, I smiled, expecting maybe a handshake. But instead, she came in for a full-on hug. With her arms wrapped around me, she whispered, "Walker, you're looking good."

She held on, waiting for me to say something back. But I

didn't. I kept my mouth closed, even though she looked pretty good herself. Especially up close.

But I knew better than to tell her that though. I was supposed to be a married man and married men aren't allowed to whisper into the ears of women they used to date.

At least that's what I thought.

When she released the hug, she stepped back and asked, "Where's your wife? I thought she'd be here with you."

Instead of answering, I asked my own question. "What are you doing here? Why didn't you call first?"

"I should have, but what's the fun in that? I was hoping to surprise you. And Abby. Both of you. Where is she?"

It wasn't any of her business where my pretend wife was, but she'd asked about her twice and expected an answer. I figured if I didn't give her one, she'd ask again. Women are like that. Relentless.

I answered in a way that I hoped would satisfy her curiosity. It wasn't exactly the truth, but it was better than telling her that she was in Miami interviewing mobsters.

"She's in town, running some errands. She'll be back soon."

"Good. I'd hate to miss her. I've got a little surprise for you and wanted her to be around when I gave it to you."

Before she could say anything else, I pointed to the Jeep. "I've got food I need to put away. It'll only take me a couple of minutes."

I walked to the passenger door and grabbed the bag with the ice cream and cupcakes and headed to the house. Anna followed me up the steps and stood behind me while I unlocked the door.

When I opened it, I turned to her and said, "I'll be right back."

I was hoping she'd get the hint that I wasn't inviting her in, but it didn't take. As soon as I stepped inside, she followed.

I headed to the fridge and put the ice cream in the freezer. When I turned around, she was standing in the living room checking out the furniture. She put her hand on the back of the couch, feeling the fabric. Then walked over to one of the side tables, and gave it a tap. Kind of like she was an appraiser on PBS's Antiques Roadshow.

Finally, she looked back at me and said, "The place came like this? Furnished?"

"Yeah, everything you see was already here."

She looked around, nodding her approval. "It's a lot nicer than I thought it'd be. When I listed it, I wasn't able to get inside. The bank told me it needed work and I figured it was in pretty bad shape. But boy, was I wrong. If I'd known it was like this, I would have told them to up the price."

She pointed to the door leading to my bedroom. "What's that go to?"

I should have thought about my answer before saying anything, but I didn't. "That's my bedroom. Abby's is on the other side."

As soon as I said it, I knew I was in trouble. Abby and I were supposed to be newlyweds. Most don't have separate bedrooms. The jig might be up.

Anna smiled. "Separate bedrooms, huh? What's up with that?"

Instead of answering her question, I changed the subject. "So you said you brought me something? You want to show me what it is?"

She shook her head. "No, not now. It can wait until Abby gets here. I'd rather both of you see it at the same time."

I didn't want to tell her it might be three hours before she showed up. I was afraid she'd want to spend the time alone with me in the house, asking questions I probably wouldn't want to answer. Wanting to avoid that, I came up with a plan.

"Anna, I'm happy to see you, but I've got work to do and it might be a while before Abby gets back. If you don't mind, I'll open the gate so you can get out. When she does get back, I'll get her to call you so you can schedule a better time for us to get together."

Anna crossed her arms and looked at me with a smirk on her face. "Walker, you're not fooling me. I know you and her aren't really married. You're not even a couple. You sleep in separate bedrooms.

"I did some digging and found out there isn't a marriage license. The one she showed me was a fake. Same with the wedding photos. Photoshop fakes.

"I'm not sure what you two are trying to pull off, but you need to be careful. You paid cash for this place and the IRS is definitely going to notice. If you used dirty money, you better get a good lawyer. As your friend, I don't want to see you go to jail."

She paused, seemingly waiting for me to say something. So I did.

"Anna, you're right. We're not married. We're just good friends. She knew I was looking for a place and when this came on the market, she knew I'd want it.

"She tried to call and tell me about it, but couldn't reach me. I was off the grid. She knew the property would sell quickly and wanted to make sure I had a chance to buy it. So on her own, she decided to make an offer in my name. She thought the only way she could, was to tell you we were married.

"She downloaded a marriage license from the web and

pasted in our details. Using Photoshop, she put together some wedding photos and had them ready when you asked to see them.

"Her plan worked. You believed we were married and wrote up the offer.

"It's a good thing you did because after seeing the place, I wanted it. I had enough money in savings and didn't need a loan. I assure you the money was clean. If the IRS asks, I can show them exactly where every penny came from.

"There's no need to worry. There's nothing wrong or illegal with the transaction. I won't be going to jail, and neither will you for making it happen."

I pointed to the front door. "It's getting stuffy in here. Let's go outside."

This time, she got the hint. After we were out on the deck, she turn to me with tears in her eyes. "Walker, I was worried you were in some kind of trouble. I didn't want to ask you about it but knew I had to. I had to know what was going on.

"I was afraid you were tied up in a money-laundering scheme and it was going to come back and bite both of us. I guess I should have known better. You wouldn't do that kind of thing. At least I don't think you would. I hope you'll forgive me for digging into your personal life."

I smiled. "Anna, it's okay. I'm glad you cared enough to come out here and tell me off. But next time, call first."

Chapter Forty-Eight

Anna and I were standing on the deck, and I was hoping she was getting ready to leave. But she wasn't. She said, "I really do have something for you in my car. Come see."

She stepped down and headed to her Lexus. I followed. When we got to it, she opened the front door and pulled out a sheet of paper. "I've been asked to bring you this. It's a cash offer to buy this place. Nine hundred thousand dollars. No strings attached. All cash, no contingencies. No commission.

"If you accept, you'll walk away with more than two hundred thousand dollars profit."

She handed me the document. "It's all there in black and white. All you have to do is sign."

I didn't bother to read it. I handed it back to her. "Anna, I appreciate you bringing me this, but I'm going to have to pass. This place is not for sale."

She looked at me, shaking her head. "Walker, I figured you were smarter than that. You are passing on an easy two hundred thousand dollar profit. Are you sure you don't want to think about it?"

I took a deep breath. The money was tempting, but I'd made a commitment to Boris and there was no way I was not going to honor it. I wouldn't live long enough to spend the money if I went behind Boris's back.

Anna didn't need to know this.

I thanked her again for bringing the offer. "It's very tempting, but I'm not selling this place. I kind of like it here."

Still shaking her head, she said, "If you change your mind, let me know."

She turned back to her car and pointed to a beat-up legal-size cardboard box on the back seat. It was taped closed and had a case number written on the side.

"That's for you."

Normally, when a Realtor closes a sale, they'll give the buyer a housewarming gift. Something to remember them by when it comes to buying or selling another property.

The gifts vary based on the amount of the commission and the kind of client involved. For people moving in from out of state, it might be a few gift cards to local restaurants, or a membership in a beach club, or if appropriate, a small kitchen appliance like an espresso machine.

I was thinking that's what Anna had in mind when she said she had brought me something. A gift card or fixture for the house. It's not that I expected or wanted a gift, but if she had gone to the trouble of getting one, I would act like I appreciated it when she gave it to me.

But when she showed me the weathered cardboard box in the back seat of her SUV, I didn't know what to think or say.

She quickly cleared up my confusion. "Walker, after closing, the bank called and said they had a box of old papers they had found on the property. When the developer defaulted on the loan, the bank sent in a crew to clean the place up.

"They had been instructed to gather up any personal items and take them to the bank to be inventoried and disposed of. That cardboard box was one of the things they found.

"At the bank, they opened the box and saw it contained property records, building permits, surveys, architectural drawings, and even some old photos. They figured the records might be important and decided instead of shredding them, they should be kept in case they were needed.

"They marked the box with the loan number and stored it away. It was forgotten until two days ago when the defaulted loan was closed. While tidying up their files, they found the box in storage. Not wanting to throw it out without first checking, they called and asked if I thought you might want it. I figured you might.

"That's why I came out here in person. To bring you the offer that you so foolishly turned down, and, thinking there was a chance you would, to see if you wanted the old records about this place.

"You want them?"

"Yeah, I do. I wonder how far back they go. Any idea?"

"No, all I know is what the loan officer told me. That the records go with the property. You want me to get them out for you?"

"No, I'll get them."

I leaned into the back seat and picked up the box. It was heavier than expected. It had to be almost full of paper. Or maybe not. Maybe half paper and half gold coins. Not likely, but you never know what someone might hide in the bottom of an old box.

One thing was for sure – I couldn't wait to see what I'd find. But I'd have to because I didn't want to start digging into the box with Anna around. It might give her an excuse to stay and see what I found.

I didn't want that. There might be things in it she shouldn't see or know about. It would be best if she left.

So, with the box in hand, I walked over to the house. Anna followed close behind. Instead of going in, I put it on the picnic table and said, "Anna, I appreciate you bringing this all the way out here. I can't wait to see what's in it. But I can't get into it right now. I've got work I have to take care of before Abby gets back, so I'll have to leave it till later.

"I don't want to run you off, but I really do need to get back to work. Let me open the gate for you so you can get out."

This time, she took the hint. I wanted her to leave. She smiled. "Walker, it's been a pleasure. Call me, now that you're single."

My Jeep was parked behind her Lexus. I had to move it before she could leave. Since the gate was locked and she wouldn't be able to get out until I opened it, I jumped in the Jeep, turned around, and led the way. At the gate, I pulled off to the side, got out, and opened it.

As she drove through, she blew me a kiss and waved goodbye.

When she was out of sight, I headed to the house. I wanted to see what kind of records were in the mystery box. But before I could do that, I had to unload the rest of the things I'd gotten at the store. Especially the beer.

It needed to be cold the next time Trudy and Clyde came over.

Chapter Forty-Nine

I'd just gotten the beer in the fridge when my phone chimed with an incoming call. The ID said 'wifey'. Clearly, Abby was having a bit of fun with our pretend marriage. Making sure I knew she was still in the game.

I figured two of us could play at that.

I answered, as if there was another person in the room with me, "Quiet, it's my wife. She doesn't know about us."

Abby played along. "If there's another woman there, ask her to take you with her when she leaves. Tell her she'd be doing me a favor."

I laughed. "It's too late Abby. She just left."

I figured that would end the joking, but it didn't. Abby followed up with, "Any chance she'll be coming back? Because I'd like to meet her. Any woman that can put up with you for more than a few minutes might be someone I want to know."

I chuckled, then said, "I'm not kidding. There was a woman here this morning. When I got back from the store, she was sitting on the deck, waiting for me. It wasn't Trudy."

This time, her voice took on a serious tone. "Really? You had a visitor? A woman? Do I know her? What did she want?"

I didn't want to get into it on the phone, so instead of answering her questions, I said, "I'll tell you all about it when you get here. How far away are you?"

"About an hour. But before I get there, I want you to move your things into my bedroom. Move everything over, including your clothes and bathroom stuff. Do it before I get there."

It was a strange request and I wanted to know more. "Are we switching rooms? You moving into mine? I'm moving into yours? Is that's what we're doing?"

"No Walker, we're not switching rooms. I want you to move into my room with me. We're supposed to be newlyweds. We should be sharing a bedroom. We're going to start doing that, tonight."

I smiled, even though she wouldn't be able to see me do it. "Sharing a bedroom? I like the sound of that. Does that mean . . ."

Before I could finish my question, she said, "No. That doesn't mean we'll be doing anything other than sharing a bedroom. No hanky panky. It's just temporary. Only for a few days. I'll tell you why when I get there. In the meantime, get your stuff moved over. And don't make a mess."

She ended the call.

I couldn't think of any reason why she'd suddenly want me to move into her room, to share her bed, but I wasn't going to spend too much time worrying about it. Just the fact that she wanted me to do it was good enough for me.

Not wanting to give her a chance to change her mind, I quickly moved the things I had in my room into hers. A few shirts, two pairs of shorts, my underwear and socks. Everything else I owned was still in the RV. It would be staying there, ready to use when I hit the road again. Which I hoped wouldn't be too far in the future.

It took me less than fifteen minutes to move everything over. It could have gone faster, but Bob and Buddy decided to help. They mirrored my every move as I went from room to room. Each time I opened a drawer, one of them would climb in. The other would stay out and play whack a mole, swatting at the cat in the drawer. When I'd open another, they'd change places and start the game anew.

I finally gave up on opening drawers. The cats had won.

After getting everything moved over, I spent a few minutes tidying up the room, then remaking the bed. Bob figured we were starting another game and quickly slid under the sheets. Buddy stayed on top, playing a game of 'whack the undercover cat'.

They played the game long after I left the room.

Eventually, they tired and joined me in the kitchen. I hadn't eaten since early morning and it was well past my lunchtime. I was tempted to put together a quick sandwich but decided to wait until Abby showed up. We could dine together and talk about the benefits of our new living arrangement.

I checked the fridge and saw that we still had fresh turkey from Publix, along with cheese, bread, mustard, mayo, and even some lettuce. Everything I needed to make a couple of sandwiches. While I waited for her return, I snacked on Sun Chips to stave off starvation.

Twenty minutes later, she rolled up in her camper van and parked near the front deck. Seeing me coming to welcome her back, she stepped out, pointed a finger at me, then held it to her lips, signaling she wanted me to be quiet.

I couldn't figure out why, but didn't question it. If she wanted me to be quiet, I'd be quiet. No need to give her a reason to make me move back into my old bedroom.

As I got closer, she signaled she wanted me to follow as she walked away from her van. It was like she thought the camper was bugged and someone would be listening to our every word.

I knew it wasn't that far-fetched of an idea.

On a previous trip, the vehicle I was driving had been tracked and monitored by an angry ex-husband. Using a radio transmitter hidden in the dash, he'd heard every word spoken by the woman traveling with me. That trip didn't end well.

Setting up a listening device like that is relatively easy. You can get them on Amazon for less than a hundred dollars. The basic ones can track a vehicle's location and post details on the web. If you pay more, you can get one with a microphone that can record everything being said.

Maybe Abby thought someone had planted something like that in her van. Or it could be, she was just being paranoid. She's been known to be that way in the past.

But then again, maybe someone really was listening. These days, you never know for sure.

I kept quiet and followed her as she walked away from her van.

We had gone about thirty feet when she stopped and whispered, "I didn't come alone. I brought someone back with me. Someone from Tony's crew. He's knocked out in the back of my van."

I wasn't sure I heard her right.

"Knocked out? You kidnapped him? And brought him back here? Are you telling me there's a mafia guy tied up in the back of your van?"

She shook her head. "No, I didn't kidnap him. And he's not tied up. He came willingly. Sort of."

I didn't like her answer.

"Abby, what do you mean by, 'sort of?' And why'd you bring him here?"

She smiled. "It's a long story. I'll do my best to make it short.

268

Chapter Fifty

We were standing about thirty feet behind Abby's van. She was starting to tell me why there was a member of Tony Duck's crew knocked out inside it.

"After the three other guys on Boris's list wouldn't talk to me, I went to the casino parking lot planning to spend the night. Right after pulling in, I got a phone call. The caller ID was blocked and I figured maybe one of the guys I talked to earlier had changed his mind and was willing to talk. So I answered.

"But it wasn't any of them. It was someone new, not on Boris's list. He said he had heard I was interested in Tony Ducks, and said he could tell me things.

"He wouldn't say more on the phone but said he would answer all my questions I had if I'd buy him dinner.

"Of course, I was suspicious. Getting a call out of the blue from someone willing to talk? I figured I was being set up. Maybe by one of the guys I'd called earlier. They warned me about asking too many questions. Maybe they were sending someone to make sure I didn't muddy up the waters.

"Still, if there was a chance the unknown caller knew something that might help us, I was willing to meet him. But only in a very public place with a lot of people around.

"I told him I was staying at the Casino and if he'd meet me there, I'd buy him dinner. He agreed, maybe a little too quickly. Kind of like he already knew where I was. He said he'd be at the front door at eight and would be wearing a boat captain's hat so I could recognize him."

"I wasn't sure he'd show, but at ten to eight, I went to the Casino's front door, and waited. The guy showed up not long after. Wearing a captain's hat and pulling a dark blue navy duffle bag behind him. The kind you see sailors toting when they go off to sea.

"He looked to be in his early seventies, about five-eight, slender build, and the kind of dark tan you get from spending too many hours out in the Florida sun. His clothes hung off his frame like he'd recently lost a lot of weight. He didn't look dangerous, but you never know these days.

"I went over, introduced myself and he did the same. He claimed to be Finn Hawkins. A name that wasn't on Boris's list. Said most people just called him Finn.

"He was hungry and wanted to eat before we talked. I was hungry too, so we headed to the upstairs buffet. After waiting in line, I paid for our meals and we found a private table near the back.

"As soon as the server brought over our drinks, Finn hit the buffet line. He loaded up his plate like it'd been a long time since he'd had a good meal. He went back through the line three times, making sure he didn't miss out on anything.

"Thirty minutes later, when he was finally full, he was ready to talk. He told me to ask him anything."

"Not wanting to waste my time, I decided to test him. Did he know the name of Tony's boat?

"He did. He said that before Tony bought it, the boat was called the Serenity. Tony renamed it to Charon.

"When I asked how he knew about the name changes, he said he had been the captain before Tony bought the boat. Captain Finn they called him.

"When Tony bought it, he was asked to stay on as the captain. He agreed and kept the job until after Tony was sent away.

"He claimed to have spent a lot of time with Tony during their trips to Key West. He said they had gotten to know each other well and had become friends. He said he was sad to see him end up in prison.

"We talked for a while, mostly about the boat and the trips to the Keys. I eventually slipped in a question about the money pit. I asked Finn if he knew anything about it.

"He thought for a moment, then smiled and said, 'Yeah, I know about. It was part of Tony's getaway plan. He spent a lot of money making sure he could get to it if he ever needed to disappear. I guess it didn't work out for him.'

"Instead of raising Finn's suspicions by asking more questions about Tony or the money pit, I asked about the duffle he had brought in with him.

"He told me everything he owned was inside it. Said he was living in a shelter in Miami and he took the duffle with him whenever he left. Didn't want anyone stealing it while he was gone.

"He said he didn't have a car and had to take the bus when he needed to go somewhere. That's how he got to the casino. By bus. It had cost him eighteen dollars and he wondered if I would cover it.

"I said I would and asked if he needed a little spending money.

"He said he always could use some extra cash, but what he really needed was a way to get out of Miami. To go somewhere else. To get away from the crime. And poverty.

"He said he missed living on Tony's boat and visiting the small town nearby. He said if he could, he'd go back there and try to get things going again.

"That's when I told him I lived near there and would be heading back in the morning. I told him I had room in my van if he wanted to ride back with me.

"I didn't tell him we lived in Tony's old place. I wanted it to be a surprise. I figured if he actually knew where the money pit was, maybe he would lead us to it.

"Instead of saying he'd ride back with me, he asked if I were with the FBI or any other federal agency. Was I investigating him? Was I going to arrest him?

"I assured him I wasn't with any agency and wasn't interested in seeing him get arrested. I just wanted to help him out.

"He said he didn't take charity, but if I would pay for his bus fare from the shelter, he would think about going back to Englewood with me. He'd let me know in the morning.

"I asked if he were going back to the shelter for the night. He said he couldn't. The buses stopped running at nine and the shelter doors closed at ten. It was too late to go back. He would just find a secluded corner and sleep in the casino. If security ran him off, he'd find a place outside to hide until the buses started running again.

"That's when I offered to get him a room. I told him it was only fair. It was my fault he had missed his ride.

"He wasn't a fool. He knew that sleeping in a soft bed was a better choice than trying to sleep on the casino floor or outside in the elements. So he agreed.

"I booked him a room and helped him get settled in. I stayed with him for about an hour and we talked about his life. Among other things, I learned he was never with the mafia. He was a boat captain. That was who he was. He was proud of it.

"I left about midnight and headed back to my van.

"The next morning, at the agreed time, I went to his room to see what he'd decided. He had showered and changed back into the clothes he had on the night before. He tried to hide it, but was clearly hungover. He had raided the mini-bar and needed coffee and food.

"We went downstairs to the cafe for breakfast. He ordered bacon, eggs, toast, and coffee. I had the same. While we waited for our food, he thanked me for the accommodations and apologized for emptying the mini-bar. He promised that when he got back on his feet, he'd pay me back.

"Then he said if my offer was still on the table, he'd be happy to ride to Englewood with me. If I wanted him to, he'd be willing to work off his debt by doing odd jobs around my house.

"I told him that sounded fair. That's why he'll be staying with us for a few days. He's sleeping in the van right now.

"When he wakes, we're going to move him into your bedroom."

Chapter Fifty-One

Abby had brought a man back with her from Miami. Someone claiming to be a part of Tony's crew and he'd be staying with us for a few days, sleeping in what was once my bedroom.

I was a little bummed he was the reason she wanted me to move and share a bed with her, but I wasn't going to complain. Sleeping next to her for any reason had to be better than sleeping alone.

At least that was what I thought at the time.

The fact the man in her van claimed to know the location of the money pit was by itself reason enough for her to bring him back with her. If he could lead us to it, and if we found the brooch that Boris was looking for, life would be good.

We were standing about thirty feet away from her camper, keeping our voices low so as not to wake the man who was sleeping inside. Abby had just finished telling me about her Miami adventure and was waiting for me to say something.

Best I could come up with was, "So you went to Miami, and came back with a new man in your life? Anything else I need to know?"

She smiled. "Yeah. I stopped at the Swamp Ape place and got the hat you wanted. It's in the van. When Finn wakes up, I'll get it for you."

It was a moderately warm day and even with the van's front windows open, it would soon be too hot to sleep inside unless we fired up the generator and turned on the air conditioner.

The generator was pretty loud, more so if you were sleeping inside what was essentially a metal echo chamber. Her camper was well insulated, but the generator was mounted right under the bed and if we started it up, the unexpected roar might give Finn a heart attack.

Abby nixed the idea.

As we stood there thinking about what to do next, we saw the van rock side to side. Apparently, sleeping beauty had woken and was trying to figure how to open the door to get out.

The Ram ProMaster chassis that Abby's van was built on, had a sliding door on the side. Opening it from the outside was easy. Just pull the handle and give it a shove to the left.

Opening it from the inside was a different story. It was hard to do unless you knew the secret steps. You first had to find the hidden handle which was at the far end of the door tucked in behind the passenger seat. Then you had to pull the handle down to unlock it. But even unlocked, the door wouldn't open unless you released the handle and let it return to its default position.

Only then could you pull the handle and shove the door to the right to get it open.

If you didn't follow the steps in the precise order, the door would stay closed. It was designed as a safety feature to keep children from accidentally opening the door and falling out.

A grand idea. Except the steps involved made it equally difficult for adults, especially those that had just woken from a deep sleep to get the door open.

The door on the back of the van operated the same way. Four steps. But in Abby's camper conversion, it was more involved. The handle was hidden by the vans' insulated walls.

Unless you knew where to look, you wouldn't find it.

From the sound and motion inside her camper, it was clear Finn wasn't too happy with the team that designed the ProMaster's locking doors. We could hear him banging on the side door trying to get it open while uttering a stream of curse words only a seasoned sailor like him would know.

Fearing he might hurt himself or damage the inside of her van, Abby rushed over and opened the side door for him. He was standing just inside, red-faced and bent over. He looked up and asked, "Why'd you lock me in?"

She apologized by saying, "I didn't mean to. The doors lock automatically when I start the motor. I guess I forgot to unlock them when I got out. Sorry about that."

Instead of stepping out of the now open door, Finn leaned out and looked around. The way the van was parked, his view was to the side of the property, toward the palm trees that lined the fence. Away from the Quonset hut.

He squinted his eyes and asked, "Where are we?"

Abby quickly answered. "At my place, in Englewood. Get out and I'll show you around."

He nodded and climbed out of the van. He was as Abby had described. About five-eight, ghostly thin, with close-cropped white hair. His skin had the wrinkled leather look of a seafarer.

His clothes were simple. Long pants, faded black, the kind worn by retirees. A white threadbare short sleeve shirt. Brown soft sole slip-on shoes. No jewelry, no tattoos.

In many rural parts of the country, Finn could have passed as a Sunday go-to-meeting preacher.

He noticed me looking at him and asked. "You with her?"

Smiling, I said, "Yes, I am. I'm her husband. She told me you might be staying with us for a few days. You want me to get your bag?"

He didn't answer right away. I could tell he wasn't sure what was going on. We were being nice to him. Maybe too nice. Maybe it scared him. Finally, he said, "No. Leave my bag in the van. I'm not sure I'm staying. I need to look around first. Get my bearings. You have any dogs that bite?"

I smiled. "No, no dogs. But there's a monkey next door. Big one, he doesn't bite. He does drink beer, though. How about you? Would you like one? There are some cold ones in the fridge."

Finn smiled and turned to Abby. "Your husband knows the magic words. Cold beer. Any chance I could get something to go with it?"

I answered for her. "How about a turkey sandwich? Does that sound good?"

"Yep, that would work."

Chapter Fifty-Two

Finn followed me around the van and toward the house. He stopped when he saw we were living in a Quonset hut.

"Ya'll live in this?"

"Yeah, we just moved in."

He stared at it, then said, "I used to know a place that had a hut like that for a house. It looked a lot like yours."

He turned toward the driveway looking back toward the gate. Then slowly did a three-sixty, taking it all in. When he turned back to Abby, he said, "This is the place, isn't it? Where Tony kept his boat. Why did you bring me here?"

Abby answered since she was the one who brought him. "We live here, that's why. After we moved in, one of the neighbors told us Tony Ducks sometimes hung out here. We wanted to know more. That's why I was asking about him. To learn the history of this place.

"If that bothers you and you don't want to be here, I can take you into town, drop you anywhere you want."

Finn stared at Abby for a moment, then pointed to the house. "You promised me a cold beer and a sandwich. Let's see how that goes before I decide whether I stay or not."

We headed to the house, Abby leading the way. At the door, I stopped and asked Finn if he was allergic to cats.

"Cats? You got cats in there? How many?"

I held up two fingers.

"Just two? That's all? That ain't nothing. I used to live with a lady that had eight. We were in a small house and those cats were into everything. Followed me everywhere I went. Even into the head. Couldn't take a poop without a cat joining me.

"I was captaining a fishing boat back then. Could have been why those cats liked me so much. I came home smelling like fish."

He paused, then said, "Your two won't be a problem. Unless they're mean. I don't like mean cats. Scratching and spitting at me. Yours like that?"

I shook my head. "No, Buddy and Bob are pretty calm most of the time. You won't have to worry about them."

We went inside where Abby had a cold beer on the counter waiting for Finn. Pointing at it, she asked, "You want it in a glass?"

"Naw, I like it from the can."

He popped the top and took a long drink. It reminded me of the way that Clyde handled his beer. Pulling the top in a single fluid motion. Like someone who had a lot of practice.

Abby told us to sit at the table while she made our sandwiches. I offered to help, but she said she'd already started and it would be easier without me being in the way.

Before we sat, Finn pointed to what used to be my bedroom. "Bathroom still over there?"

I nodded.

"Mind if I use it?"

"No, go ahead. And while you're there, check out the bedroom. That's where you'll be bunking if you decide to stay with us."

He got up and walked toward the bath. It was the first time I noticed he had a limp. Could have been due to old age or an ancient injury.

I wouldn't be asking him about it.

Abby was putting sandwiches on the table when he came back out to join us. He waited for her to take a seat before he sat. Then with all three of us sitting, he asked if it was okay to say a prayer.

We didn't object.

He bowed his head and thanked the Lord for the meal and for the new friends he had met.

It felt good to hear him say those words.

We finished our sandwiches fairly quickly. When we were done, Abby asked Finn if he would like me to get his duffle and put it in our guest room.

Shaking his head, he said, "Don't make a special trip. I can get it on my own."

He paused, then said, "But if you're going out there for something else, it won't bother me if you bring it back in with you."

Abby wanted me to get her bag which was still in the van, so I went out and got both. When I picked up Finn's duffle, I was surprised at how light it was. There couldn't have been much in it. Maybe just a change of clothes and a few toiletries.

I guess he traveled light.

Back inside, Abby had me put it in what had been my bedroom but was now the guest room. She told Finn to make himself at home and said if he needed anything let us know and we'd get it for him.

So far, the cats had stayed hidden.

While he settled into his new room, Abby had me follow her into her bedroom. As soon as she stepped in, she saw the tattered cardboard box that Anna had dropped off earlier. It was on her bed, hard to miss.

Pointing to it, she asked, "What's that? And why is it on my bed?"

I told her how Anna had brought it over, along with an offer to buy the property.

"She offered you how much!"

I repeated the amount. "Nine hundred thousand dollars. All cash. No contingencies."

Shaking her head, she said, "That's crazy. Somebody must really really want this place. Did you find out who?"

"No, the buyer's name was shown as a corporation. One that I never heard of."

"You turned it down, right?"

"Of course I did. Boris has already made me a better offer."

She nodded as if she knew about my deal with Boris. Even though it was supposed to be a secret, I wasn't surprised she was in the loop.

Again, she pointed at the box, "Tell me why it's in here."

I smiled. "It's full of records about this place from way back when. Surveys, permits, receipts, photos, and more. I thought if we went through it, we might find something that could lead us to the treasure."

Abby pointed over her shoulder toward Finn's room. "He's our best lead. He said he knows where the money pit is. Let's find out if he really does."

Chapter Fifty-Three

Leaving Abby's bedroom, we found Finn in the living room sitting on the couch with Bob in his lap. Buddy was beside him trying to squeeze his way in. Bob was purring, apparently enjoying the pets he was getting.

Bob prefers women. He almost never allows a strange man to get close to him. Finn was the exception.

We went over and sat in the two chairs across from the couch. Finn looked up. "I found your cats. Soon as I sat down, they came over to check me out. This big one came first. The little one followed. Hope you don't mind me petting them."

Abby smiled. "No, not at all. Pet them all you want. I'm glad they like you. They're generally a pretty good judge of character, and the fact they like you is a good sign.

She pointed to the door. "Walker and I are thinking about taking a walk, maybe down to the boat dock. You want to join us?"

Finn looked down at Bob, then back up at us. "Yeah, a walk sounds good. But one of you is going to have to come over and get this big lunk off my lap."

Since it was Bob weighing him down, it was my job to get him off. Instead of going over and picking him up, I went to the kitchen, got out his bag of treats, and shook it.

He was off Finn's lap and at my feet in a flash. I threw a treat across the floor and he took off after it. Buddy wanted in on the action, so I threw him one as well.

Both cats liked to give chase when I tossed their kitty

treats. To them, it was a lot more fun that way. I guess in their minds, they were training for the day they'd come across a live mouse or lizard. Something even more fun to chase than treats.

With Bob out of his lap, Finn got up from the couch, told us he'd be right back and went to his bedroom. Two minutes later, he returned, wearing his Captain's cap and a pair of dark sunglasses. He was ready to walk.

Outside, the weather was Florida fall perfect. Partly cloudy with a slight breeze off the Gulf.

Abby had decided our destination would be the boat dock. That way, Finn could see if it had changed much since he last saw it. Knowing about his bum leg, we kept a slow pace. We weren't in any hurry, and neither was he.

Along the way, our guest marveled at how much the trees had grown and how the areas that had once been clear, were now covered with brush.

It took us about ten minutes of slow walking to reach the dock. Upon seeing it, Finn smiled and said, "It hasn't changed much. The seawall has held up well. I'm surprised about that. The dock used to be made of wood, but this new one is much better. With the safety rails and all, it'll be a lot easier to board a boat."

He paused, then said, "I lived here for almost four years. In the Charon. Those were some of the best times of my life.

"My crew cabin was the nicest of any boat I've been on. Even had my own private head. Tony's stateroom was nicer. With a king-size bed, a large wardrobe, a desk to work from, even a tub in his private bath.

"As Captain, I did all the maintenance on the boat. It was my job to keep everything up and running and make sure the pantry was well-stocked, and the fuel tanks full. Tony wanted me to have it ready to go on a moment's notice. I never knew when he might show up and want to head out, so I kept it in tip-top shape, ready to go.

"It was a real beauty. Sleek, modern, and when needed, it could go plenty fast. It handled beautifully. Even in rough seas. I wonder if it's still around."

I could have answered his question, but didn't. Not without first getting permission from Boris, the current owner of the yacht.

On our way back to the house, Finn paused at the trail that led to the other two Quonset huts. He turned to Abby and said, "Back at the casino you asked about the money pit. If you want to see it, I can show it to you now. It's close."

Abby and I both were surprised at how casually he brought it up. I think we both thought it was a big secret and that no one was supposed to know or talk about it.

But apparently not, at least when it came to Finn.

Trying not to seem too eager, Abby said, "I guess if it's close, we ought to go see it. As long as you don't mind showing it to us."

"No, I don't mind at all. I can't promise that it'll still be there. But I can show you where it was. Follow me."

Finn led the way, with Abby close behind. I brought up the rear.

About a minute after leaving the main trail and taking the path leading to the two older Quonset huts, Finn walked up to the shelter that covered the decrepit boat we'd seen the day before. He stopped and said, "I can't believe it. It's still here. The Money Pit."

Chapter Fifty-Four

The three of us were standing just a few feet away from the open-air Quonset hut that provided minimal shelter for the broken-down cabin cruiser we had seen earlier. Finn had just told us it was the location of the Money Pit.

I assumed he meant that the pit was in the ground somewhere under the Quonset hut. Probably hidden under the boat.

I was wrong.

I learned this when Abby asked, "It's under the boat? Is that where it is?"

Finn shook his head. "No, I thought you knew. The Money Pit is the name of the boat. It's on the back unless the paint has faded away."

Abby looked at me, then said, "Go check. See what it says."

The ground around the boat was heavy with weeds and filled with broken glass and parts that had fallen off the vessel during the twenty years it had sat unused. There was no way to get to the backside without wading through overgrown tropical brush and becoming a meal for whatever small critters might be hiding within.

I was wearing tennis shoes, thin socks, and pants that ended above my knees. I wasn't in any hurry to expose the bare skin of my legs to whatever was lurking in the dense bush.

Instead of wading in, I turned to Finn and said, "Tell me about the boat. How'd it get here?"

He didn't hesitate. "This is the first boat Tony bought. He had planned to use it to get to the Keys. But after the first trip down, he realized it was too small for what he wanted to do. The boat could make it, but in heavy weather, it was no fun. He needed something bigger.

"That's when he bought the Charon. He kept the Money Pit and used it for day trips or when he took his friends out fishing. It was perfect for that. Back then, we kept it docked behind the bigger boat.

I nodded. "So, how did it get the name Money Pit?"

Finn smiled. "He didn't know anything about boats when he bought it. He just liked the way it looked and paid the asking price. Didn't even bother getting a marine survey. It was used, and like most used boats, it needed a little work.

"He took it to the local marina and told them to fix everything that was wrong with it. While they were at it, he wanted them to update the electronics, put in radar and autopilot, and make it like new.

"It took them about two months to get everything taken care of. But when finished, the boat looked great. They had done everything he had asked and hadn't scrimped on anything.

"When he got the bill, he was shocked to see that it was almost twice what he had paid for the boat. So when they asked him if he wanted a name painted on the back, he immediately thought, 'Money Pit'.

"As it turned out, the money he put into was well worth it. The boat was safe, reliable, easy to handle, and great for cruising the Intracoastal, even for medium offshore trips. After that first big bill, it never needed to go back to the marina, except for fuel."

I nodded, thinking about the rumors of Tony having a

Money Pit filled with gold. Was it possible the treasure was stored in the boat? And was it still there?

I decided to ask a few questions that might give me the answers without giving away my hunt for treasure.

"So, Finn. You said that Tony kept the boat in the water at the dock so he could use it at a moment's notice. Does that mean he kept his gear in it? Or did he have to bring his things down here and put them in every time he wanted to take the boat out?"

Finn thought about for a moment, then said, "Most of the gear stayed in the boat, ready to be used when needed. The bigger items were stored in the lockers under the front bunks. Usually in waterproof cases. Anything he needed for a short trip would be there. Except food and drink.

"To keep thieves from stealing stuff while the boat was at the dock, he kept the storage compartments locked. Only Tony had the key.

"They're probably still locked. We were in such a hurry to get away when the Feds picked Tony up, that all we could do was to get the boat on the trailer and parked under the shelter.

"I was hoping we wouldn't be gone for long. That he'd get out and we'd come back here. But it didn't go that way.

"On Tony's orders, I took Charon to Key West and stayed with it for two years. When he was sentenced to prison, I knew my days on it were numbered. His attorney arranged to sell it privately, and I was out on my own."

He took a deep breath, look at the Money Pit, and shook his head. "Such a shame."

Abby patted his shoulder and said, "Maybe we ought to head back to the house. I have a surprise there for you."

I had no idea what she had in mind and really didn't care. All

I could think about was we had found the Money Pit, and there might be something of value hidden inside it.

Boris would want to know. I needed to call him.

Chapter Fifty-Five

Back at the house, Abby said for us to wash our hands and meet her back at the dining table. It was a simple request and I did as I was told.

When I got back to the table, I saw that she had set out a bowl of ice cream and a cupcake for each of us. A small candle had been put in the one in front of Finn.

When he looked up, he was smiling. Abby started singing the happy birthday song, and I finally understood what was going on. It was Finn's birthday and she had put together a small party for him. Complete with cake and ice cream.

I didn't know how she knew it was his birthday, but I was glad she had found out. The cake and ice cream put us all in a good mood.

After we finished our little celebration, Finn retired to his room to take a nap. Abby decided to do the same. She'd been on the road for a couple of days and was probably tired. As she headed to her bedroom, she didn't bother to invite me to join her.

I could have been disappointed, but I wasn't. I had other things on my mind. I needed to call Boris and let him know what we'd found. And since I didn't want our guest hearing what I was going to tell Boris, I was going to make the call from the privacy of my RV.

Outside, I was surprised it was almost dark. The day had gone by quickly. I went over to my RV, unlocked the door and went inside. Then pulled out my phone and made the call.

Boris answered on the third ring, sounding like I was interrupting something when he barked, "Find anything?"

I knew he would be pleased with my answer. "Yeah, I did. I found the Money Pit."

His gruff tone immediately went away. "Really? You found the Money Pit? Was there anything in it?"

This time, I knew my answer wasn't going to make him happy. But he had to know. "Boris, the Money Pit is the name of a boat. It's stored here on the property. It's been out in the elements for twenty years and is in pretty rough shape. I haven't gone through it yet, but will first thing tomorrow morning."

I figured he'd ask why I hadn't immediately searched it. It was a logical question and I had my answer ready. I would tell him the boat was in such bad shape I didn't dare go into it in the dark of night. As soon as the sun was up, I'd start my search.

Surprisingly, the question I expected never came. Instead, he asked, "How'd you find out? That the Money Pit was a boat?"

I took a deep breath, then said, "Finn told us. He's one of the guys Abby met in Miami. He claims to have worked on the Charon back in the day."

Boris paused before he asked his next question. Then, "Does he know about the gold? Did you tell him you were looking for it?"

"No, we haven't told him anything. We didn't want to scare him off. He's staying with us for a few days, so we'll be able to find out more."

"Staying with you? There at Duckville? How'd that come about?"

This time, it was me who paused before answering. I wanted to be sure I got the story right. If he asked Abby the same question, our answers needed to match. After thinking about it, I said, "He was living in a homeless shelter in Miami when he contacted Abby. After she was convinced he knew about Tony and had spent time with him at Duckville, she invited him to come stay with us for a few days. He agreed and he's here now."

Boris immediately asked, "You think she's safe around him? You're not leaving her alone with him are you?"

It was a good question and I hoped my answer would be acceptable. "He seems pretty safe, and from what I can tell, he doesn't have any weapons. Abby spent last night alone with him in Miami and most of today here without any problems. She seems to trust him."

He grunted, then asked, "You say he worked on the Charon? In what role?"

It was an easy question, one that I knew the answer to. "He was the Captain. His job was to make sure the boat was always ready to go at a moment's notice and he was with Tony on every trip he made to the Keys.

"When the feds stepped in, he took the Charon to Key West and stayed with it until it was sold. I don't know what he did after that. All I know for sure is he was living in a shelter in Miami when Abby found him."

Boris's tone softened. "It sounds like this Finn guy knows the Charon inside and out. I need to meet him. Keep him there until I arrive."

He paused, then said, "Search the boat. Do it first thing in the morning. Don't let anything stop you. Tony gets out in two days and he'll probably pay you a visit. You'll want to find the treasure before he shows up. I'll try to get there before Tony does."

Another pause, then, "Let me know if you find anything."

He ended the call.

I was relieved it had gone so well. Also relieved that Boris was going to pay us a visit and might be with us when Tony Ducks showed up. Having both of them at Duckville at the same time should help keep the peace.

That is, unless one or both brought a trigger-happy crew to back them up.

Rather than dwell on that possibility, I looked around the inside of the motorhome. I had been living in my house on wheels for almost three years, and already missed being on the road. Hopefully, that would change soon.

Remembering that I had to search the Money Pit in the morning, I went to the bedroom closet and pulled out the steel-toed boots I'd gotten a few months earlier. They would be a lot safer to wear while crawling through the broken-down boat than the tennis shoes I usually wore.

While rummaging through my closet, I looked for and found the pair of military camo pants I wear when working under the RV. They were designed to protect your legs in the roughest terrain and I figured they'd be good to have on when I crawled through the Money Pit.

Along with the boots and pants, I'd need to wear the gloves I'd picked up earlier at Babes. And a mask. The paper ones I'd gotten for Covid would probably be good enough to filter out the fiberglass dust I would be stirring up during my search.

Instead of taking all the gear with me back to the house, I left it piled up on the couch. I'd get it in the morning before I trekked over to the boat.

Stepping out of the RV, I intended to go back to the house, but stopped when I remembered the front gate. I had left it open so that Abby could get through when she came back from Miami and hadn't closed it after her return.

Since I didn't want to leave it open overnight, I grabbed a flashlight and hiked down to the gate, closed and locked it, and headed back to the house.

When I got there, Abby and Finn were outside sitting at the picnic table I'd put together. They both had beers and seemed to be enjoying each other's company. Seeing me heading their way, Abby held up her can and pointed to it. She was asking if I wanted her to get me a cold one.

I shook my head. A cold beer sounded good, but water was what I really wanted. I went inside, grabbed one out of the fridge, came out and took a seat next to her at the table.

As soon as I sat, she said, "Tell Finn there really is a beer-drinking monkey living next door. He doesn't believe me."

Smiling, I, took a sip of water and said, "A monkey? You think there's a monkey living next door? Abby, you may need to cut back on your drinking."

I was joking, but she didn't think it was funny. She punched me in the shoulder and said, "Walker, I'm serious. Tell him about Clyde."

It might have been funny to keep telling her it was all in her head, that there was no monkey. She would have surely punched me again, probably harder. It was funny and would have been worth it.

But, I held back, not because I didn't want to get punched, but because Trudy and Clyde were walking down our driveway, heading in our direction.

There would soon be no doubt we had a beer-drinking monkey as a neighbor.

I stood and waved them over. When Abby turned to see who was coming, she smiled at Finn and said, "Here comes your proof."

Chapter Fifty-Six

We had two cold beers waiting for them when they arrived. Trudy took one and Clyde the other, but not before handing me another one of the small purple flowers he seemed to be fond of.

I introduced both to Finn, explaining that he used to live on the property and would be staying with us for a few days. After they exchanged their hellos, Trudy turned to me and asked, "Did you see the two guys out here late last night?"

I shook my head. "No, I didn't see anyone. Are you sure they were here?"

She nodded. "Yeah, I'm sure. There were two men. With shovels. They climbed over your gate and followed your fence line about halfway to the water. They stopped there and started digging. Clyde was the one who heard them first. He alerted me and I followed him over to where they were.

"We hid in the bushes and watched as they dug. After about ten minutes, Clyde couldn't stand it any longer and started growling and hissing. Loud enough to scare them off. They left, leaving their tools behind."

She continued. "The dirt must be soft there because they dug a pretty deep hole. One of them had gone down into it, trying to get something out. Clyde scared him off before he could get it.

"Figured you'd want to know."

I was stunned. The front gate had been closed and locked. The no trespassing signs were everywhere. What kind of people would sneak in after dark and dig holes on my property? I needed to find out.

"Trudy, thanks for telling me. I definitely need to put a stop to this. If you see them again, come get me, no matter what time it is."

She nodded. "I will."

She paused, then said, "They parked their truck on my property. How about I flatten their tires next time so they can't leave. You okay with that?"

I was. "Yeah, do that. Flatten their tires. If they complain, tell them to talk to me."

She nodded again and stood. "I need to get back to my place. Thanks for the beer."

Clyde high-fived me and then he and Trudy headed back the way they had come.

When they were gone, Finn was the first to speak. "Sounds like you have a problem with trespassers. You want me to stand watch tonight?"

I smiled. "No, but I appreciate the offer. Clyde and Trudy will be on the job. That monkey knows his way around this place in the dark better than any of us. If they come back, he'll sniff them out."

Abby had kept quiet while Trudy was telling us about the trespassers. But no longer. She had something to say. "I want to go see where they were digging. Right now."

She stood, ready to leave. But I stayed seated.

"Abby, wait. I want to go too. But it's too dark. We'll be hiking through a tangle of weeds and thorny bushes. Dealing with whatever animals come out at night. I'm not sure it's a good idea. I think it'd be better to wait until the morning. When the sun is up and we can see what's going on."

She crossed her arms. "You afraid of the dark?"

"No, Abby, I'm not. It's just that living this far out, we have to be careful. We don't need any of us to get hurt. The nearest hospital is at least an hour away. If one of us fell and broke a leg or got bitten by a snake, we'd be in trouble. I don't want to risk it."

She shook her head. "Walker, you're turning into a pussy. You know that?"

I laughed. "Yeah, right. Just because I don't want to see you go out there in the dark and get hurt, you think I'm getting soft. I assure you I'm not. I'm as tough as ever. But it's not just about me anymore. I have to think about you. I care too much to see you get hurt."

She laughed. "Oh, that's good. Saying you care. I'll have to make a note of that in my diary. Walker says he cares."

Finn, who had kept quiet, had heard enough. "Abby, I think he's right. You won't be able to see much in the dark. You could definitely get hurt. I'd hate for that to happen."

She took a deep breath, sighed, and said, "I guess you're right. It'd be better in the morning."

Instead of sitting back down, she pointed to the house. "Probably time to eat. How about pizza?"

We both gave her a thumbs up.

"Good, I'll have it on the table in fifteen minutes."

She looked at me, smiled, and mouthed the word, "Pussy." Then she went inside.

Fifteen minutes later we were at the table eating pizza. Abby had taken one from a box in the freezer, juiced it up with extra toppings, and cooked it to perfection. It was one of the better frozen brands, and thanks to her additions, it tasted a lot like take-out, maybe even better.

After eating, Finn thanked us for our hospitality and said he was going to turn in early. We agreed to meet for breakfast the next morning and talk about our plans for the day.

Since it looked like we were all in for the night, I locked the outside doors, topped off the kitty bowls, and went to join Abby in her bedroom. As soon as I stepped in, I noticed the bed was covered with pages pulled from the box Anna had dropped off earlier.

Abby picked up one of the pages, handed it to me and said, "Look at this."

It was a property survey. From 1937. Of Duckville. Back when it was just raw land. There were no buildings, no fences, just an outline of the property.

She picked up another page. "Now look at this one. Another survey, fifteen years later."

The newer one had the same property outline, with notations showing the location of the three Quonset huts, the driveway, the well and septic tank, and the fence along the property border.

I was still looking at it, when Abby said, "Compare the two. Other than what has been added, what else has changed?"

It took me a minute, but I finally spotted it. I tapped the first survey. "This one has a small area shown as a swamp. The second one doesn't."

She nodded. "Look closer. On the second one, what does it say where the swamp used to be?"

The words were too small to read without getting closer. Leaning in and squinting, I could just barely make out the second word.

"It says 'pit', right?"

She nodded. "Now read the word in front of it."

I looked closer, but it was too small for me to make out. I hoped her eyes were better than mine. "I can't read it. What does it say?"

She smiled. "It says, 'bone pit.'"

Chapter Fifty-Seven

"Bone Pit? Are you sure that's what it says?"

"Yeah, I'm sure. Now look at this third survey."

It was dated twenty years after the second one. Probably ordered by the bank before it loaned the money to the failed developer.

Abby tapped the page. "What do you see?"

I looked again, figuring she wanted me to look where the swamp had been. This time, I didn't have to squint. I saw the difference. "There's no bone pit or swamp. They're both gone."

She nodded. "Yep, they're no longer there. You want to know what I think?"

Before I could answer, she told me. "I think that sometime after the first survey, the swamp probably dried up. Maybe from the drought they had back then.

"Before that, it could have been a spring, like Manatee Springs in Chiefland or Warm Mineral Springs over in North Port.

"If it were a spring, it was probably used as a watering hole by animals that used to roam around here. Gators for sure, but maybe even mastodons and bison.

"It probably had a mud bog near the edges, especially in the dry season. Some of the larger animals would surely get stuck in that bog, and their bones will still be there."

"When the farmer bought the place back in the thirties, it could be that all that was left of the spring was a small patch of wet mud. The surveyor saw it and put it down as a swamp.

"There was a drought after that and the mud eventually dried up. When it did, it's possible that something uncovered some of the bones that were in it. Maybe that's why the spot that was first labeled as a swamp, was later shown as a bone pit."

So far, I was following along, thinking that what she was saying was reasonable. But she wasn't through yet.

After taking a deep breath, she continued.

"Sometime later, the bone pit was covered up. Maybe by the developer. He wouldn't want potential investors to see bones on the property. Or the words 'bone pit' on the survey.

"He had that small tractor and could have used it to cover the pit with dirt."

She stopped and pointed to the location of the bone pit on the second survey. "You see where it is?"

I nodded, but said nothing. I wanted her to continue with her story.

After a moment, she did.

"It's pretty much where Trudy said those guys were digging last night. That means they could have been looking for bones."

I again nodded, thinking that so far, everything fit.

She continued.

"If there are fossils there, and if they are old, they could be valuable. Especially if they are rare."

She stopped talking and pulled out her phone. After scrolling to a web page, she handed it to me and said, "Check this out."

The headline on the page said, "Rare saber-tooth tiger skull could bring one million dollars at auction."

Below the headline was a picture of the fossil in question, along with a story about how it was found and how collectors might bid the price up to well over a million.

Abby held out her hand, wanting her phone back. I handed it to her and said, "You think there is any chance there might be something like that in our bone pit?"

Instead of answering, she scrolled to another page and held the phone so I could read the headline. It said, "Sabre Tooth Tiger was a Florida native."

She pulled the phone away before I could read the rest of the story, but told me what it said. "According to this, saber-tooth tigers lived around here. They went extinct about ten thousand years ago. There's fossil evidence. Mostly jawbones and vertebra. But no full skulls have been found yet.

"If one were found intact, it'd be worth a lot of money. Maybe a million or more. That would definitely give a person a reason to go out digging at night hoping to find one."

Finishing her story, she paused, giving me a chance to think about what she had said. Looking at the three surveys, it made sense. There had been a swamp on the property. When it dried, the surveyor had noticed bones and marked the location. On the final survey, the swamp and bones were no longer shown. They had probably been covered with dirt.

I couldn't see any flaws in her logic. There was a good chance there were bones on our property and they might be worth something. The fossils were the most likely reason someone was coming over our fence at night, trying to dig them up.

We needed to find out for sure.

"Abby, I think you might be right. We need to see where they were digging. Let's go now."

She shook her head. "No, we're not going out there. Not now, and it's your fault. I was ready to go earlier but you said it was too dangerous to go out in the dark. You said you didn't want me to get hurt.

"So have you changed your mind? You don't mind if I get hurt now? You don't care if I fall and break a leg or get bit by a snake? Is that it? You don't care anymore?"

Not waiting for my answer, which was probably a good thing, she pointed to the papers on the bed. "While you're putting those away, I'll be getting ready for bed."

She turned and went into her bathroom, locking the door behind her. While she was in there, I put all the papers back in the box except for the three surveys. I kept them out in case we needed them later.

When she came out of the bathroom, she was wearing just a tee-shirt and panties. Seeing the look in my eyes, she waved a finger and said, "Stay on your side of the bed tonight. No touchy feelie allowed. Break the rules and you sleep on the floor."

She crawled under the sheet, rolled onto her side, and issued her final order for the day. "Turn off the lights."

I did.

Chapter Fifty-Eight

The next morning I woke to the smell of bacon. Abby was curled up on her side of the bed, still sleeping. She couldn't be the one in the kitchen. I eased out of bed and made a quick bathroom stop being careful not to wake sleeping beauty. After washing up, I went out to see who was cooking.

Finn. He was at the stove, working two skillets. One with bacon, the other with eggs. When he saw me, he said, "Hope you don't mind, but I'm making breakfast. It'll be on the table in five. Let Abby know."

I left him to his skillets and went back to tell her. She'd already smelled the bacon and was up when I reached the bedroom. She'd made the bed, put on her daytime clothes, and combed out her hair. All in less than the two minutes I'd been gone.

I was impressed.

Seeing me come in the room, she said, "I hope you came to tell me breakfast is ready."

"It is. Follow me."

Back up front, Finn had just plated the eggs and told us to take our seats at the table. There, we found each setting of silverware had been carefully tucked into a paper towel that had been folded to look like an elegant napkin. Emily Post would have been proud.

As soon as Abby was seated, Finn brought a plate over and placed it in front of her. He apologized that there was no coffee. He hadn't found any in the pantry nor a coffee maker. He had found orange juice in the fridge and hoped that was acceptable.

We told him it was.

After bringing my plate and asking if there was anything either one of us needed, he joined us at the table and had us hold hands while he said a short prayer.

After that, we ate.

The food was delicious, the eggs were perfect, sunny side up with bright yellow yolks. The bacon was as it was supposed to be, crisp, but not burned. The buttered toast with raspberry jam had been cut into triangles, and neatly stacked on the side of our plates. The presentation would have made Gordon Ramsey smile.

Abby and I both complimented Finn on the meal, telling him how much we enjoyed it. When I asked where he'd learned to cook, he said, "In the Navy. I started out as a dishwasher, but they soon taught me to cook. First, doing easy things like hash browns. Putting frozen potato patties on a cookie sheet and then into the oven. It was hard to mess that up.

"Then they trained me on the griddle. Had me cooking eggs, sausages, hotcakes, whatever was on the menu.

"We were feeding about three hundred hungry sailors every meal. I was told if we messed up their food, they'd toss us overboard. It never happened, so I guess we did all right.

"After a year, they moved me up to the officer's mess. That's where I learned about table settings. Up there, they were real particular about how the table looked and how the meals were served. Everything had to be just so. If you messed up, you'd end up back downstairs, washing dishes.

"I must have had an angel on my shoulder. Never had a problem with the food and never got sent back down. When my time was up, I left the Navy and it didn't take me long to find a job as chief steward on a private yacht.

"That angel must have still been looking out for me because the owner of the yacht took me under his wing and helped me get a captain's license. That's how I eventually ended up on the Charon."

He took a deep breath and smiled. "Maybe that angel is still with me. Maybe he's what led me back here. To get a fresh start."

He paused, then said, "I won't be staying with you folks long, but while I'm here, I'd be happy to take over the kitchen duties. It's the least that I can do."

Abby shook her head. "Finn, you're not here to work. You're our guest. There's no need for you to cook for us."

He nodded as if he understood. But then said, "I need to be doing something to get my head straight. Cooking and planning meals will help me do that. I don't see it as work. It's rehabilitation. So please, let me take it on."

Abby smiled, then said, "Okay, you can handle the meals. But remember, you are a guest here. You don't have to do anything unless you want to. If you want to skip a meal, just let me know. I'll get Walker to feed us."

I knew she was kidding. If I were cooking, it'd be something from a box found in the freezer.

After we helped Finn clean up the kitchen, Abby said it was time to go look at where the trespassers had been digging. She invited Finn to join us and he said he would.

We left the house with Abby leading the way. She had studied the surveys and said if we followed the fence line at the edge of the property, it would take us right to where they had been. She was assuming the bone pit was their target.

And she was right.

When we got there, fresh dirt was piled up next to a six-foot-deep hole. A discarded shovel lay nearby.

Looking down into the pit, I was surprised they were able to dig that deep without hitting hard limestone or coral. But if the area had once been a spring, it made sense. The water would have come from deep in the earth, creating a void that was now filled with soft dirt.

Digging into it would have been fairly easy.

Abby pointed into the pit. "There's something down there. On the side. Sticking out. It might be a fossil."

She looked at me. "Go down there and see what it is."

I shook my head. "Nope. Not without a ladder. It's too dangerous. I might not be able to climb back out without one. If I got stuck, how are you going to get me out?"

She shook her head and started to call me the p-word again, but stopped. Instead, she asked, "So what's your plan?"

I pointed over my shoulder. "I'll check in the workshop. See if there is a ladder there. If I don't find one, I'll get one when I go into town this morning."

"You're going into town? What for?"

I smiled and said. "I'm going to get an electric fence. Tractor Supply has them in stock. A solar-powered kit with everything you need.

"I figured putting a hot wire around the hole, about waist high, would be a nice surprise for nighttime visitors if they return. Let them walk into the wire in the dark and they'd light up real nice. What do you think?"

Abby smiled. "I like it. But I'd like it more if you didn't have to go into town. How long you think you'll be gone?"

I thought before I answered, taking into account the location of Tractor Supply and likely snowbird traffic. Finally, I said, "Probably take me about two hours to get there and back. Anything you need me to get for you?"

She nodded. "Yeah, food. But I'm not leaving that up to you. How about this? You stay here. Finn and I will go into town and buy groceries. When we get back, you can go to Tractor Supply. That work for you?"

It did. Boris wanted me to search the Money Pit and I could do that while they were gone.

"Yeah, Abby. That works. I'll stay here until you get back."

Back at the house, she and Finn went through the pantry and made a shopping list. They left soon after in her van.

With them out of the way, I headed to the RV to suit up for the search. I had just gotten inside when my phone chimed with an incoming call. No caller ID, but I knew the number. It was Boris.

Reluctantly, I answered, thinking he would want to know how far I'd gotten with the boat.

I was right. His first question was, "Have you searched it yet?"

I answered truthfully. "No. But I'm heading over there now."

There was a pause, then words I didn't expect to hear. "Walker. Listen carefully. Forget about the search. Leave the boat alone. Don't touch it. And don't let anyone else get close to it. Not even Finn. Keep him busy until I get there. Whatever you do, don't let him leave. Understand?"

I was surprised to hear him tell me to call off the search. And relieved. It meant I wouldn't have to climb into the old vessel and breathe in fiberglass dust while standing shin-deep in broken glass.

I'd gotten a reprieve.

I should have wondered why he didn't want me to search the boat. But really, I didn't care. I was okay with his decision. In fact, I was very happy about it. I tried not to show it when I said, "Yeah, I understand. You want the boat left alone. You don't want anyone to get close to it. Including Finn. And you want me to keep him around until you get here. Anything else?"

"Yes. Don't worry about Tony Ducks. I've got that taken care of. Keep Finn there and stay away from the Money Pit."

He ended the call.

A wave of relief washed over me. My day had just gotten a hundred percent better. I wouldn't be risking my life looking for treasure in a broken-down old boat that might crumble away under me.

I didn't have to worry about Tony Duck's hidden treasure. I could concentrate on something far more interesting.

The bone pit.

Chapter Fifty-Nine

Leaving the RV behind, I headed over to Quonset hut number three. The workshop. I was hoping I'd find a ladder there.

We'd left the door unlocked on our last visit; I didn't need a key to get in. I stepped inside, flipped on the lights, and looked around. I didn't see a ladder right away but did see a large raccoon eyeing me suspiciously. He was probably wondering what I was doing in his home. I was wondering the same thing. What was he was doing in my Quonset hut and how he was able to get in?

We'd both have to figure that out later.

With a show of teeth, he hissed in my direction, then darted under the workbench on the back wall. From there, he quickly disappeared behind a row of old cardboard boxes. I watched to see if he was going to come back out.

He didn't. He had chosen to flee rather than fight.

I applauded his decision.

With the raccoon no longer a concern, I continued my search. Looking around, I could see that most everything inside was covered with a layer of dust. Its grayness masked the color and obscured the identity of the thing I was hoping to find.

But a ladder is hard to hide. Even under an inch of dust. There are only so many ways you can store one. Stand it up, and it'll stick out above just about everything else. Lay it horizontally, and the ends invariably give it away.

The one I saw was leaning vertically on the wall to my

right. A six-footer made entirely of wood. Not a folder and not an extension. Just a simple straight ladder, probably homemade many years earlier.

I walked over for a closer look. The wood was old, and worn in several places, but not rotten. The rungs were round, and when I put a little weight on the bottom one, it held without complaint.

Picking it up, I was surprised at how heavy it was. It was probably made of hardwood. Designed to last. With the ladder in hand, I headed for the door. Stepping outside, I looked back to see if the raccoon had come out of hiding.

He had and bid me a farewell hiss.

I hissed back, "Same to you."

I carried the ladder to the house, checking to see if Abby and Finn had made it back. I didn't figure they would have, but I had to check. They'd be mad if they were home and I went over to the bone pit without telling them.

As it turned out, I didn't have to worry. They were still gone.

I figured it'd be at least another hour or more before they got back. They were shopping for food and kitchen supplies and it might take a while.

Still carrying the ladder, I headed over to the bone pit.

When I got to the hole, I went ahead and lowered it into the recently dug hole. There was no reason not to. It didn't make sense to carry the ladder that far and just lay it on the ground waiting for Abby and Finn to give me permission.

The pit was about five feet wide and looked to be about six feet deep. With the ladder in it, only the top rung showed above the surface. Clumps of dirt gave way when I leaned it against the edge of the pit. Not enough to worry about, though.

I decided that since the ladder was in the hole, I should at least test it by climbing down and seeing if I could find the suspected fossil that Abby had pointed out on our earlier visit.

I wasn't a hundred percent sure it was a good idea to be climbing down into a pit dug in soft soil, but since there was no one there to talk me out of it, I went ahead and did it.

Stepping over the top rung, I put my foot on the next one down and tested with my full weight. The ladder sunk a bit, maybe two inches into the soft soil at the bottom of the pit. But seemed to stay steady after that.

Feeling confident that I could make it all the way down and then back up, I went rung by rung, until I reached the bottom. Stepping off into the soft dirt I was happy to learn it wasn't quicksand. But it might not be as firm as it felt.

Soft dirt piled over an ancient spring could easily collapse into a deep sinkhole. With that in mind, I decided not to spend too much time in the pit. Not without having a rescue rope and people to haul me out if needed.

I scanned the dirt walls and quickly found the object that Abby had wanted me to examine. It was off-white, covered in dirt, and was sticking out about three inches from the wall. It had a slight downward curve and ended in a dull point.

Wiping away some of the dirt, I could see it was very old and had a porous texture. It could have been a bone or a tooth.

Wanting to see if I could get it out, I used my finger to dig around it, trying to loosen it up. After clearing away about an inch of dirt above and below, I tried to wiggle the object free. It didn't come out. It was stuck.

I tried again, this time pulling a little harder. The object didn't move, but my effort triggered a shower of dirt to come down on me from above.

I didn't think I was in immediate danger but didn't feel like spending too much more time in the pit. Still, I didn't want to leave without documenting what I had found.

Pulling out my phone, I shot several close-up photos of the suspected fossil from different angles. I wanted to have proof it existed in case the pit collapsed in on itself.

Just as I was shooting the last photo, another shower of dirt told me it was time to get out. After stowing my phone, I climbed up the ladder, brushed dirt off my shoulders, and headed to the house.

On the way over, I started thinking about what I'd found and wondered who might be able to tell me what it really was.

Then I remembered the woman who I had met back at Oscar Scherer. She had told me her daughter was a paleontologist, a specialist in bone identification.

I needed to get in touch with her. Unfortunately, I didn't have either her or her mother's phone number.

But I knew who did.

Chapter Sixty

It was probably good that Abby and Finn weren't back when I got to the house. I was covered in dirt and Abby wouldn't want me tracking it inside leaving a mess.

Knowing this, I didn't go in. Instead, I went to my RV, stood outside, and stripped off my clothes. I had just pulled off my underwear when I heard applause from behind me.

Turning around, I saw that Trudy, with Clyde at her side, was standing about ten feet away. Embarrassed, I quickly pulled on my shorts and waved.

Trudy, with a big grin, said, "Mighty Mouse? Really?"

At first, I wasn't sure what she was talking about. She'd just seen me naked. I hoped the mouse comment wasn't a reflection on the size of my manhood. Working six feet underground had caused a bit of shrinkage. At least that was what I was going to tell her if she asked.

Still grinning, she pointed to my shorts. "Mighty Mouse? That's what you are wearing?"

I looked down and realized my underwear for the day featured a large graphic of Mighty Mouse, the hero from a seventies Saturday morning cartoon series. His catchphrase was 'Here I come to save the day.'

If only he had got to me before Trudy showed up.

I nodded and said, "Yeah. Mighty Mouse. That's what I'm wearing today."

Seeing that Clyde was pulling a utility wagon filled with what looked like metal poles, and wanting to change the subject, I asked, "So what's in the wagon?"

Trudy, still grinning, said, "That's twice you've been naked in front of me. If you keep it up, I might think you're doing it on purpose. Trying to win me over."

I shook my head. "I didn't know you were there when I took my clothes off. I was covered in dirt and planning on taking a quick shower in the RV. Didn't want to track it inside. That's the only reason I got undressed. So I could shower."

She smiled. "Yeah, right.

"Anyway, I was out for my walk this morning and ran into Abby as she was leaving. I asked if there was any action at the dig site last night and she said it didn't look like it. She mentioned you were going to go into town and get an electric fence to put up around it.

"I told her I had one I wasn't using and if you wanted it, I could bring it over. That's what's in the wagon. Electric fence parts. I can help you set it up if you want."

I was still standing in front of her in my Mighty Mouse boxers. I needed a shower and needed to put more clothes on. But if she was willing to give me an electric fence and it actually worked, it would save me a trip into town and a couple hundred dollars. Those savings would be a fair payback for the free peek show she had just gotten.

"If you're sure you don't mind letting me use the fence, I'll take it. Along with your help to set it up. But I need to shower first. If you want, I can meet you on my deck in about twenty minutes. There's cold beer inside in the fridge. The door is unlocked and you're welcome to go in and get some for you and Clyde."

She looked over at her monkey. "You want a beer?"

He let out a whoop and smiled. A cold beer sounded good to him.

"Yeah, we'll meet you over on the deck."

Then she waved and said, "Bye-bye, Mighty Mouse."

As soon as they turned and walked away, I bent over, picked up my pants, and retrieved my phone. After going into the RV, I called Anna, my Realtor friend.

She answered on the fifth ring. "Walker, I was hoping you'd call. Did you finally come to your senses? Are you gonna take that offer?"

"No Anna, still not going to sell. But I need a favor."

"Okay, ready to help."

"You know that lady I met in the campground? The one I sent to you?"

"Yeah, Carol Davis. I'm helping her and her husband find a place. Thanks to you."

"Good, because I need her phone number."

Anna paused, then said, "Walker, she's married. You can't be hitting on married women."

Anna, I just need her number. You have it?"

She did, and after a bit of back and forth, she agreed to text it to me. It arrived a minute after we ended the call.

Instead of calling Carol Davis right away, I took a quick shower and changed into clean clothes. My new underwear for the day had a holiday theme. Red candy canes and yellow lollipops. That particular pair wouldn't have been my first choice, but they were at the top of the clean pile, so I put them on.

Fully dressed, I called the number Anna had sent me.

Carol answered on the second ring. "Hello?"

"Carol, this is Walker. We met at Oscar Scherer. You were folding my laundry. Remember?"

Hesitantly, she said, "Yes, I remember. Why are you calling?

Is there more laundry to fold?"

I laughed. "No, I've got that under control. But I remember you telling me that your daughter, Cassie I think, was into bones. Old ones. You said she was a paleontologist, right?"

"You've got a good memory. Yeah, her name is Cassie and yes, she is a paleontologist. Are you calling to ask her out?"

"No, that's not it. This is about bones. On this property I bought, we found an old survey that has a spot marked on it as a 'bone pit'. We checked it out and it looks like it was an old spring that dried up. Someone has been digging in it and pulling fossils out. Really old ones.

"I was wondering if maybe I could get Cassie to come take a look and tell me what she thinks. I took a photo of one of the things I found in the pit this morning. Maybe she'd like to see it."

Carol thought for a moment, then said, "Send me the photo and I'll send it to her. If she thinks it's important, she can call you. I'll give her your number if that's okay with you."

"Yes, please give her my number. I'll text you the photo."

Instead of ending the call, I asked, "How's the property search going?"

She answered right away. "It's going well. Anna found us a place that we really like. It's a little more than we wanted to spend, but I think it's worth it. We've already made an offer and it looks like they are going to accept. We'll find out later today."

"That's great news. If there is anything I can do to help, just let me know."

We ended the call and I sent her several photos of the object I found in the bone pit.

Remembering that Trudy and Clyde would be waiting for

me at the house, I headed over to join them. When I got there, they were on the deck, sipping beer. Clyde had parked his wagon full of fence parts near the front steps.

Trudy looked me over and asked, "So, are you still wearing Mighty Mouse?"

I didn't really want to talk about my underwear, but since she had already seen me in them, it was hard to avoid the subject.

"Sorry Trudy, Mighty Mouse has been retired for the day. Replaced with just plain boxers. I promise you won't be seeing them."

She laughed. "Well, that's a disappointment. Still, the early show was pretty good."

She pointed to the wagon. "You ready to do some fencing?"

I was.

After going into the house to grab a cold water, the three of us went over to the dig site and spent about an hour setting up the electrified strand of wire. We mounted the solar panel and charger on one of the existing fence poles. Then put a circle of shorter metal poles around the hole, each with a glass insulator. Then we ran a single strand of bare electrical wire to each, forming an unbroken circle.

The charger that Trudy had was designed to keep cattle within the wire. It would deliver a 5,000-volt shock when touched. That was twice the voltage recommended for use on humans.

There was no way to turn it down, but Trudy said even though it would pack a punch, it wouldn't kill anyone. She'd walked into it once and survived. She claimed it'd knocked her down and her hair had stood on end for a couple of days, but other than that, there were no lasting ill effects.

I asked her about Clyde. "How do we keep him from getting shocked?"

Shaking her head, she said, "Don't worry about Clyde. He knows about the wire. He won't touch it. He's learned his lesson."

I was about to ask her what she meant when my phone notified me of an incoming text. It read, "When can I come look?"

It was from Cassie.

Chapter Sixty-One

Before I replied to Cassie's text, I decided it would be best to let Trudy know we might have a visitor. She had said she didn't want too many people knowing about Clyde.

From what I gathered, the state considered him an unregistered exotic animal and would take him away if they found out he was living with her. And I didn't want to be responsible for that.

Pointing to my phone, I said, "Trudy, I sent a photo of a fossil I saw in the bone pit to a friend. She's a paleontologist. She wants to come here and take a closer look.

"Before I tell her where we're located, I thought you'd want to know."

Trudy nodded. Then asked, "Is she with the state? Working for the government?"

I shook my head. "No, I don't think so. But I'll call and ask."

She nodded and said, "Let me know what you find out. Right now, me and Clyde are going back home. His favorite soap starts on the TV in a few minutes."

I thanked her for the electric fence and watched as they walked away.

When they were out of sight, I dialed the number the text had come in on.

A woman answered right away and said, "Tell me about the fossil"

No 'hello', or 'how you doing' or 'thanks for calling'. Just 'tell me about the fossil'.

I wasn't going to tell her anything, not before she answered a few of my questions.

"Uh, are you Cassie?"

"Yes. My mom sent me some photos. Said you found them on your property. Tell me about them."

"Cassie, I'll get to them in a minute. But first, I need to know more about you. Do you work for the state, in any capacity?"

"No, why do you ask?"

"My neighbors are concerned. Most of them don't trust the government and they wouldn't be too happy if I invited government agents onto my property."

She laughed. "Yeah, I know what you mean. People don't want anyone coming on their land with a bunch of new rules and regulations. I totally understand why. I wouldn't want the state coming onto my land either if I owned any.

"But no, I'm not with the state or any government agency. Until recently I was working as a paid researcher for FSU at the Salt Spring dig, but the grant there has run out. So right now, I'm what you call between jobs."

That was good to hear. Maybe Trudy would approve.

"So Cassie, I just bought a place in Grove City. We were looking at an old survey and found a spot marked 'bone pit'. On an earlier survey, the same spot had been shown as being a swamp.

"The latest one shows nothing. The swamp is gone. The bone pit has been covered up. But someone has been sneaking in at night and digging where the bone pit was. Two nights ago, they dug down almost six feet.

"My neighbor heard them and was able to run them off.

When we checked, I saw what looked like a bone poking out of the side of the pit. It looked old and I thought someone who knew about bones should take a look.

"That's why I asked your mother if you'd be interested."

Cassie waited a moment, then said, "I've seen the photos you sent, and I am definitely interested. I'm in North Port. About twenty miles from Grove City. I could come over now if that works for you."

I thought about it before I answered. I wondered what Abby would think about me bringing another stranger onto the property without first asking her about it. And what about Boris? How would he feel about someone digging holes in Duckville?

Still, it was my name on the deed. It was my property and in the end, it was up to me to decide who could come through the gate and what they could do once they got on the other side of it.

"Cassie, come on over. I'll pin you the location. When you get to the gate, call me and I'll open it for you."

She said she would and we ended the call.

With the electric fence set up, my work at the dig site was done, at least until Cassie arrived.

I decided to head back to the house to see if Abby and Finn had gotten back.

They hadn't.

They'd been gone about three hours, a lot longer than I expected. I guess their grocery list was pretty long.

I went inside, washed up again, then topped off the cats' food and water bowls. Upon hearing the kibble drop, both cats came running. Bob got to me first. He rubbed up against my ankle, inspected the food, and chirped his approval.

Buddy did the same, he was learning from Bob about how to act around people. I didn't know if Abby would think having him as a teacher was a good thing. The younger cat might pick up some of the Bob's bad habits. If he did, she would blame me.

With the cats fed, I headed to the couch and waited for Abby, Finn, and Cassie to show up. Wondering who would arrive first.

I didn't have to wonder long. A few minutes later, Abby pulled up in her van and parked near the door. She and Finn got out, grabbed a grocery bag each, and headed inside. When she saw me, she pointed back to the van and said, "There's more. If you'll bring it in, Finn and I will sort it out in here."

Figuring I had the easier job, I went out and started hauling bags into the house. It took six loads. In addition to groceries, they'd bought a few small appliances. A rice cooker, a toaster, a slow cooker, a hand mixer, and a few other things I couldn't identify.

I had just put the last of the items on the kitchen counter when my phone chimed with a call from Cassie. She was at the front gate. Apparently, Abby had closed it when she came through. Good for her.

I gave Abby the Cliff notes version of why Cassie was visiting and went out to let her in. Instead of walking, I headed over in my Jeep. It was quicker.

Cassie was driving an older Toyota FJ Cruiser. It was covered with mud and showed signs of heavy off-road use. The kind of thing you'd expect a bone hunter to be driving.

After opening the gate, I waved her through, and as she passed by, I told her to follow me to the house.

When we got there, I parked beside Abby's van; Cassie parked behind me. She got out, walked over and introduced herself. She looked to be in her late twenties, had short hair that was dyed purple, a deep tan, and stood about five foot six. Dressed in safari pants, a National Geo shirt, work boots, and a blue bandanna around her neck, she had the outdoorsy look down pat.

After shaking her hand, I pointed in the direction of the dig site. "It's over there. About fifty yards from here. There's an electric fence around it, so we'll need to be careful."

She nodded back toward her Toyota. "Let me get my tools. Then you can show me."

While she was at her SUV, Abby came out to see what was going on. I let her know that Cassie and I were going to the dig site. She nodded and said, "I'm going with you. Introduce me before we go."

With a duffle bag slung over her shoulder, Cassie walked over to us. The bag looked heavy, so I offered to carry it. She said thanks, but she could handle it herself. She didn't need my help.

She smiled at Abby and before I got a chance to introduce her, the two women exchanged names and said their hellos. Abby told her she was living on the property but didn't say anything about us being married and just referred to me as being a good friend.

I was surprised at the designation but wasn't bothered by it. As a friend, I had more leeway than as a husband.

Or so I thought.

I led the way to the dig site with Abby and Cassie staying a few steps behind me. They spoke to each other along the way, sometimes whispering, sometimes laughing. I couldn't hear what they were saying, but it sounded like they were enjoying each other's company.

When we got to the site, I pointed out the electric wire we had strung around the boundary of the old spring. To make sure none of us got shocked, I went over and pushed the hidden switch that Trudy said would disable the charge.

To make sure it wasn't live, I tapped the hot wire quickly with my finger. There was a slight tingle, probably from residual energy, but nothing to worry about. We'd be able to work around it without fear.

Cassie put her duffle on the ground, bent over and pulled out what looked like a paintbrush, then looked down to the pit. After testing the soft dirt around the edge, she pointed to the ladder. "You've been down it, right?"

She was looking at me when she asked the question. "Yeah. Climbed down this morning. No problem."

She smiled, pulled her bandanna up over her nose, and headed down. When she reached the bottom, she looked around and quickly found the object I'd sent her pictures of.

She pulled out her phone and shot a few of her own photos. Then putting the phone in flashlight mode, she leaned in to get a closer look. Apparently happy with what she saw, she gave us a thumbs up.

Then she used the brush from her duffle to clear away dirt and continued to do this for about five minutes. From where we were standing, it didn't look like brushing was doing any good. Finally, she put the brush away, shot a few more photos, and climbed back up to give us her opinion.

At the top of the ladder, Abby reached out and took Cassie's hand to help her get her footing. Once out of the hole, Cassie stood next to Abby and said, "It looks like a Miocene Rhino tusk. I've never heard of one being found this far south, but that's what it looks like to me.

"If it is, it's a major find. But I could be wrong. I won't know for sure without further excavation.

Still looking at Abby, she said, "I'd need permission from

the property owner to do that. After getting it, I'd have to set up camp nearby so I could preserve and protect the site.

"I would also need to get some kind of funding. To cover expenses. Maybe a grant to get me through the several months it might take to fully explore this area."

Facing Abby, she continued. "This could be an important discovery. But we won't know until we dig. My schedule is currently free, but I can't start working on this without permission and funding."

Both women turned toward me. Abby spoke first. "Walker, you said you wanted to find out what's down there. Here's your chance. Give her permission to explore the site."

She looked at me, a special kind of smile on her face. One that I hadn't seen before.

The truth was, I did want to find out what was in the bone pit. And Cassie seemed to have the right qualifications to get the job done. But, I didn't want her to get funding from outside sources. I didn't want any government agency or anyone else having a say on what was being done on my property.

I had a solution in mind but needed to know more.

"So Cassie, what will it cost to do this? In dollars? Exactly how much?"

She shook her head. "There's no way to know for sure, but to start, it has to be enough to cover my labor and living expenses. And since I'll need a helper, it will have to cover theirs as well. I own most of the tools I'll need, but we'll need to rent a small tractor or excavator. If it takes longer than a few weeks, I'll have to come up with a small camper I can put close by, so I have shelter in case a storm comes up or I need to stay over."

I frowned. She hadn't given me a dollar figure yet. That's what I was interested in.

"Cassie, break it down for me. How much to cover just your expenses? How much per month?"

She thought, then said, "I can probably get by on two thousand a month. That covers travel, my labor, meals, and incidentals."

I nodded. "So if you have a helper, it'll probably be another two thousand, right?"

Before she could answer, Abby butted in. "Cassie, can I volunteer for the job? As your assistant? I'm here all the time. I'd like to help. I don't mind hard work, just ask Walker."

Cassie smiled. "If you don't mind digging in the dirt, you're probably as qualified as the last volunteer I had. So yeah, if you want the job, you can have it."

Abby turned to me. "Walker, I'll be her assistant. You won't have to pay me."

I liked the sound of that. It meant other than Cassie, there wouldn't be another stranger coming on the property working on the dig.

"Abby, that'll work. But I have two more questions."

I turned to Cassie. "If you find something, who owns it? I mean if it's valuable, who does it legally belong to?"

Cassie didn't have to think about it, she already knew the answer. "Usually the property owner has first right of ownership. But that depends on how the dig is funded. If there is a grant involved, the grantee might have an ownership claim."

I nodded. "So, if I fund the project myself, and if the dig is on my property, anything you find belongs to me, right? I'm not trying to be greedy or anything, I just want to be sure we understand ownership rights."

She nodded. "I understand completely. If you fund it, and

if the dig is on your property, you will legally own anything we find. We will document everything, and store all finds here on the property in the secure location of your choice."

I nodded again. I had one last question. "You said you might need to park a camper nearby. Shelter in case a storm comes up. Do you already have one?"

She shook her head. "No, I wish I did, but I don't."

Abby smiled. "Hey, that's not a problem. There are a lot of campers for sale around here. You and I could have fun looking for one."

She had more to say. "We have a tractor with a front-end loader here on the property. We could probably get that up and running in no time. Would that work as an excavator?"

Cassie nodded. "Yeah, as long as it's not too big. Does it have a mower attachment? It'd be nice to have a path cut in so I could drive back here."

Abby smiled. "As your assistant, I'll get that taken care of."

Then she turned to me. "Walker, when do you want her to start?"

Chapter Sixty-Two

The two women didn't wait for my answer. After telling me to turn the electric fence back on, they headed to the house excited about working together on the upcoming dig.

It was going to cost me a few thousand a month, but the rent Boris was paying me for Abby's lodgings, would easily cover that and more.

I just hoped it was going to be Abby who broke the news about the dig to Boris. He liked her and would probably go along with pretty much anything she wanted.

I doubted it would be the same with me.

When I got to the house, the two women were at the dining table working on a list of things they needed before they could start moving dirt. The list was pretty long.

Abby told me not to worry, they would be putting together a budget and would present it to me when it was ready. I could then start writing checks.

Finn was in the kitchen working on a dinner plan. He and Abby had loaded up on groceries and he was putting together a special meal. Abby had invited Cassie to stay for dinner, and she said she would.

Since it would be an hour until we ate, and Abby and Cassie didn't seem to want me around, I decided to go check on the old tractor. It would give me an excuse to be outside away from them, and maybe even let me find out how much work was needed to get it up and running again.

When I reached the hut where the tractor was stored, I was careful not to bother the raccoon I'd seen earlier. Instead of using the shop door, I raised the garage door where the tractor was stored.

From a distance, it didn't look too bad. But up close, you could tell its best days were behind it. Three of the four tires were flat, there was a small puddle of oil underneath it, and vermin had eaten the stuffing out of the seat.

But it wasn't all bad news.

The tractor was diesel-powered, which meant as long as the motor wasn't locked up, it would probably start after adding fresh fuel and a new battery.

On closer inspection, the tires didn't look rotten. I could use the portable air compressor I kept in the RV to find out if they held air. Hopefully, they would. Because tractor tires can be expensive.

An old bush hog mower sat on the floor behind the tractor and looked to be in relatively good shape. There was a good chance it would still get the job done.

Next to it, a metal fuel can with the word 'diesel' painted in green letters. I'd be taking it with me when I went into town to get a new battery. To be sure I got the right one, I pulled out my phone and shot a close-up photo of the old one.

Being optimistic that I could get the tractor running again, I went outside, closed the roll-down door, and headed back to the house.

Abby was outside with Cassie, giving her a tour of her van. They were both smiling as they climbed inside. Not wanting to horn in on their fun, I went in the house to see Finn.

He was sitting at the dining table, pencil in hand, making a list. Seeing me, he nodded and said, "Be about twenty minutes. Until then, have a seat."

I sat across from him and he showed me the list he'd been

working on. The first item was 'Weber Genesis II'.

Without me asking why, he said, "Living out here, you really need a good grill. With the weather as nice as it is, you could cook almost every meal out on your deck."

The second item was 'outdoor shower'.

Smiling, Finn said, "That one was Abby's idea. She wants a way to wash off before coming back in. She says you can get a shower kit at HomeDepot or Lowes that would work. That's the way I'd do it."

I agreed, a kit would be the way to go. It would be quick and easy and require no carpentry skills.

The other items on the list seemed to be mostly decor-related. Frilly stuff that Abby would want to buy without me being around.

At least, that's what I hoped.

Thirty minutes later, we sat at the table as Finn served up our plates. We were having Dijon baked Salmon, with a side of roasted Brussels sprouts. Lemon wedges over parsley added color to the dish.

After filling our glasses with wine, Finn took a seat at the table and had us hold hands as he said a short prayer.

Then we ate.

Most of the conversation was between Cassie and Abby. It was almost like they were on a first date, trying to learn about each other's likes and dislikes and past history. They were obviously enjoying each other's company, especially after Finn refilled our wine glasses.

After eating, I stayed inside with him to help clean up, while the two women went out to talk on the deck. They topped off their wine glasses before heading out.

Finn washed dishes while I dried. When he asked what my

plans were for the next day, I told him about the tractor and how I was going to try to see if I could get the diesel motor started.

That's when he said, "You know, almost every boat I worked on had diesel motors. On some of them, I was responsible for keeping them up and running. A lot of little things can make a difference in whether they start or not. If you want, I'd be glad to help you with the tractor."

We agreed that after breakfast we'd both go look at it, then go into town and pick up any parts he thought we needed.

A half-hour later, the girls were still outside. Abby had come in once and gone back out with what was left of the second bottle of wine.

Finn retired to his bedroom, leaving me alone in the living room, to think about everything that had happened in the four short days since I left the goat farm.

It'd been crazy. And it was about to get a lot crazier.

Chapter Sixty-Three

Around bedtime, Abby came in and told me that Cassie was staying the night. They'd finished off the second bottle of wine, and both agreed it wouldn't be safe for her to drive home.

She'd be sleeping in Abby's camper and Abby would be joining her. There were two beds in it and plenty of room for both of them. They'd have everything there that they'd need, as well as each other's company.

Before going back out, she went to our shared bedroom, washed up, and left carrying her pillow. She smiled and said, "See you in the morning."

Then she was gone.

She was out the door before I had a chance to say anything about the surprise sleepover. That was probably a good thing. Anything I said would have either sounded stupid or offensive.

And really, I was happy she had a new friend. Someone about her own age who lived in the area. They'd soon be working together at the dig site, and it was good they were getting to know each other.

It was getting late and I decided it was time for bed. My normal nighttime routine involved locking up the house, but with the two girls out in the camper, I decided to leave the front door unlocked. Just in case one or both of them decided to come back in during the night.

After topping off the cat's food bowls, I headed for bed.

Both cats soon joined me.

Finn was up early the next morning. He had whipped up blueberry pancakes and let me know just as they were coming off the griddle. When I came out of the bedroom, Cassie and Abby were at the dining table, halfway through their buttery stacks.

Both smiled and said their good morning's when I came to join them.

While I ate, Abby said she and Cassie were going into town to pick up some things from Cassie's place. Then they were going to look at a camper they had seen for sale on Facebook Marketplace.

She said they'd be gone for at least four hours but would be back before dinner. Cassie would be spending the night again, in Abby's van.

After they left, I helped Finn with the dishes, and then we went out to look at the tractor.

After he checked it over, he said, "It doesn't look too bad. If we change the oil, clear the gummed-up fuel lines, and add fresh diesel and a new battery, we'll probably be able to get it up and running."

He paused, then said, "We could probably get everything we need at AutoZone. If you want to go there now, I'm ready."

We went back to the house, locked everything up, including the front gate, and headed out in the Jeep.

At AutoZone, Finn picked out the parts we needed. The store had everything on his list, except diesel. Since we knew we'd need fresh fuel, we added a five-gallon gas can to our purchases. After I paid, we left and went to the nearby Walmart for diesel fuel.

I asked Finn if there was anything he needed from inside the store. He nodded and said, "I could use a pair of gloves. Maybe some clean socks and underpants. They probably have them in there."

I was sure they did. Walmart has everything.

Before we went in, I told him that since he was helping me with the tractor, I'd be paying for whatever he bought.

It was only fair.

He picked up a few inexpensive clothing items, a new toothbrush and toothpaste, a bar of soap, some deodorant, a razor, and shaving creme. The basic necessities of life.

After leaving Walmart, we went back to Duckville. On the way in, I stopped at my RV and grabbed the portable air compressor. I put it in the Jeep and drove over to the shed, pushing down a new path through the overgrown brush as we went.

After unloading everything, Finn started working on the diesel motor while I put air in the tires. I was pleased to see that all three held air and there were no leaks.

It turned out that Finn was a wizard when it came to working on diesel motors. Without much hesitation, he disconnected the injectors, blew out the fuel lines, cleaned the three glow plugs, and did an oil and filter change.

After priming the motor, he closed the blend valve and said, "When the glow plug light goes off, crank it for about five seconds."

I did. The motor spun but didn't start.

"Do it again."

I did. Same result. The motor spun but didn't start.

Finn repeated himself. "Again."

This time, the motor actually started. It ran a little rough at first, then settled into a noisy idle. Black smoke poured out the exhaust for about thirty seconds, then it mostly cleared.

Finn smiled. "Turn it off. We'll check for leaks."

There was only one small leak and Finn said it was typical of diesels. Nothing to worry about.

Since the bush hog was parked behind the tractor, he suggested we hook it up to see if it worked. It took us less than five minutes to get it connected. After starting the tractor, I engaged the PTO and the mower blades on the bush hog spun to life.

Proud that Finn had gotten the tractor up and running, I suggested he be the one to drive it to the house. Without hesitation, he hopped up on the seat, put it in gear, and took off.

I followed behind in the Jeep.

When we got to there, I saw that we had visitors. Trudy and Clyde. And Tiny.

Finn pulled the tractor up close to where they were standing and killed the motor. When he climbed down off the seat, Tiny walked over and shook his hand, then the two men hugged.

It was obvious they knew each other.

When I walked over to them, Tiny nodded and said, "This is one of the greatest guys you'll ever meet. He saved my life more than once and still refuses to take credit. I'm sure glad to see him. Especially here."

I nodded, then asked, "So how do you know Finn?"

He put his arm around his shoulder and said. "Twenty-five years ago, a punk kid walked into my store with a gun. I had my back turned and didn't see him. Finn was there, near the coolers, getting beer.

"When the punk pointed the gun at me and cocked the hammer, Finn didn't wait. He took him to the ground and got the pistol. Saved my life.

"After we dealt with the kid, Finn and I became friends. I saw him just about every day that he wasn't out to sea. I was either taking groceries to him on the boat or he was coming into the store to get beer.

"I sure was sorry when he left town. Always wondered where he went. Now he's finally back. Ain't that something?"

He turned to Finn. "Where have you been all these years?"

It was clear the two men had a lot of catching up to do; I left them to talk in private. Before walking away, I asked, "You two want a cold beer?"

They both did. So did Trudy and Clyde.

I went inside, got everyone a beer, and handed them out. Tiny and Finn moved to the picnic table, where they could sit and talk. Trudy wanted to go to the dig site to see if there had been any changes.

On the way over, I told her about Cassie. That she would be working the site and I would be funding her efforts. It would be a private dig and there would be no involvement with any government agency or school. No one else would be coming on the property except for Cassie. We'd be pulling a camper close to the site so she'd have shelter if a storm came up.

Trudy nodded, then asked, "Did you tell her about Clyde?"

"No, I didn't. I never tell anyone about him. It's nobody's business."

She nodded, then said, "If she spends time here, she's going to find out about him. How are you planning on handling that?"

I thought for a moment, then said, "We'll let Abby tell her. But only after you two get together and come up with a story about why Clyde is here. Something that will keep Cassie from asking questions or telling others about him."

Trudy frowned. "Think she can keep a secret?"

I shrugged. "I don't know. But I'll put a non-disclosure in the contract I'm going to have her sign. It'll say she can't tell anybody anything about what she sees or discovers on the property. If she does, we can sue her for breach of contract.

"That should give her some incentive to keep quiet about Clyde."

Trudy didn't seem convinced, but there wasn't much more I could do or say. Maybe after she met Cassie, she'd be able to win her over.

Leaving the pit, we headed back to see how Finn and Tiny were doing. They were still on the deck, talking. Two empty beer cans on the table in front of them.

Trying to be a good host, I went inside and got four more cold ones and a water for me.

Everyone thanked me. Including Clyde. He gave me a purple flower along with a grin and a hoot when I handed him his brew.

For the next hour, I listened as Finn and Tiny talked about what life was like when Tony and his crew were hanging out at Duckville. The tales were interesting and quite revealing.

But there was no mention of hidden treasure.

Clyde was getting a little antsy. It was almost time for the weather girl on Wink News and he didn't want to miss out. Trudy could tell he was ready to leave. She stood, thanked me for the beer, and turned to go.

Tiny also stood. He turned to Finn and said, "Come by the store. We'll talk more."

After saying his goodbyes, he followed Trudy and Clyde as they walked away.

It was mid-afternoon when they left.

Abby and Cassie had yet to return from town.

Chapter Sixty-Four

About an hour later, Abby rolled up in her van. She and Cassie got out and came into the house. They were both smiling and seemed to be pretty happy. Abby walked over to me, pulled out her phone, and said, "Look at this."

It was a photo of an older Airstream trailer with a 'for sale' sign taped to the door. While I was looking at it, she said, "It's the perfect size for the dig site. It's a little dented up, but really nice inside. We talked to the owner and he said everything worked like it's supposed to. After looking it over, we decided it was worth the asking price, and we bought it. Just five thousand dollars. That includes delivery.

"They'll be bringing it here on Monday. What do you think?"

She smiled and waited for me to say something. I knew better than to say anything negative about the trailer or the price. From the photo, it looked decent. I figured that since Abby lived in her own camper, she probably knew enough about them to check out the things that were important. The roof and windows for leaks, the fridge, and the air conditioner to see if they work, and the plumbing for leaks.

If those things were good, the trailer should be fine.

I tapped the photo. "I always liked Airstreams. It sounds like you got a good deal. Did you already pay for it?"

She shook her head. "No, not in full. I gave the guy a deposit. Told him he'd get the rest when he delivered it. And don't worry, I'll be paying for it. Not you."

She pointed over her shoulder, "I see you've got the

tractor up and running. Any chance you'll be able to mow a path to the dig site before the Airstream gets here?"

It was Friday. That meant we had three days before the trailer was supposed to show up, giving us plenty of time to get a path mowed. Of course, that depended on the tractor. If it kept running, we could get it done.

"Yeah, we can probably mow one for you. Anything else you need?"

She smiled. "No, I think that's it. I'm spending the night at Cassie's tonight. Tomorrow we're going to Montbrook dig show near Gainesville so Cassie can show me what a professional dig looks like. I'll be back late Sunday."

Cassie tapped Abby on the shoulder. "I'm going on over to my place now. I'll meet you there later."

They air-kissed, and Cassie left.

As she drove away, Abby said, "We had fun today. Going places, buying things, looking at campers. If that Airstream works out like I think it will, I might be able to talk Cassie into moving into it full-time. Would that be okay with you?"

I nodded. "Yeah, no problem. Cassie is welcome to stay, but with one condition."

Abby frowned and crossed her arms. "What do you mean, condition?"

I smiled. "It's about Clyde. If the wrong people find out he's here with Trudy, they'll come and get him. They'll take him away and he'll never be free again. We don't want that to happen.

"So you have to make sure Cassie tells no one about him. She has to promise not to let the authorities or anyone else know there's a monkey living out here. If she can't do that, if she can't promise to keep quiet about Clyde, we can't have her around. Understand?"

Abby nodded. "Yeah, I get it. And I agree. We don't want to do anything to hurt him. I'll talk to Cassie about it tonight. I'll make sure she understands."

She pointed to the bedroom. "I'm going to get a change of clothes. Come with me, there's something I want to talk to you about."

I followed her to the bedroom, and after she closed the door, she turned to me and said, "Walker, we're not going to pretend we're married anymore. That's done with. From now on, if anyone asks, we're just good friends. More like brother and sister.

"Your Realtor friend already knows the truth. You can let Finn know in the morning. I don't think there's anyone else who thinks we're married. If there is, tell them we're not.

She continued, "Don't take this wrong. You're a nice guy. You really are. But you're not the marrying kind. At least not now. Maybe that will change in the future. But right now, neither of us needs to have people thinking we're married.

"So if anybody asks, we're just good friends. Roommates, living in the same house like brother and sister."

I nodded. "That's fine with me. I never wanted to be pretend married in the first place. It was your idea."

She tapped me on my chest. "You mean you're not broken-hearted about losing your pretend wife?"

I laughed. "Abby, it hurts, but I think I can get over it. Give me five minutes."

She punched me in the arm, grabbed some clothes from her closet, and waved as she walked out the door. Before stepping outside, she said, "See you Sunday afternoon."

A few minutes later, she was in her van, leaving Duckville to spend the weekend with Cassie.

After she left, I explained the situation to Finn. "Abby and I aren't really married. We never were. It was just something she told our Realtor. It was just a little white lie.

"But now it's over. We don't have to pretend. We're just good friends who trust each other."

Finn scratched his head, then said, "She sure fooled me. I guess she's good at pretending. A lot of women are."

He turned to the kitchen and said, "You ready to eat?"

I was.

He whipped up a quick meal of chicken burritos, stuffed with beans, shredded cheese, and sour cream. Served up with peach salsa and blue corn chips.

As expected the food was good.

After dinner, I helped him clean up the kitchen. With everything put back where it belonged, Finn said he was tired and was going to go read in bed. He said we'd be having eggs for breakfast.

That sounded good to me.

With Finn in his room and Abby gone for the weekend, it was quiet in the house. For the moment, the cats were my only company. When I sat down on the couch, Bob quickly jumped up onto my lap. He had missed out on a lot of attention during the day and wanted to catch up.

I petted him until he couldn't take it anymore. The signs were easy to see. His little tail would start twitching and his ears would fold down. When he did that, I knew he had had enough and was moving into bite mode if I didn't stop petting him.

Not wanting to feel the sting of his sharp teeth, I pulled my hand away and said, "Bob, time to go play."

He jumped down off my lap, ran over to Buddy, and bonked him on the head with his paw. Then he took off running. Buddy got the hint. He chased after Bob swatting at his tail. They ran through the kitchen, then disappeared into the bedroom.

It was too bad that Abby wasn't around to see the cats playing. I think she would have enjoyed the show.

Thinking of her, I wondered if she'd remembered to close the gate when she left. She was in a hurry and probably hadn't.

I didn't want to leave it open, making it easy for uninvited guests to come onto the property. I grabbed my flashlight, went out, and locked it.

When I got back to the house, I bid Finn good night, went to the bathroom, washed up, and climbed into bed.

It had been a long day and I fell asleep quickly. I probably would have slept through the night had it not been for the panicked screams and stream of profanities coming from the direction of the dig site.

Our midnight visitors had returned.

Chapter Sixty-Five

Hearing the screams from outside, I rolled out of bed, quickly dressed, grabbed a flashlight, and ran out the door toward the dig site. About halfway there, I regretted not having mowed a path when we had the tractor out. It would have made my run in the dark a lot easier. As it was, my bare legs were getting cut up by the thorny underbrush.

But I didn't stop, I kept running.

When I got to the site, Trudy was already there. She was pointing a large caliber pistol at a middle-aged man dressed in black. Black pants, black shirt, black work boots, and a black bandanna. His hands were above his head, and he wasn't saying anything.

Trudy glanced at me and asked, "Should I go ahead and shoot him now, or do you want to wait till later?"

Her question caught me off guard, but I figured she was trying to put a scare into the guy, so I played along by saying, "I don't know. If you shoot him here, we'll have to drag his body down to the water. Be easier to walk him down there, then shoot him. We can roll his body over the edge and let the tide take it out."

She nodded. "Yeah, that sounds like a better idea. We'll shoot him later."

She pointed her gun at the hole. "There's another one down there. He's the one who walked into the hot wire. You probably heard the scream over to your place.

"When those five thousand volts hit him, he dropped to the ground like a bag of wet cement. I was hiding on the other side of the fence. Saw the whole thing.

"He was rolling around, screaming, the wire getting tangled around his leg. Every time he moved, he'd get hit with another bolt of lightning. It kept sparking him until the battery died.

"He's still groaning, which means he ain't dead yet. He'll be another one we have to walk to the water before we do him in."

"This guy here, he didn't see the wire and didn't know what was going on with his partner. All he knew was he was down in the pit screaming like he'd been bit by a gator. He didn't know whether to run or try to help the other guy climb out.

"Wouldn't have done him no good to run. I flattened the tires on their truck right after they pulled in. It's not going anywhere.

"Funny thing about that truck though. It's got a sign on the door. For a business. Guess what kind."

She was talking to me. Wanted me to make a guess. I wasn't in the mood though. So I said, "Grave robber? Is that the business they're in? Going out at night, robbing graves?"

She chuckled. "Could be, but that's not what it says on their truck."

She waved the gun at the man, "The sign says they are property surveyors. Probably the ones who surveyed this place before you bought it. Most likely, they're the ones who put those flags on your corners.

"It don't seem right, them coming back here in the middle of the night with a pick and shovel, digging holes, and stealing who knows what."

The man started to say something, until she raised her gun and said, "Shut up and listen.

"Here in Florida, they call it home invasion. That's when you sneak onto someone's property carrying a weapon, with intent to cause harm. I'm pretty sure both of you qualify for the charge. Those shovels and picks you brought are definitely weapons.

She continued. "The law in Florida says a homeowner has the right, maybe even an obligation, to shoot suspected home invaders. It saves the court and the legal system a lot of time and money when the perps end up dead."

She paused, then looked at me. "We have the legal right to shoot them. They're home invaders."

I nodded like I agreed.

The man spoke up. "It's nothing like that. We didn't come here to hurt anyone. We just like to dig fossils. That's it. You can't shoot us."

From the hole, we heard a weak voice say, "Dad, get me out of here. I want to go home."

The man made a move toward the hole. When he did, Trudy cocked the pistol.

Thinking she might fire, I said. "Stop. No shooting. Not yet."

I turned to the man. "Don't move. We'll get your son out in a bit. Right now, listen to me.

"You broke the law coming onto my property. You know it, and I know it. It's not the first time either. You've been out here before. Digging in this bone pit. Stealing fossils. No telling how many you've taken. They're probably worth thousands. That makes it grand theft."

He started to say something. I pointed my finger at him and said, "Don't say a word. Just listen."

"I can call the Sheriff right now. He'll come here and arrest you and your son. In the morning, it'll be on the news. People will learn that your company is using land surveys paid for by your clients, to come back and steal from them.

"When the state finds out, they'll pull your license. You'll be out of business, and you'll probably spend some time in jail. Your son will get charged too, and at the very least, end up with a criminal record."

"I can make the call right now. Start the ball rolling."

I paused, then said, "But, there's another way we can handle this. Are you married?"

He nodded.

"Good, you have your phone with you?"

He nodded again.

"Good, call her, tell her to come get you."

He shook his head. "Can't. She's at work. She's a nurse and can't leave. But we don't need her. We've got our truck. Even with flat tires, we can leave in it."

I shook my head. "Nope. That truck is not going anywhere. It's not yours anymore. You lost it when you came to steal from me.

"If you have a problem with losing it, call the sheriff. Let's get him out here and talk about it. I'm sure he'll be interested in your story. About how you are using your surveyor credentials as a cover to steal from your clients.

"The sheriff might not believe me. But he'll want to investigate anyway. He'll want to contact everyone you work with - bankers, title agents, realtors, and of course, owners of properties you've surveyed. He'll want a list of names so he can talk to them. To check if anything of theirs was missing after you did a survey.

"That should do wonders for your reputation. So yeah, go ahead and call the Sheriff. Let's get him out here. Call him now."

I crossed my arms and waited.

He didn't make the call. Instead, he said, "You can have the truck. The keys are in my pocket."

Trudy handed me the gun. "If he moves, shoot him."

She walked over, spun the guy around, and checked to see if he was armed. Not finding anything, she said, "Slowly reach into your pocket. Get your keys. If you come out with anything else, you'll get shot. Understand?"

He nodded and slowly lowered his right hand, slid it into his pants pocket, and pulled out a key fob. Before handing it over, he said, "Can't we do this a different way? Let me buy this place. I made an offer earlier this week, but you turned it down. How much will it take?"

His question was directed at me. By asking it, he was telling me he was the one who had made the crazy high offer that Anna had brought me.

Now that I had him at gunpoint, maybe I could find out why he was willing to pay so much and where the money was coming from. I decided to see if I could.

"Let's say a million. That's my price. You have the money?"

He nodded. "I can get it. I have a backer ready to pay. You ready to sell?"

Instead of answering his question, I asked one of my own. "You have a backer? Why does he want this place? No way the bones in the pit are worth that much?"

The surveyor relaxed. "He doesn't know or care about the bones. They are not worth anything to him. It's the safe harbor he's interested in. Your boat dock. It'd be a perfect place for a marina. He could build it out and rent slips and sell fuel to boats traveling up and down the Intracoastal. And add high-end waterfront condos nearby. It's the perfect place for it.

"So yeah, he'll give you your million, no problem. I can get you the paperwork by the end of the day. All you have to do is sign and the money is yours."

I shook my head. "No. Don't bother. The property is not for sale. Not at any price."

Trudy stepped over and handed me the truck keys. She took her pistol back and pointed it at the surveyor. "Can I shoot him now?"

I was tempted to say 'yes', but I didn't want to deal with the bodies. Instead, I looked at the man and said, "Get your son out of the pit."

He put his hands down and walked over to the hole they had dug. The ladder I had placed in it earlier had been knocked over when his son fell in. With both of them working together, they got it upright and his son climbed out. He looked to be about twenty-five. Old enough to know better.

Trudy kept the pistol pointed at both of them.

With his son no longer in the hole, I turned to the surveyor and said, "Tell your backer there is someone a lot more dangerous than me who has a vested interest in this property. If you or him or anyone else, does anything to interfere with his interest, you will regret it in ways you can't imagine.

"I can't state this strongly enough. You do not want to cross this individual."

I turned to Trudy. "Should we call the sheriff and let him take over? Or should we just keep their truck and send them on their way?"

She smiled. "I still think we should shoot them."

I nodded. "I know you do. But not today. If they come

back, you can shoot them then."

She shook her head. "Be easier to shoot them now. That way, we'll know for sure they won't be coming back."

"You're right, if we shoot them now, they won't come back. But wouldn't it be better if they decided on their own to stay away, and not tell anyone they were ever here and to never have anything to do with this place again?"

She shrugged. "I guess that would be better, but would you trust them to keep their word?"

We both looked at the surveyor. He put his arm around his son and said, "We're never coming back, I can assure you of that. It was a mistake to come here in the first place. One that I sincerely regret. I've never done anything like this before with any other property and will never do it again. I promise I won't be coming back. Ever. Neither of us will."

He surprised me with what he said next.

"It's not all my fault, though. My backer was so confident he would be buying this place, that he told me I could come out here whenever I wanted. But I shouldn't have listened to him. It was my mistake and again I apologize. I promise we won't be coming back. I'll cut my ties with him immediately."

I nodded but had a question. "What's his name? Your backer?"

Without hesitation, he said, "Brandon Berber. He's the man behind all this."

I turned to Trudy. "What do you think? Still want to shoot them?"

Looking disappointed, she said, "I guess not. But we're still keeping the truck, right?"

"Yeah, we are."

I turned to the surveyor. "Don't report it stolen. If anyone asks, you sold it to me. Mail me the signed title within a week. Don't make me come looking for you."

Holding his palms up in front of him, he said, "No problem, the truck is yours. I'll get my stuff out of it on our way out. Can we leave now?"

I looked at Trudy. She shook her head. "I still think we should shoot them."

I nodded. "Next time we will. But for now, let's escort them off the property and make sure they leave the truck behind."

Twenty minutes later, it was over.

On our way back to my gate, I asked Trudy about Clyde. "You didn't bring him?"

She stopped and whistled. Almost immediately there was a rustle in the palms and Clyde came out to join us. Trudy rubbed his head and said, "He's been shadowing us all the time. I didn't want the trespassers to see him, so I told him to stay hidden. He's good at that.

"If either one of them had made a move on me, Clyde would have destroyed them."

I didn't doubt it one bit.

Chapter Sixty-Six

Finn was still asleep when I got back to the house. I wanted to sleep too, but I knew it was a lost cause. I was too wound up.

Instead of bed, I grabbed my laptop and headed out to my RV. I wanted to do some research and I was worried if I stayed in the house, the clicking of my keyboard might wake Finn. Out in the RV, I wouldn't have to worry about making noise. I could do whatever I wanted. No one would hear me.

It was still dark out with no moon, just a sky full of stars. The air smelled of seawater and greenery. The only sounds were of nature. The buzzing of insects, and the rustle of palm fronds in the breeze. An owl hooted in the distance.

When I got to the RV, I unlocked it and went in. Going through the door, I was met with the familiar feeling of being home. I'd spent almost every day of the past three years living in the motorhome. Everything I owned was inside it.

All my recent memories revolved around my life living and traveling in an RV. Including the people I met, the places I visited, the good times and the bad.

Being back inside, it truly felt like I was home.

All that was missing was Bob. He would normally meet me at the door and rub his furry body around my ankles while telling me about his day. I'd checked his food and water, and we'd stay close until it was his nap time. Then he'd trot to the back and slip under the pillow fort on my bed.

But not that night. He was back in the house, probably enjoying his sleep. I'd have to give him an extra pet the next time I saw him.

Firing up my computer, I went to Google and searched for Brandon Berber. According to the surveyor, he was the money man with dreams of turning Duckville into a commercial wasteland.

People like him, people with money who are used to always getting their way, rarely give up without a fight. I expected the war between us was just getting started.

I needed to learn all I could about my enemy. To see if he had an Achilles heel. A weakness I could use to keep him away from Duckville. A poison pill that would kill his interest in the property.

Google gave me a starting point. Links to web articles where his name was mentioned. Most were in the Sarasota's Herald Tribune. The newspaper of record for Sarasota county.

Clicking through the links, the Berber name popped up often in the society section of the paper. There were photos of him smiling, wearing a tux surrounded by others in formal wear.

He looked a lot younger than I expected. Probably in his mid-twenties. He didn't look like someone with a lot of experience taking on major construction projects. But if he was going for the rich playboy look, he had it nailed.

Scanning through the articles, I found one that mentioned his marriage to the daughter of one of the richest men in Texas. According to the story, it had been a whirlwind romance. They had met, dated a few times, and Berber had proposed.

The wedding was a major event, attended by wealthy friends of the bride's father. Berber claimed he was an orphan; there was no family on his side of the aisle. After the wedding, the newlyweds honeymooned in Saint Tropez.

The next mention of Berber was his announcement that he had started a creative investment fund. Unlike other such funds, his would only invest in initial public offerings from new companies. The risk was high, but he explained that the rewards would be worth it. He expected those who invested with him, would see thirty percent returns within a year.

He was wrong.

The returns weren't there. In the first twelve months, he had burned through the entire fund, averaging a negative fifty percent return. His investors lost everything.

Having failed in that venture, he turned to real estate development. Even though he personally was broke, his wife wasn't. She had money through her father and pledged to provide her husband with as much as he needed to launch his new business.

According to a press release from his newly formed company, he would be concentrating on acquiring underutilized waterfront properties and turning them into commercial successes. To assist in this, he would be offering a finders fee to those who brought him potential properties to invest in.

That explained why the surveyor had gotten involved. The lucrative finder's fee. Who better than a surveyor to find investment potential properties.

I decided to see what was being said about Berber on social media. I started with Facebook as it was the easiest to search.

Several posts popped up, mostly links to the same articles I had found on Google. They told of his glamorous lifestyle, his attendance at society events, and his support of various causes. There was nothing negative – which was surprising, considering how many people had lost money investing with him.

Either those posts had been scrubbed, or no one dared to publicly defame him. Things were different on Reddit. There, anyone could post anything about anyone and stay anonymous.

A quick search found a subReddit where his name was mentioned. People who had dealt with him and lost money weren't keeping quiet. They were tracking his activities. Hoping to catch him doing something that would bring an end to his free ride on his father-in-law's money.

Reading the posts, it sounded like they were getting close to hitting pay dirt.

According to a poster going by the name of Slurp151, Berber was seen checking into a hotel in Tampa with a woman who wasn't his wife. The hotel had confirmed Berber paid for the room. He had checked in at eleven in the morning and checked out at three that afternoon.

There were several similar posts. All involved him out during the day with different women. Almost all were described as being young, blonde, and not his wife.

Unfortunately, there were no photos to back up the claims. Without them, the posts were simply rumors started by people who held a grudge against the man.

But rumors often turn out to be true.

Using one of my throw-away email addresses, I posted the following message.

```
$250 reward to the first person who can
provide proof Berber is cheating on his
wife. Must include time, date, location,
photo(s), and name of woman. Strictly
confidential.
```

I knew that Brandon Berber needed to stay in the good graces of his wife and his father-in-law to keep the money flowing in his direction. It was his Achilles heel.

Without them, he would soon be broke.

I packed up my laptop and headed back to the house confident that I would soon have what I needed to defeat my enemy.

Chapter Sixty-Seven

Bob was waiting for me at the door. He twined his body around my ankles, then walked away, looking back over his shoulder to make sure I was following him.

He trotted to his food bowl, nudged it with his nose, then looked up at me and meowed.

We both knew what he wanted.

"Yeah, Bob. I know. Your bowl is almost empty. Let me take care of that for you."

I topped it off, rubbed his big head, and watched as he trotted away, not bothering to touch his food. He wasn't hungry. He just wanted his bowl to be full so that when he did get hungry, there'd be plenty for him to eat.

Bob is a prepper. He wants to be prepared in case things go south. I'm the same way. I like to have a pantry full of food, a tank full of gas, and enough cash on hand to get me through an emergency. The last thing I ever want is to have to depend on the government to feed and house me while I bend my knee to their rules.

Finn had been cooking for us during his stay and I figured it was time for me to take a turn at the stove. Whatever I put together wasn't going to match what he'd been serving, but it would be edible.

Scrambled eggs were the easiest. It was hard to mess them up. I fired up the stove, cracked two eggs into a cup, added a bit of water and a pinch of salt, and put them in the skillet.

While they cooked, I put bread in the toaster, filled a glass with orange juice, and got the butter out of the fridge.

Using a spatula, I worked the eggs toward the center of the pan until the top side looked done, then flipped them over to finish them off.

My timing was pretty close. The toast came up just as the eggs were finished. I buttered the top side of the bread and laid the scrambled egg on it. It looked pretty good.

Bacon would have been a nice touch, but the eggs were ready to eat, and I wasn't going to let them get cold while I cooked anything else.

I had just finished eating when Finn came out of his bedroom. I nodded and said, "You want me to fix you some eggs?"

After looking at my plate, he said, "I think I'll cook my own. You want me to make enough for you?"

"No, but if you're cooking bacon, I could eat a couple of strips."

He worked his magic, and six minutes later he was at the table eating eggs, toast, and bacon. His eggs looked a lot better than mine did.

The bacon was perfectly cooked. Crisp, but not burned. I finished off the three strips and wished I'd asked for more.

After breakfast, I helped him clean the kitchen, then went outside to check the weather. If the ground was dry, and there was no morning dew, the plan was to use the tractor to mow a path to the dig site.

If it didn't break down, we'd mow a path to the docks and clear brush from a couple of other trails we frequently walked. It made sense to use the tractor as much as we could, while it was still running.

Finn came out with me. Right away he said, "Boss, we have a problem."

When I turned to see what he meant, he was pointing at the tractor. Two of the tires had gone flat. They were old and cracked, and all four would need to be replaced. But that would have to wait. My goal for the day was to get a path mowed to the dig site.

Turning to Finn, I said, "I'm going to the RV to get my air compressor. Maybe the tires will hold air long enough for us to mow."

He nodded and pointed back to the house. "I'll be inside. Come get me before you start the tractor."

We headed in different directions. Me to the RV, Finn to the house.

At the motorhome, I got the compressor out and started back to the tractor. But then I remembered the message I had posted on Reddit and decided to check to see if there had been any responses.

I went inside, fired up my laptop, and checked the throw-away email address I had used. It'd only been a few hours since I'd posted and I really didn't expect any replies.

But there were. Six so far. All from the Reddit subgroup.

The first three were spam. Advertisements for male enhancement products, single females looking for love, and life insurance.

I quickly deleted them.

The fourth message was different. The subject line was, 'Dirt on Berber.'

The message was as follows:

`"Photo proof as requested.`
`Taken on September 19 at 2:15 PM, at Hampton Inn Sarasota`
`Woman's name – Hanna Davis`

Berber paid for the room, checked in
with Miss Davis. He left two hours later."

Attached to the email were four photos. Each clearly showed Berber and a woman who wasn't his wife. In one he had his hand on her butt. In another, he was kissing her.

I saved the email in a folder labeled 'Berber'.

Checking the other emails, I found two more that included photos, along with time, location, and comments. They showed Berber with different women at different times and different hotels. I saved those as well.

I replied to the three emails, asking how payment should be made. Paypal, Venmo, or other means.

Then I logged into Reddit and deleted my original post. The three emails I had received gave me everything I needed.

I had just closed my laptop when my phone chimed with an incoming text message. I figured it'd be from Abby, telling me about her weekend adventure with Cassie.

But I was wrong. There was no sender name and I didn't recognize the number. The message was short. It said, 'Come to the dock. Bring Finn. No one else."

Chapter Sixty-Eight

The text had to have come from Boris. He was one of the few people who knew about the dock and knew that Finn was staying with us.

I hadn't heard his boat pull in, but it could have happened overnight. Whether it was there or not, didn't matter.

I had been summoned to the dock and there was no way I wasn't going to show up. And I was definitely bringing Finn with me.

I went into the house and found him on the couch with Buddy in his lap. The cat was on his belly, and Finn was rubbing his head. Hearing me behind him, he looked up and asked, "Tractor ready?"

I shook my head. "No, not yet. But there's something outside I want you to see."

He lifted Buddy off his lap and set him down on the cushion next to him. After he stood and stretched, he asked, "Is this going to take long?"

I nodded. "Yeah, it might."

He pointed to the bathroom. "I probably ought to pee. I'll meet you outside."

Three minutes later, he came out into the yard, wearing his work clothes and his captain's hat. He looked around, saw that the tractor tires hadn't been aired up, and said, "They're still flat."

I nodded. "Yeah, something came up before I could get to them. Let's take a walk."

With Finn close behind, I led the way to the trail that would take us to the dock. About halfway there, I started to hear the low rumble of the twin diesels. If Finn heard them, he didn't say anything. At his age, his hearing probably wasn't as good as it once was.

Near the end of the trail, where the tropical foliage gave way to the open space adjacent to the dock, the boat came into view. Finn pointed at it. "Nice boat. Wonder what it's doing here?"

Then before I could say anything, he said, "Wait, is that the Charon? It sure looks like it. What's it doing here?"

Excited to see his old boat, he quickly walked over to the dock. I followed, wondering what would happen next.

It didn't take long to find out.

Just as he reached the boat, the same man who I had seen last time and presumed to be the captain, came out on deck and waved us over. He opened the entry gate and stepped out onto the dock.

When Finn got to him, the man smiled, introduced himself as Captain John York, and welcomed him to the Charon. He pointed to the open gangway and said, "Please, come aboard. We have refreshments ready for you in the salon."

Finn pulled off his shoes and cap, set them behind him on the dock, and stepped onto the yacht. I started to do the same, but the captain closed the entry gate before I could. He held up his hand and said, "Mr. Chesnokov said it would be in your best interest to stay ashore. He will explain later. Until then, he wants you to return to the main house and wait for his call."

I was surprised I was being turned away. But if Boris didn't want me to be privy to whatever was going on on the boat, he likely had a good reason.

I saluted the captain, turned, and headed back to the house. When I got there, I pulled off my shoes, laid down on the couch, and tried to catch up on the sleep I had missed out on the night before.

Two hours later, my phone chimed me awake with an incoming text. Same return number as before. The message said, "Your presence is requested at the dock."

I quickly pulled on my shoes and went out to see what Boris and his crew wanted.

When I got there, Boris, Finn, and an older man I didn't recognize were waiting for me. Boris didn't bother to introduce me to the stranger. Instead, he said, "We'd like to see the Money Pit. Please lead the way."

I nodded and took them to the derelict old boat. When we got there, the old man shook his head and said, "Yep, that's it. Sure hate to see it in that condition."

He nodded at Finn. "You think you can get it?"

Finn smiled. "Yeah, if someone will give me a boost, I can climb over the rail and get it for you."

Since I was the youngest one around, I stepped forward to give him the boost he needed. Like a lot of older men, he was skinny and couldn't have weighed more than a buck forty. I had no problem getting him into the boat.

He made a beeline to the door leading to the front berth and disappeared within. The boat creaked with his movement; each step he took raised a plume of fiberglass dust.

From somewhere within the hull, I heard him say, "Found it." Then he reappeared on the splintered deck lugging a dust-covered suitcase with a bright yellow first aid logo on the front. He hefted the case up onto the deck rail and said, "Walker, help me get this down."

I reached up, grabbed the handle and lifted the case over the rail and quickly set it on the ground. It was quite heavy. Then I helped Finn get out of the boat. He dusted the fiberglass off his hands and legs, and said, "That was a lot easier than I thought it would be."

He turned to the older man who I had yet to be introduced to and asked, "Where next?"

The man rubbed his chin and said, "The old workshop. That's where I put it."

The workshop was close and it took us less than a minute to get to it. The door was still unlocked from my last visit. I started to go in, but Boris stopped me. "Walker, stay out here with me."

Finn and the old man went in alone. Two minutes later, they came back out, with Finn carrying a metal tackle box.

Boris turned to me. "Go back to the house. You don't want to be involved in this."

I knew better than to ask questions. I turned and headed back to where my day had started.

Two hours later, Finn showed up at the house. He went to his bedroom and came out a few minutes later carrying his duffle bag. Walking over to me, he offered his hand. I shook it, not knowing what to expect.

Grinning, he said, "I've been offered a job on the Charon. Doing what I love. They have a crew cabin ready and waiting for me. I'm moving over there now. Hate to leave you on such short notice, but I can't pass this up. Thanks for letting me bunk here for the past few days. I really appreciate it. Tell Abby I'll miss her. Be careful around that tractor."

He saluted and headed out the door. That was the last time I saw him.

Thirty minutes later, my phone chimed with another text. This one was from Boris. It said, "Meet me at the dock."

Chapter Sixty-Nine

Boris was waiting for me when I got to the dock. He had a large manila envelope in his hand and said, "We need to talk."

I smiled. "Sure, what about?"

He nodded toward the trail we had taken earlier. "We found what we were looking for. Everything except the brooch. It should have been in the tackle box we took from the workshop. But it was missing. The box had been opened."

"The question is, who opened it?"

He paused, then continued. "I know you've only been here for a few days, but can you think of anyone other than you and Abby who's been in that building?"

He waited for my answer.

I thought, then said, "As far as I know, it's only been me, Abby, and Finn. I was with each of them when they went in. We didn't stay long and while we were there, we didn't see or touch a tackle box.

I paused, then said, "Trudy, my neighbor, told me she went in once. Before I got here. She said she was looking for Clyde. He had somehow gotten in and couldn't get out. She heard his cries and was able to get the door unlocked to get him."

Boris nodded. "Clyde? He's the monkey, right?"

"Yeah, he lives with Trudy."

He smiled. "Interesting. If you get a chance, ask her about the brooch. Maybe she knows something."

Again, nodding toward the trail, he said, "Abby says you found a bone pit. Tell me about it."

I filled him in, including how Abby's new paleontologist friend, Cassie, was going to research the site to see if there was anything significant in it. I mentioned that I was funding the dig.

He shook his head. "I'm not sure how I feel about someone digging here, but since Abby thinks it is a good idea, I'll go along with it. But I'll be the one funding it. Through Abby. It'll be cleaner that way.

He paused, then said, "Speaking of her, she tells me she really likes this Cassie woman. Would you do a background check on her for me? Let me know if you find anything that's not on the up and up."

I nodded. "Will do."

He held out the envelope he'd been holding. "Here's the signed contracts we talked about, along with the payments for the first year's rent and the option to buy. Everything is made out in your name.

"I know about the offer you received for Duckville. It was a lot of money. But you were smart to turn it down. You won't have to worry about getting any more offers from Berber. His money has dried up."

He didn't explain and I didn't ask.

He took a deep breath and said, "Let's get back to Abby. As you might have figured out, she's like a daughter to me. I am quite fond of her. But she has a wild side. One that has caused me grave concerns. I've worried about her living alone on the road in her small van. Recent news suggests that this can be very dangerous for a young woman.

"That's why I'm happy she's off the road, living here. It's only been a few days, but I think she likes it. It would be ideal if she settled down here. At least for a while.

"Maybe Cassie is the key to her doing that. Abby seems to be quite taken with her. I know they've bought a small trailer and will be moving it on the property next to the dig site. Cassie plans to live in it. That's fine with me, but I'm afraid that won't last long. From what I hear, there won't be running water or electricity at the trailer. Living in it won't be fun.

"Abby has hinted she'd like it if Cassie could move into the house with her. But there are only two bedrooms, and one of them is yours. The two women could share a room, but that might be stressful and could lead to Cassie moving out. If she did, I'm afraid Abby would soon move back into her van and go out on the road again. I would not like that. I want her to stay in Duckville.

"This is where you come in. If you were to tell Abby you miss living in your motorhome, and you planned to move back into it, it would solve the problem. You could still live on the property. It's yours, you own it. You even could move your RV down to the dock if you wanted to. There are electric and water hookups there. Or you could leave the RV where it's parked now.

"The choice would be yours. Of course, if you prefer, you could stay in the house. All I want is for Abby to stay off the road until things settle down in the outside world. If you can help in any way, I would appreciate it."

I started to say something, but Boris wasn't quite finished. He smiled and said, "There is a good chance I will execute the option to buy this place after twenty-four months. When I do, you'll get your investment back along with a significant profit, while avoiding a major tax hit.

"I only mention this so you can plan for it."

I smiled. He was telling me that my time at Duckville was

limited. Probably just two years before I was completely out of the picture. It wasn't like I was getting kicked out, though. I was going to get all my money back plus a decent profit.

It had been Abby's plan for me to buy the place. Not mine. Still, living in Duckville, even for the short time I'd been there, was turning out to be a nice break from life on the road.

But I knew going in, it wouldn't last forever. It wouldn't be long before I wanted to start traveling again.

"Boris, I actually prefer living in my RV. So when Abby gets back, I'll tell her I'm thinking of moving into it and see what she says. I'll tell her I won't be moving off the property, not right away. I'll stay and help her and Cassie with the dig and whatever else they need me for until they don't need me anymore. Then I'll get out of their way.

"If for some reason, Cassie moves out, I'll stick around until Abby finds someone else. That sound good to you?"

He nodded. "Yes. I think that will work."

He shook my hand, smiled, and said, "We're leaving in the morning. If you get a chance to talk to that Trudy woman about the brooch, please let me know what you find out.

"And Walker, I very much appreciate how you've handled this. If you need my help on anything, just ask."

He reached into his pocket and pulled out three coins. "I've been asked to give you these. As a small reward for taking care of Finn. You'll find another little bonus in the envelope."

He turned and walked back to his boat.

Without looking at the coins, I put them in my pocket and headed back to the house.

Chapter Seventy

It was lonely when I got back to the house. Both Abby and Finn were gone. It was just me. And the two cats.

I'd missed a lot of sleep the night before, and decided that since there was no one there to bother me, I'd take a short nap. But first, I wanted to take a closer look at the coins Boris had given me.

From the size and weight, I figured they were probably gold. Pulling them out of my pocket, my assumptions were confirmed.

But they were much more than just gold. They were Spanish shipwreck treasure coins. Escudos Reales. One ounce each. Worth far more than their weight in gold. Maybe as much as twenty thousand dollars per coin.

I was grateful to receive them as a gift. I smiled, knowing that they were most likely from a much larger collection of coins recovered that day. That larger collection would certainly help fund a comfortable retirement for the stranger who I hadn't been introduced to, but who I was certain was Tony Ducks.

After putting the coins away, I joined Bob on the bed and settled in for a nap.

Two hours later, I was woken by a knock on the door. Thinking that maybe Boris had come to talk to me again, I got up to see him.

But it wasn't Boris. It was Trudy. With Clyde.

She smiled and said, "You've had a busy day. Lots of company. Mind if we come in?"

I was still half asleep and didn't know why they were asking, but invited them in any way.

Trudy looked around, then said, "Abby's gone, right?"

I nodded.

"So it's just you?"

I nodded again.

"Good, because I believe Clyde has something that belongs to you. But before he gives it to you, I have to make a confession.

"When all those people showed up today in the yacht, Clyde and I were watching. We were hiding in the trees, trying to figure out what was going on.

"We saw you lead them to the old boat, then to the workshop. Both times they came out carrying something. I'm not going to ask who those people were or what they came to get.

"But I think Clyde might know. He took something from the workshop when he was locked in there and gave it to me when I rescued him. I put it away, thinking it was just a trinket he had found. He brings me things all the time. Things he finds lying around.

"Anyway, when I saw those people going into the workshop, it occurred to me that the thing Clyde had given me, might be what they were looking for. So I dug it out and brought it over to you.

"I was going to let Clyde hand it to you, but I was afraid he might damage it."

She reached into her pocket and pulled out the brooch. The one Boris had been looking for.

Smiling, she said, "I'll trade you this for a beer. One for me and one for Clyde."

I was so happy to finally see the brooch, I didn't hesitate. I pulled out four beers and gave two to Clyde and two to Trudy. Then said, "I can't thank you enough for bringing this over to me. One of the people on the boat has been looking for this for more than twenty years.

"I need to call and tell him it's been found. He'll want me to bring it over to him. I don't want to rush you off, but I need to do it now."

She nodded. "I understand. We'll be going. Thanks for the beers."

After they left, I called Boris and gave him the good news. I told him I'd meet him at the dock with the brooch.

He was waiting for me when I arrived. Smiling he said, "I can't believe you found it. I thought for sure it was lost forever. Let me see it."

I pulled it out of my shirt pocket and handed it to him. He stared at it for a full minute. Then looked up and smiled, tears in his eyes.

"Walker, I can't thank you enough. You found it. After all these years, you found my mother's brooch."

He looked at it again, then back at me. "I am certain there is something in your life that you want, but can not afford. "Whatever it is, let me know. I will get it for you. When you decide, just tell me.

"And thank you again. I would like to stay and talk, but I must go and put this somewhere safe. I would invite you to join us on the boat, but it would be in your best interest not to meet my guests. I hope you understand."

I did.

He shook my hand and went back onto his yacht.

I smiled, knowing that this latest adventure was almost over.

Epilogue

Over the next few weeks, there were a lot of changes. Abby and Cassie worked on the dig site, spending a lot of time together. They found a number of rare fossils, none of which turned out to be worth much. Still, they continued their search, hoping that sooner or later they'd find something significant.

As the two women grew closer, it was obvious to me that I was a third wheel in their relationship. Even though Abby acted like she didn't want me to leave, I was pretty sure she was happy when I moved out of the house and back into my RV. Soon after, Cassie moved into the house with her.

Bob moved into the RV with me. My fears about him missing Buddy were for naught. He seemed to enjoy being the sole focus of my attention again.

Buddy, on the other hand, missed having someone around to play with. Cassie solved the problem by adopting a female Siamese from the same shelter Buddy had come from. After a rough start, the two cats got along well.

Abby introduced Trudy and Clyde to Cassie and they became regular visitors at the dig site and the house. Clyde liked being surrounded by the three women and would give flowers to each of them every time he visited.

Tiny was surprised to learn his old friend Finn had left on the boat but was happy knowing he would no longer be living on the streets. He kept up with what was going on at Duckville, getting regular updates from Trudy.

I never did do anything with the photos showing

Brandon Berber cheating on his wife. It turned out she didn't need them. She filed for divorce a week later. I still paid the three people who had sent them as I had promised.

The surveyor and his son never returned to Duckville. He did send me the title to his truck, though. I signed it over to Abby and told her having a truck was a must on a dig site.

The old tractor ran long enough for me to clear paths around the property. I hid the key to keep Abby from using it while I was away. It was old and cranky and dangerous.

Kind of like what I'd be in my old age.

Right after Christmas, Bob and I hit the road. A super low tide was coming up, and I'd heard rumors it might expose an ancient shipwreck on Crescent Beach, near St. Augustine. I wanted to be there when it did.

As it turned out, it was the start of another crazy adventure for me and Mango Bob.

One that I plan to write about later.

Author's Notes

I'm supposed to say that the people, places, and events mentioned in this book are not real. So that's what I'm going to say.

But if you search Google, you might find a few similarities between some of the characters within and the things they've done. I'm not saying the book is based on them, just that much of what I write about in the Mango Bob series is based on the people and places I encounter while on the road.

If you've ever traveled in a motorhome, you probably know how this works. You check into a park, meet people and see things you never expected. Very often, these things can change your perspective on life.

Anyway, if you liked this book, please post a positive review on Amazon. Good reviews help book sales and keeps me writing new volumes of the adventures of Mango Bob and Walker.

Should you visit Florida and see a big orange tabby sitting on the dash of an RV going down the road, wave. It might be Mango Bob. He likes all the attention he can get.

As always, thanks for your support.

Bill Myers

The adventure continues . . .

If you liked Mango Road, please post a review at Amazon, and let your friends know about the Mango Bob series.

Other books in the Mango Bob series include:

Mango Bob

Mango Lucky

Mango Bay

Mango Glades

Mango Key

Mango Blues

Mango Digger

Mango Crush

Mango Motel

Mango Star

Mango Road

You can find photos, maps, and more from the Mango Bob adventures at http://www.mangobob.com

Stay in touch with Mango Bob and Walker on Facebook at: https://www.facebook.com/MangoBob-197177127009774/

Made in the USA
Middletown, DE
18 January 2022

58994036R10214